STO

W9-CZX-095

Date Due

LEGENDS OF THE
UNITED NATIONS

❧   ❧   ❧

Legends of the United Nations

❧ ❧ ❧ ❧ ❧ ❧ ❧

BY FRANCES FROST

WHITTLESEY HOUSE

New York   MC GRAW-HILL BOOK COMPANY, INC.   London

LEGENDS OF THE UNITED NATIONS

Copyright, 1943, *by* FRANCES FROST

All rights reserved. This book, or parts thereof, may not be reproduced in any form without permission of the author.

NINTH PRINTING

PUBLISHED BY WHITTLESEY HOUSE
A division of the McGraw-Hill Book Company, Inc.

Printed in the United States of America

C257973

CO. SCHOOLS

McClung 1.82

To My Son

PAUL BLACKBURN

Introduction 🖋 🖋 🖋 🖋

THE SELECTION AND RETELLING OF THESE LEGENDS and folk tales of the United Nations was undertaken in order to give children and grown-ups a conception of the essential spirit of the countries allied with us in the fight for freedom. In choosing the stories, I have tried to present those which seemed to me most representative of the national characteristics of each country. Whether the tales are romantic, fantastic, moralistic, humorous, or courageous, all are indigenous and a part of the inheritance of children for generation after generation, and a part of the essential integrity of the men and women into whom the children grew.

The source material from which I drew the stories is hereby gratefully acknowledged: "The Blue Fairy Book," by Andrew Lang; "Chinese Fairy Tales," by Norman Hinsdale Pitman; "Paul Bunyan," by Esther Shepherd; "Told Again," by Walter de la Mare; "Russian Fairy Tales," by Palevoi; "The Shoemaker's Apron," by Parker Fillmore; "Popular Traditions of Scotland," by Chambers; "The Art of the Story-Teller," by Marie L. Shedlock; "The Boy Who Could Do Anything," by Anita Brenner; "More Celtic Fairy Tales," by Joseph Jacobs; "Once in France," by Marguerite Clément; "The Master Wizard and Other Polish Tales," by Josephine B. Bernhard and Frances Le Valley; "The Laughing Prince," by Parker Fillmore; "Fairy Tales from the Far North," by Asbjornsen; "Wonder Tales from Windmill Lands," by Olcott; "Tales of the Silver Lands," by Charles Finger; "Folk Tales of all Nations," by F. H. Lee; "Folk Tales of Flanders," by Jean de Bosschère; "The Brazilian Fairy Books," by Elsie Spicer Eells; "Black Genesis," by Samuel Gaillard Stoney; and "Canadian Fairy Tales," by Cyrus MacMillan.

I wish to acknowledge my indebtedness for their kind assistance in research to Mrs. May Lamberton Becker of the *New York Herald Tribune,* and to Miss Helen H. Morgan and Miss Vaughn Cunningham of the Jackson Square Branch of the New York Public Library. I also wish to thank Mr. Karl M. Schultheiss for his delightful illustrations of the legends.

F. F.

Contents ✒ ✒ ✒ ✒ ✒

GREAT BRITAIN

Dick Whittington and His Cat — 1

The Black Bull of Norroway — 13

Arthur in the Cave — 19

The Children of Lir — 25

POLAND

Mr. Whirlwind, Shoemaker — 34

Saint Stanislaw and the Wolf — 44

The Jester Who Fooled a King — 49

CHINA

The Gods Know — 55

The Blue Rose — 63

Yu-Kong and the Demon — 69

NORWAY

The Squire's Bride — 76

The Golden Bird — 79

RUSSIA

The Flying Ship — 89

The Harp That Harped without a Harper — 99

GREECE

Demeter and Persephone 114
The Lion, the Tiger, and the Eagle 120

CZECHOSLOVAKIA

The Devil's Little Brother-in-law 127

INDIA

The Unforgiving Monkey 142
The Magic Lamp 147

UNITED STATES OF AMERICA

Johnny Appleseed 154
The Creation of Man (Indian) 161
Paul Bunyan 165
How Br'er Wasp Got His Small Waist 174

NETHERLANDS

The Legend of the Golden Helmet 177
Green Grass on the Wall 181
Three Hundred and Sixty-five Children 183
The Mermaid of the Moving Sands 186

MEXICO

Tepozton 190
The Cow That Cried 199

FRANCE

Ys and Her Bells 215
"Geneviève! The Huns Are Coming!" 223
The Faithful Little Squire 230

· x ·

YUGOSLAVIA

The Little Singing Frog   240
The Best Wish   245
The Silver Tracks   250

BRAZIL

Rairu and the Star Maiden   263
The Protection of the Devil   269
The Three Horses   273

CANADA

The Boy of the Red Twilight Sky   278
The Tobacco Fairy from the Blue Hills   283
How Glooskap Made the Birds   287

AUSTRALIA

Wayambeh, the Turtle   295
Goolahwilleel, the Topknot Pigeon   297
Dinewan, the Emu, and Wahn, the Crows   300

BELGIUM

The Choristers of Saint Gudule   302
Sugar-candy House   309
A Drum Full of Bees   312

Great Britain ❧ ❧ ❧ ❧

ENGLAND

DICK WHITTINGTON AND HIS CAT

IN THE OLDEN DAYS IN ENGLAND, THERE LIVED A little boy named Dick Whittington. His parents were dead and the only friend he had in the world was his young black cat. Dick called his cat Thursday, because that was the day on which he found her crying at the edge of the forest, a forlorn kitten as lost and hungry as he.

Dick wandered about the countryside with his kitten, doing what odd jobs the farmers gave him and somehow managing to keep alive. At night he and Thursday would curl up in a haystack or in a shed or under a hazel bush and go to sleep. Thursday grew up into a fine high-tailed, green-eyed cat and learned to feed herself on field mice and barn mice and wild birds. Dick called her his "following cat," for she followed at his heels wherever he went, meowing for him to wait for her if he walked too rapidly. He thought she was the most wonderful cat in all England.

·1·

One day as he stopped at a roadside spring for a drink of water, a passing wagoner halted to water his horse, and Dick asked him where he was going.

"To London Town," answered the man, "where the streets are paved with gold."

"What's it like?" Dick asked, all eyes and ears.

"Oh, it's a fine city!" the wagoner said, grinning. "Full of rich men and beautiful ladies and big houses. And there's the river with bridges and boats and the stalls and shops loaded with things to buy."

"Could I make my fortune there?" asked Dick, picking up Thursday, who began to purr as he stroked her head and scratched behind her ears.

"To be sure you could," said the wagoner. "Whoa up there, you've had enough," he said to his horse, yanking on the reins.

"Could I go along with you?"

The man laughed. "I'll let you walk all the way beside my wagon without paying anything for your journey." He climbed up on his wagon and shook the reins.

"That's very kind of you," said Dick, tucking Thursday inside his jacket and taking his place beside the wagon.

Thursday rode inside Dick's jacket for a while, her black head sticking out under his chin; then she wiggled and wanted to get down, so he set her in the dust of the road. She ran off into the grass and came back and followed along at his heels until she grew tired. She meowed anxiously, and Dick picked her up again. His own legs were tired, too, by then, and he thought it was certainly a long way to London Town.

At last they came to the city, and the wagoner drove off without even saying goodby. Dick's feelings were hurt as he stared after the departing wagon, but he knew the man had done him a service in letting him walk beside the wagon without paying for his journey. Thursday, her head sticking up from his jacket, rumbled loudly and washed his chin affectionately, and Dick felt better. Tattered and hungry, he began to wander about the great city in a daze of delight. He gazed at the churches and marvelous houses, at the million glittering things in the shop windows, at the rich men passing on foot or on horseback or in splendid coaches. Occasionally someone stared at the ragged country boy with the black cat whose green eyes were as wide and astonished as her young master's.

Dick screwed up his courage and asked a tall man where he could find work.

But the man said angrily, "Be off with you! We don't want pickpockets here, you young rascal!" He raised his stick as if to strike Dick, and Thursday growled and spat.

Dick scurried out of the way. He wandered on, knocked at the doors of houses and asked for work. But the women slammed the doors in his face. Miserable and very hungry now, he found himself in the narrow dirty alleys where beggars lived. There was no work anywhere for a penniless, grubby boy.

He heard the bells of the city ringing as the blue twilight crept over the misty town, and he loved the sound of them. But his stomach felt like a cavern and his heart like a boulder in him. Darkness was falling when he came to a large warehouse and sat down on the doorstep. He huddled there, aching with weariness, while Thursday stepped nervously over the cobblestones, exploring the neighborhood. Finally Dick fell asleep, curled up on the stone step, his thin, grimy cheek resting on one torn sleeve.

Thursday left him on silent paws and did some excellent exploring this time. She hurried down the street and found a butcher's stall. There she stole a piece of mutton, slipped back to the warehouse with it, and had a satisfying feast. When she had washed her face and cleaned her whiskers, she felt fortified and much more confident. So she skirted the warehouse, caught a big gray rat, and brought it back to Dick, for she knew he was hungry too. But Dick slept soundly on. Thursday put the rat down on the step where he would be sure to see it first thing in the morning. She stretched, yawned, sneezed delicately, curled up close to Dick's chest, and went to sleep herself.

The next morning the merchant who owned the warehouse walked down the cobbles to find a dirty-faced boy asleep on his doorstep, a black cat beside the boy, and a dead rat lying near by. The merchant chuckled, for he liked boys and cats. He shook Dick gently by the shoulder. "Here, boy, wake up!" he said. Thursday opened one green eye and then the other, and Dick sat up so suddenly he nearly spilled Thursday from the step.

"Good day, sir," he murmured sleepily, rubbing his eyes. He remembered his manners and sprang to his feet. "Oh, sir, is this your warehouse?"

The merchant said that it was and asked Dick where he had come from. His voice was so kind that Dick told him his story at once. He was faint with hunger and he swayed as he told the merchant that he had been unable to find work.

"How would you like to work here in my warehouse?" asked the merchant. "I have plenty for a boy to do, and your cat, I see, is a good mouser, or should I say ratter? She will find enough mice and rats here to set herself up in business. How long is it since you've eaten, boy?"

"Three days," Dick answered in a low tone.

"That will never do," said the merchant firmly. "We'll soon settle the matter of your stomach and then we'll get to work."

So Dick became apprenticed to the merchant and promised to work for him for seven years. For a long time he was happy in the warehouse, and Thursday grew as sleek and well fed as any cat could wish to be.

Dick himself ate in his master's kitchen. But at night he lay down on a pallet in a corner of the big warehouse and listened to the wash of the river tide at the wharf on which the warehouse was built. Thursday hunted mice and rats in the darkness, and Dick could hear the scamperings and squeakings; but in spite of Thursday's company, he was lonely. And in the spring he became restless and homesick for the countryside and the fragrance of the woods.

One moonlit night he could bear it no longer. Forgetting his promise to the merchant and the merchant's unfailing kindness, he put Thursday inside his jacket and slipped out of the warehouse. He ran through the cobbled streets in the moonlight, away from the salt smell of the river, on through the sleeping city. Out of breath, he stopped running and began to trudge, and at last he was outside of London Town.

In the early dawn he sat down in the young dew-wet grass on the hill of Highgate and breathed deeply of the good smell of the ground. He looked around at the new leaves just breaking forth, tender and green on the trees and bushes, and sighed happily. Thursday high-stepped daintily through the damp grass, paused to chew a grass-blade, returned to Dick and meowed uneasily. Just then the bells of London Town began to ring. Dick heard their music far and sweet, blowing toward him on the cool wind.

He remembered his broken promise to his master, and the countryside did not seem quite so marvelous. He plucked a blade of grass and nibbled the white root, and as he listened to Bow bells, it seemed as if they were calling to him:

> *Turn-again-Whittington!*
> *Turn-back-Dick-Whittington,*
> *Thrice-Lord-Mayor-of-London-Town!*

Thursday washed hard behind her ears, came and put both black front paws on Dick's knee and gazed up into his face, her green eyes questioning him. It was as if she reproached him for taking her away from her life of catching gray velvet mice in the shadowy warehouse. Dick stroked her head but she refused to purr. Once more he heard the bells of the city calling him:

Turn-again-Whittington!
Come-back-Dick-Whittington,
Thrice-Lord-Mayor-of-London-Town!

His conscience was hurting badly now, so he got to his feet, took a last reluctant look around at the soft green mist of the woods, and set out for London with Thursday at his heels. He reached the warehouse before his master came to begin business, and he was so relieved to be back that he worked harder than ever. Thursday fairly outdid herself catching mice, and *she* worked so hard for the rest of the week that by Sunday she was exhausted and slept all day long without so much as opening an eye or twitching a whisker.

One day the merchant called Dick to him and asked, "How would you like to see the world, Dick?"

Dick gasped, "Why, I'd like to, sir."

"Very well. You've served me honestly and faithfully for a year. I've a ship, the *Unicorn*, sailing for the Indies next week. How would you like to go on her as a cabin boy?"

"That would be fine, sir! But what about Thursday?"

"You may take Thursday," said the merchant, smiling. "Ships have rats, too."

The *Unicorn* sailed on the evening high tide. The Thames was purple and silver, and Dick and Thursday leaned on the vessel's rail, gazing backward at England. Then Dick went to work, filled with joy at the sight of the sea ahead and at the sound of the creaking masts above his head.

Thursday had a wonderful time chasing the ship's rodents. It was a bit more difficult to catch them on board than on shore, for the *Unicorn* rolled from side to side. Sometimes, just as Thursday was about to pounce on a rat, the deck veered so violently that she slid in one direction while the rat got away in another.

At length the *Unicorn* hove in sight of an island ruled by a powerful blackamoor. The sailors dropped anchor, and the next day the Captain went ashore to trade with the King, who had vast stores of gold, precious stones, and splendidly carved ivory.

When he returned to the *Unicorn*, the Captain said, "You never in your life have seen so many rats! The island's overrun with them, and the King has to keep special servants watching over him while he sleeps, for fear they'll bite him. When we were feasting, they snatched the food on the banquet board right from under our noses!"

Dick hesitated a moment, and then he stepped forward. "By your leave, sir, may I go ashore with Thursday and see the King? Perhaps she can help him."

The Captain gave his permission. Dick put Thursday in a bag, and one of the sailors rowed them to the beach, where great palm trees were rattling in the seawind. Dick found the King taking his afternoon nap on the royal couch under a scarlet and gold pavilion. Five black slaves were waving peacock-feather fans to keep the rats and mice away from His Majesty. But the rats and mice paid no attention to the fans and scurried merrily about everywhere. One impudent mouse popped up over the King's shoulder and gave him a smart nip on the nose, at which the King awoke in a howling rage. Holding onto his nose, he glared at Dick and shouted something unintelligible.

Dick held out the bag in which Thursday was kicking and fighting like ten cats. "Your Majesty, my cat will help you get rid of these creatures."

The King didn't understand a syllable. He sent for his old witch doctor, who bobbed his white head at Dick and interpreted Dick's words to the King. The King rubbed his nose and talked rapidly. The witch doctor told Dick that the King wished to see what was in the bag.

Dick freed Thursday, who sprang upon the rats, and before you could say *scat*, thirteen rats and seventeen mice lay dead around the King. The King clapped his hands for joy; the slaves cried out; the witch doctor jumped up and down with glee and got a Charley horse in his left leg.

Thursday was a bit out of breath, so she sat down at the King's feet, looked up at him smugly, and calmly began to wash her face. Dick had to laugh at her.

The King was very excited and sent for the Queen to come and see this astonishing cat who dispatched rats and mice so swiftly. He moved over on his couch so that the Queen could sit down. Thursday washed thoroughly behind her ears and gave her whiskers a good going-over before she sprang into the Queen's lap. She purred loudly, rubbing her black head against the Queen's black hand. Dick showed the Queen how to stroke Thursday's sleek fur, and the Queen and Thursday purred together.

The King wanted to buy Thursday at once. But Dick shook his head.

"Yes," said the King, through the witch doctor.

"No," said Dick politely but firmly.

"Yes!" said the King.

"No!" said Dick.

"*Yes!*" demanded the King.

"*No!*" said Dick. "But I will lend her to you for one year, and she will have your island free of rats and mice in that time."

The King was delighted and said he would give Dick fifteen casks of pearls and gold and precious stones and three big bundles of ivory for the loan of the cat. He agreed to take good care of Thursday and to give her cocoanut milk three times a day.

Dick said goodby to Thursday, rubbing his cheek against her head and giving her ears a final scratch. The King loaded the boat with the casks and the ivory, and Dick returned to the *Unicorn*, pleased with his bargain but already missing Thursday very much.

When the *Unicorn* once again reached London Town, the merchant was delighted with Dick's good fortune. Dick wished to give his master the casks and the ivory, but the merchant would have none of it. Instead, he took Dick home with him, had him bathed, had his hair curled properly, and brought him a rich suit of fine clothes. Dick turned out to be a handsome young man, well mannered, if still a little shy. The merchant presented him to his charming daughter, Alice, and Dick promptly fell head over heels in love with her.

Dick and the merchant traded together, and Dick's wealth increased. The following year when the *Unicorn* returned from her voyage to the Indies, Thursday came home, too, along with twenty casks of pearls and gold and precious stones and nine bundles of ivory sent by the grateful King. But Dick was so glad to see Thursday again that he picked her up and put her inside his fine jacket and walked away from the wharf talking to her, paying no attention to his new wealth, while Thursday purred so hard she became positively hoarse.

The merchant and Dick became more and more prosperous, until Dick was the greatest merchant in London Town. He married Alice, the merchant's beautiful daughter, and they were very happy.

Before long, Dick was made Lord Mayor of London Town, and he was loved and respected by all men. And he was Lord Mayor not once, but three times. When Thursday became too old to hunt, Dick and Alice always had special dishes prepared for her, such as tender young roast chicken with all the bones taken out, or a delicious mouse-tail stew served in a golden porringer. And Thursday would thank them with a very affectionate *purr-urp* and a long look out of her great green eyes, before she washed her face and strolled to the hearth rug of the Lord Mayor's mansion and went to sleep with her paws tucked in.

SCOTLAND

THE BLACK BULL OF NORROWAY

Langsyne in Norroway in Scotland lived a lady who had three lovely daughters. One day in spring the eldest of them said to her mother, "Mother, bake me a meal cake and roast me a bit of meat, for I'm going away to seek my fortune."

Her mother did that; and the daughter went off to an old witch wife and said she wished to seek her fortune.

The witch wife said, "Bide here this day, and go and look out of the back door and see what you see."

The girl saw nothing the first day. And the second day she saw nothing. But the third day she saw a coach-and-six coming along the road. She ran into the house and told what she saw.

"Ah, well, that's for you," said the witch wife, "and it means you will wed well and have great good fortune."

So the eldest daughter was taken into the coach, and the horses galloped off.

Then the second daughter said to her mother, "Mother, bake me a meal cake and roast me a bit of meat, for I'm off to seek my fortune."

Her mother did that; and the daughter went off to

the old witch wife and said she wished to seek her fortune.

And the witch wife said, "Bide here this day, and go and look out of the back door and see what you see."

The second girl saw nothing the first day and nothing the second. But on the third day she saw a coach-and-four come rollicking along the road.

"Ah, well, that's for you," said the witch wife, "and it means you will wed a good man and have a lifetime of laughter."

So the second daughter was taken into the coach, and away the horses pranced.

The third daughter said to her mother, "Mother, pray bake me a bannock and roast me a collop, for I'm going away to seek my fortune."

Her mother did that; and the youngest daughter went off to the old witch wife and said shyly she wished to seek her fortune.

The old witch wife said, "Bide here this day, and go and look out of the back door and see what you see."

The girl did so, but she saw nothing. On the second day she saw nothing. On the third day she ran in to the witch wife and said, "I see nothing but a handsome Black Bull roaring along the road."

"Ah, well, he's for you," said the old wife, "and what it means I cannot tell."

The girl grew pale with terror, but she was lifted up and set on the Black Bull's back, and away they went.

On they journeyed and on they traveled, till the girl grew faint with hunger. But the Black Bull told her to eat out of his right ear and drink out of his left ear; and she did as she was told and felt marvelously refreshed.

Long they paced and far they raced till they came in sight of a great fair castle. "Yonder we'll stay this night," said the Black Bull, "for my eldest brother lives there."

At the castle they lifted the girl from the back of the Black Bull and took her in; and the Bull they sent to a field for the night.

In the morning they gave the girl a beautiful apple, and told her never to break it till she was in the greatest trouble ever mortal was in, in this world, and the apple would save her. And they lifted her upon the Black Bull's back.

Again they paced and far they raced until they came in sight of a greater and fairer castle than before. "Yonder we'll stay this night," said the Black Bull, "for my second brother lives there."

At the castle they lifted her down and took her in; and the Black Bull they sent to a field for the night.

In the morning they gave the girl a wonderful pear, telling her never to break it until she was in the greatest trouble ever mortal was in, in this world, and the pear would save her. And they lifted her upon the Black Bull's back.

Long they paced and far they raced until they came in sight of the greatest and fairest castle they had seen yet. "Yonder we'll stay this night," said the Black Bull, "for my youngest brother lives there."

And they lifted her down and took her in; and the Black Bull they sent to a field for the night.

In the morning, they gave the girl a fine plum, and told her never to break it until she was in the greatest trouble ever mortal was in, in this world, and the plum would save her. And they lifted her upon the Black Bull's back.

Again they paced and on they raced till they came to a dark and lonely glen. The Black Bull stopped and told the girl to get down.

Then he said to her, "Here you must stay while I go to fight the Devil. Sit on that stone and move neither hand nor foot till I return, else I'll never find you again." He turned his gentle dark eyes on her and said, "Remember this—if everything turns blue around you, I shall have conquered the Devil. But should everything turn red, he will have overcome me."

The girl sat down on the stone and cried after him, "I shall not move, and I shall watch for all things to turn blue!"

The Black Bull went on steadfastly into the darkening wood, not looking back.

The girl sat very still for a long time, not moving hand nor foot, and suddenly the trees, the wild grass, the flowers, the leaf-spattered sun itself, turned blue. So glad was she that the Black Bull had conquered the Devil, that she forgot her promise and shifted her feet, lifting her right ankle over her left ankle. The Black Bull returned and sought for her but could never find her.

Long she sat and long she worried, waiting, but the Black Bull did not come back into her sight. At length she arose and walked away, not knowing where she was going nor why, her heart sore within her. Through the glen she wandered and on, till she came to a great hill of glass. She tried to climb it but could not. Around the foot of the glass hill she went weeping until she came to a smith's house, and to him she told her sorrow.

"If you'll serve me for seven years," the smith said, "I'll make you a pair of iron shoes so that you can climb the hill."

To that she agreed and that she did, and at the end of the seven years she climbed the hill and found herself at the old witch wife's house.

The witch wife's servant told her of a brave young knight who had given in some bloody socks and had said that whoever washed the socks clean would be his wife. The old wife had washed them herself until she was tired. She'd sent then for her own daughter, who had scrubbed and rinsed and scrubbed, while the witch wife helped, but neither of them could remove the stain.

"I'll try," said the stranger girl to the servant.

The servant told the witch wife, and the witch wife sent to the kitchen for the girl. In one water the girl put the socks and in another water rinsed them and they came out clean and pure.

When the gallant knight returned, she saw him from the back door and fell deeply in love with him. But the witch wife told him that her own daughter had washed the socks clean. He replied that to keep his promise he would marry the daughter.

The stranger girl was distracted at the thought of it,

and recalled the apple given her by the Black Bull's eldest brother. So she broke it, and it was filled with gold and precious stones.

"All these I will give you," she said to the daughter, "if you will put off your marriage for one day, and allow me to look upon him while he is sleeping."

The daughter agreed. But the witch wife prepared a sleeping-potion and gave it to the knight, who drank it unknowing and never awakened until morning. Night-long the girl wept and sang:

> *Seven lang years I served for thee,*
> *The glassy hill I clamb for thee,*
> *The bluidy socks I wrang for thee:*
> *And wilt thou no wauken and turn to me?*

The following day the stranger girl was stricken with grief. She broke open the pear then, which the Black Bull's second brother had given her, and it was filled with richer jewels than the apple had been. With these she bargained for a second night in the young knight's room. And again the witch wife gave him a sleeping-drink, and once more he slept until morning. All night the girl sobbed and sang, and she nearly lost all hope.

But on the third day, while the knight was out hunting, one of his men asked him the cause of the weeping and moaning in his bedchamber. The knight replied that he had heard no noise. His man insisted that there had been; so the knight resolved to stay awake and listen.

That evening when the witch wife brought his drink, he required that there be sweetening in it. While she went to fetch honey he poured out the drink, and when she returned he said he had drunk it.

Meanwhile the girl broke open the plum given her by the young brother of the Black Bull, and it was filled with the richest jewels she had ever seen. She bargained with the daughter for a third chance to look upon the knight while he was sleeping, and went to his room, where he lay in the moonlight, pretending to be asleep. Again she looked at him and sobbed and sang:

> Seven lang years I served for thee,
> The glassy hill I clamb for thee,
> The bluidy socks I wrang for thee:
> And wilt thou no wauken and turn to me?

He heard and turned to her and sprang up, and told her he had been the Black Bull of Norroway, enchanted by the old witch wife. He told her all that had happened to him; she told him all that had happened to her. And they were wed, and are living happy to this day, for aught I ken.

WALES

ARTHUR IN THE CAVE

Once a Welsh drover boy named March was strolling along London Bridge in the late afternoon, his hazel staff in his hand. He'd come to London in charge of a herd of black Welsh cattle, for his master trusted him. The cattle he had sold at a profit, and the money belonging to his master he had carefully hidden on his person, but he had a few coins of his own jingling in his pocket. Wandering happily along, he looked at the shops on the Bridge, and at the afternoon sun going down into the molten water.

As he paused to gaze at a stall of mutton pies, wondering whether or not he was hungry enough to waste a penny on his stomach, his hand on his hazel staff tingled. He glanced up to find a man gazing at his staff with a long, fixed look. He clutched his staff tighter, forgetting the pies.

The man stepped toward him and asked, "Where do you come from, lad?"

March was on guard. "From my own country," he answered, and his voice held an edge of anger. The stranger looked as if he coveted the hazel stick, and no man could take that staff from March, who had cut it himself.

"Don't be annoyed at my questions," the stranger said. "Do you recall where you cut that stick?"

"What difference does it make where I cut it?" March asked suspiciously.

"It makes a great deal of difference, because there's great treasure hidden near the place where you cut it. If you can take me to the spot, I'll show you riches enough to make you prosperous for the rest of your life."

The drover boy knew then that the stranger was a sorcerer, and the hazel staff throbbed in his hand.

Tempted by the thought of treasure, still March was afraid to have anything to do with the powers of darkness. At length, however, the sorcerer prevailed upon him to lead him to the place where he had cut the hazel staff.

Reluctantly March said, "Come along, then, and I'll show you," although he would rather have stayed longer strolling on London Bridge and eating mutton pies and gazing at the brilliant shops.

March and the sorcerer journeyed then to Wales. The boy led the stranger to Craig y Dinas, the Rock of the Fortress, at the head of the Neath Valley, near Pont Nedd Fechan. There the boy, pointing to the root of an old hazel, said, "This is where I cut my staff."

The sorcerer nodded three times and said, "Now we must dig."

March borrowed two shovels from his master's toolshed, and he and the sorcerer dug and dug beside the hazel root. At last they came to a broad, flat stone.

The sorcerer pried up the stone and there were stone steps leading downward. March followed him down and along a passage until they came to a massive door.

Here the sorcerer paused and looked sharply at the boy. "Are you brave, Welshman?" he asked. "Will you come with me?"

March gripped his hazel staff, which was now throbbing so that it made his arm ache. He shivered a little and answered, "I will."

They pulled open the door, and a vast cave opened before them, filled with a faint red glow. They came to an enormous bronze bell.

"Don't touch that bell!" commanded the sorcerer.

"Why not?" asked March.

"Do you want to die?"

"Not yet," said March.

"Then come ahead."

As they went further into the cave, March saw that it was filled with thousands of soldiers lying down. Each soldier wore bright armor, the steel helmet of each one was on his head, the great shining shield of each was on his arm, the sword of each was at his hand, and every soldier was sound asleep. March stared in wonder.

In the center of the cave stood an enormous round table, where sat warriors whose splendid build and noble faces and richly emblazoned armor proclaimed them no ordinary men. Each of these, too, had his head bowed in sleep.

On the further side of the round table, on a golden throne, sat a mighty king, gigantic in stature and with features both heroic and kindly. In his hand he held a magnificent sword, its scabbard and golden haft studded with sparkling gems. On his head was a crown set with precious stones that flashed like fire and stars. And sleep lay upon him also.

The drover boy could scarcely believe his eyes. "They're asleep," he whispered.

"Yes," said the sorcerer. "But if you touch the brazen bell, they will awake."

"Have they been asleep long?" March asked, blinking.

"For over a thousand years."

"Who are they?" March clutched his hazel staff tightly.

The sorcerer looked at the boy with a smile. "They are Arthur's warriors, waiting for the time to come when they shall destroy all the enemy of the Cyrmy and repossess the strand of Critain, establishing their own king once more at Caer Lleon."

March looked toward the center of the cave. "Who are the men sitting at the round table?"

"Arthur's knights," replied the sorcerer.

"And on the golden throne?" The boy's voice was hushed.

"Arthur himself," said the sorcerer, "and that is his sword Excalibur in his hand."

March felt his heart grow big within him as he gazed at Arthur and his knights and felt as if he had been swept back into the past a thousand years.

But the sorcerer was impatient. He hurried to an enormous heap of yellow gold on the floor of the cave, gathered up as much as he could carry, and told March to do likewise. March put a fistful in his pocket, and followed the sorcerer toward the door.

The boy was entranced, however, by the vision of the countless warriors in the glittering armor, all asleep, and wished he could see them awake. When he came to the bronze bell, he hesitated a second, then struck it with his hazel staff, and it rang throughout the cave. March gulped, for at once the thousands of warriors leaped to their feet and the ground beneath them shook with the clashing sound of their arms.

A great voice demanded from their midst, "Who rang the bell? Has the day come?"

The terror-stricken sorcerer shouted, "No, the day has not come! Sleep on!"

Fascinated, March watched the mighty host in motion, and his eyes were blinded by the ranks of glittering steel arms which flashed in the cave like flames.

"Arthur!" said the voice. "Awake, Arthur the Great! The bell has rung, and the day is breaking!"

"No," cried the sorcerer, "it is still night. Sleep on, Arthur the Great!"

But Arthur was standing on the golden throne, the jewels in his crown shining like glittering stars above his army.

Strong and sweet as the sound of a thousand waters was his voice as he said, "My warriors, the day has not come when the Black Eagle and the Golden Eagle shall go to fight one another. It is only a seeker after gold who has rung the bell. Sleep on. The morn of Wales has not yet dawned."

A peaceful sigh swept over the cave, and again the soldiers lay down and slept and the knights at the round table slept, and sleep sealed once more the eyes of Arthur the Great.

The sorcerer hurried toward the door of the cave, but March put his hand in his pocket and took out the gold and left it behind him in the cave of Arthur. When they had moved the stone back in its place, the sorcerer van-

ished, and March went back to his master's, his heart
still dazzled with what he had seen. In his hand was his
hazel staff, which served him well for the rest of his
happy life.

IRELAND

THE CHILDREN OF LIR

When the five kings of Ireland met to choose which
of them should have the chief kingship over them, they
chose Dearg, son of Daghda, because Daghda had been
a great Druid and Dearg was the eldest of his father's
sons. But King Lir of the Hill of the White Field had
expected that he would be elected; and he left the council and went home to the Hill of the White Field in
displeasure. The other kings wanted to follow Lir and
wound him for not yielding obedience to Dearg.

But Dearg said, "Let us not fight, but bind Lir to us
with bonds of kinship, so that there may be peace in
the land. Tell him that he may choose for wife one of
the three most beautiful maidens in Erin, one of the
daughters of Oilell of Aran, one of my three foster
children."

So the messengers went to Lir, and Lir was glad, and
set out the following day with fifty chariots from the
Hill of the White Field. And he came to the Lake of
the Red Eye near Killaloe. And he chose Ove, the eldest
and noblest of the three daughters. And Lir and Ove

were married and returned to the Hill of the White Field.

There were born to them twins, a son and a daughter, and Lir named them Aod and Fingula. Then two more sons were born, Fiachra and Conn. When they came, Ove died, and bitterly Lir mourned for her and would have perished of grief had it not been for the great love he bore his children.

Dearg the King grieved for Lir, and sent a message to him: "We weep for Ove for your sake, O Lir; but that our friendship may not be lessened, I give you her sister, Oifa, for a wife."

And Lir married Oifa and took her to his house on the Hill of the White Field.

At first Oifa felt affection for the children of Lir and her sister, but soon she began to grow jealous. Lir doted upon his little ones; they always slept in beds in front of their father, and each morning he arose at dawn and lay down among his children. Oifa was gnawed by jealousy, and she regarded the children with hatred and enmity and resolved to do them evil.

One day she caused her chariot to be yoked, and she took the children of Lir into it and drove to the Lake of the Red Eye. There she said to the servants, "Kill the four children of Lir, and I will reward you marvelously."

But the people refused, for they loved the children of Lir. She would have raised a sword and killed them herself, but her own weakness prevented her. So she commanded the children of Lir to bathe in the lake.

And as soon as they were in the water, Oifa struck

them with a Druid's wand of spells and wizardry, and changed them into four beautiful white swans. And she sang this song over them:

Live now upon the wild waves, children of Lir!
Henceforth your cries shall be with the flocks of birds!

And Fingula, the little daughter of Lir, answered:

We know you now, O wicked witch!
We shall be driven from wave to cold green wave,
And sometimes we shall rest upon the headlands.
But nothing can stop your punishment or save
Your soul from demons! Though our bodies be
Upon the windy lake, our thoughts will fly
Home to our father, Lir, whom we shall love,
Despite your evil spell, until we die!

And again she spoke, "Tell us how long must last this woe you have brought upon us."

Oifa laughed and said, "Never shall you be free until the woman from the south marries the man from the north, until Lairgnen of Connaught is united to Deoch of Munster, nor shall any man have power to release you from the bodies of swans. Nine hundred years must you wander over the lakes and rivers of Erin. This only will I grant you: that you retain your own speech, and there shall be no music in the world equal to the plaintive music you shall sing."

Then Oifa rode on to the hall of Dearg the King. When the nobles of the court asked the whereabouts of the children of Lir, she replied, "Lir will not trust them to Dearg the King."

But Dearg suspected that she had played some treachery on Lir and his children and straightway he sent messengers to Lir, to the Hill of the White Field.

"Why have you come?" Lir asked the messengers.

"To fetch your children, Lir," they answered.

"Have they not reached you with Oifa?" said Lir anxiously.

"They have not," said the messengers, "and Oifa said you would not let the children go with her."

Then Lir knew that Oifa had done some wrong to his beloved children, and his heart grieved, and he set out toward the Lake of the Red Eye.

When the children of Lir saw him coming, Fingula began to sing.

> *Let us move to the shore, O Aod,*
> *Fiachra and comely Conn.*
> *Here is our father come to seek*
> *Where his little ones have gone.*

When King Lir heard the swans speaking with human voices, he asked them who they were.

And Fingula answered, "We are your own children, O Lir, changed into swans by your wife, our mother's sister, because of her jealousy and hatred of us."

"How long must this spell be upon you?" asked Lir.

And Fingula replied, "Until the woman from the south and the man from the north come together, until Lairgnen of Connaught shall wed Deoch of Munster, and we must wander the lakes and streams of Erin for nine hundred years."

Then Lir and his horsemen lamented greatly, and they stayed by the shores of the lake listening to the wild sweet music of the swans until the swans flew away. Then Lir rode on to the halls of Dearg the King and told Dearg what Oifa had done to his children. And Dearg was angry, and he put his Druid's power on Oifa and commanded her to say what shape on earth she considered the worst of all. She said it would be the form of an air demon.

"Then become one," said Dearg, and he struck her with his Druid's wand of spells and wizardry, and she changed into an air demon and flew away. "You shall be an air demon forever," said Dearg, "and none may ever release you."

The children of Lir lived on the Lake of the Red Eye and delighted the clans with the sweet music of their songs. But at last the appointed time came for them to leave the Lake of the Red Eye; and Fingula sang a farewell lay.

> *Farewell, O Dearg, the Druid King,*
> *With your brave sword and glittering shield!*
> *Farewell, beloved father, Lir,*
> *Lord of the Hill of the White Field!*
>
> *We go to pass the appointed time*
> *Far away from the haunts of men*
> *In the rocking current of the Moyle,*
> *And we shall not return again*

Till Deoch come to Lairgnen. So,
Fly up, my brothers, let us leave
The tribe we love behind who stands
On the green shore and loudly grieves.

And Aod and Fiachra and Conn rose into the air after their sister, and the four white swans flew high out of sight. At last they reached the Moyle, between Erin and Albain.

The men of Erin were filled with sorrow at their departure, and it was proclaimed throughout Erin that henceforth no swan should be killed.

The swans were alone, filled with cold and grief. Then a tempest came upon them, and Fingula said, "Brothers, in case the winds should separate us, let us choose a place to meet again."

And Conn said, "Let us meet, O sister, at the Rock of the Seals."

The winds roared and lightning flashed, thunder rolled down the heavens, and the waves rose up black and stormy, and the children of Lir were scattered over the tempest-battered sea. When the storm was over at last, there came a calm, and Fingula, solitary on the waters, sang plaintively.

Woe on me that I am still alive!
My wings are frozen by these bitter weathers!
O beloved three, O beloved three,
Who hid beneath the shelter of my feathers!
Until the dead return unto the living,
I and the three shall never meet again!

And she flew to the Lake of the Seals and flew down
to the Rock of the Seals to wait. Soon she saw Conn
coming toward her slowly and with drenched feathers,
and Fiachra also, cold and wet and faint, and they were
too exhausted to speak. Then Aod came, and she put
him under the feathers of her breast, and Fiachra under
her right wing, and Conn under her left wing, and sang
them to sleep.

When the time came for the children of Lir to leave
the Moyle, they flew to the Bay of Erris, and remained
there until the time of their fate. Then they flew to the
Hill of the White Field, but all was desolate and empty.
There was no dwelling place; there were only green
tangles and forests of nettles. And Fingula and her three
brothers came close together and wept, and she sang
a song of grief.

> *Uchone! How bitter is the heart*
> *Beneath my snow-white wings,*
> *To see our father's place forlorn,*
> *No feasts, no valiant kings,*
>
> *No drinking-horns, no happy songs*
> *Within the vanished door!*
> *Uchone! Our father, Lir, the King,*
> *Lives on earth no more.*
>
> *Much have we suffered, much endured,*
> *But this is the sharpest thorn—*
> *There lives no man who knoweth us*
> *In the house where we were born.*

So the children of Lir flew away to the Glory Isle of Brandan, the saint, and they settled upon the Lake of the Birds, until holy Patrick came to Erin and holy Mac Howg came to Glory Isle.

The first night that Mac Howg came to Glory Isle, the children of Lir heard the sound of his bell ringing matins, and they were terrified at the strange voice of the bell. The brothers flew up and down in fear, and Fingula called, "What is it, beloved brothers?"

"We do not know what strange voice it is we hear," said Fiachra.

And Mac Howg came down to the shore and said to them, "Are you the children of Lir?"

"We are," said Conn.

"Thanks be to God!" said the saint. "It is for your sakes I have come to this Isle beyond every other island in Erin. Come now to land and put your trust in me."

So they came to shore, and he made for them chains of bright silver, and he put a chain between Aod and Fingula, and a chain between Fiachra and Conn.

Now it happened that at this time Lairgnen, prince of Connaught, was to wed Deoch, the daughter of the King of Munster. Deoch had heard of the four swans and she said she would not marry until she possessed the marvelous birds of Glory Isle. Lairgnen sent to Mac Howg, demanding the swans, but the saint refused to give them up. So both Lairgnen and Deoch traveled to Glory Isle.

Lairgnen went to seize the birds from the altar, but the instant he touched them, their feathers fell off, and the three sons of Lir became three withered old men, and Fingula a withered old woman. And Lairgnen and Deoch hastened away. But Fingula chanted this lay:

> *Come and baptize us, O Saint,*
> *For this day I see our grave.*
> *Place Fiachra and Conn at my sides,*
> *And on my breast, between my two arms,*
> *Place Aod, my beautiful brother.*

And the saint baptized them, and they died, and were buried, Fiachra and Conn on either side of Fingula, and Aod before her face. And the saint raised a cairn for them and on it he wrote their names in runes, Fingula, Aod, Fiachra, and Conn, the beautiful children of Lir.

Poland ❧ ❧ ❧ ❧ ❧

MR. WHIRLWIND, SHOEMAKER

IN A CITY IN POLAND THERE LIVED AT ONE TIME A slender shoemaker who was nicknamed Mr. Whirlwind. He was called Mr. Whirlwind because, no matter how slowly he started to do something, he kept going faster and faster and faster until he was thoroughly exhausted and had gotten himself into amazing trouble.

When he started out for the market to buy himself a little meat or cheese, he walked slowly at first. He made himself walk very slowly, but then he began to think about the leaves on the trees or what made cats purr or why the little birds' throats wobbled in and out as they sang—and the first thing he knew, he was walking faster, and then faster, and still faster, until he had overtaken and left behind the horses and the cabs and the trolley cars, and was tearing along like the wind.

Sometimes the people who saw him racing down the street like a leaf in a gale thought he was chasing a thief, and chased with him. Mr. Whirlwind, intent on his own thoughts, left them far behind, out of breath and out of temper.

Sometimes people thought Mr. Whirlwind himself was a thief trying to escape, and they started chasing *him*, shouting for the police and hurling vegetables and stones at him. But usually Mr. Whirlwind, thinking about his cat's new tiger kittens, or the sound grass made when it grew, or why bird shadows seemed to fly faster than the birds, soon outdistanced his pursuers and their vegetables and ran on until he remembered that he was running. Then he was ashamed of himself and took himself to task: "Oh, my awl and nails, here I've been a whirlwind again!"

C257973

GO SCHOOLS

Two or three times when he was streaking along, he stumbled and fell, and all the people behind him fell on top of him, so that he nearly smothered. Although he was by nature a merry soul, this acceleration of his made Mr. Whirlwind very sad.

When he was at home and began to cobble shoes, it was even worse. He would nail the heel lightly at first, hammering very gently—then his hammer went a little faster, then faster, then faster still and harder, until the heel was smashed to fragments and the shoe was useless. Stricken by remorse, Mr. Whirlwind would take off his apron and hurry out to buy new shoes for his customer. The art of cobbling, therefore, brought Mr. Whirlwind no profit.

The same thing happened when he spoke. He began very slowly and clearly, so that every word was understood. But in a minute he was speaking faster, and then faster, and faster still, until all his words ran together and he sounded as if he were humming instead of talking.

It worried Mr. Whirlwind very much, but he couldn't seem to do anything about it.

Mrs. Lovepenny, a rich but stingy widow, lived on the same street, uphill from the cobbler's shop, in a large, impressive mansion. One fine spring day she sent her housemaid to Mr. Whirlwind with a pair of shoes to be soled. When Mr. Whirlwind looked at the shoes, he sat down on his bench with a thump. They were patched upon patches, and each patch was patched three times, and he grew quite dizzy staring at them.

The maid asked him to have the shoes ready on the morrow, for her mistress had no other shoes to wear when she wished to go out. Mr. Whirlwind started to nod his head but caught himself in time and said, "The grass is growing." It was a good thing that the maid left the shop in a hurry, or else he would have said so rapidly that the grass was growing, she would have heard it growing right out of the floor of the shop.

Mr. Whirlwind took one shoe and started to work. He nailed and sewed, sewed and nailed, nailed and sewed; sewed and nailed, working faster, and then faster, and faster still, until there wasn't a scrap of shoe left. Surprised and worried, Mr. Whirlwind took the other shoe to another cobbler and bought a pair of shoes the same size.

The next morning he set out for the home of Mrs. Lovepenny with the pair of new shoes, and since she lived just up the street, he didn't have time to begin rushing. He went up the front steps and rang the bell.

There was a letter box on the right-hand side of the

door, and on the left-hand side there was a small round opening covered by a brass plate. Anyone inside the house could move the plate aside and see who was ringing the bell.

No one opened the door for Mr. Whirlwind. The servants were out and Mrs. Lovepenny never answered the bell herself. Mr. Whirlwind became impatient and began tapping on the brass plate with his fingers. Mrs. Lovepenny heard the tapping, and it was such an unusual sound that she thought she would take a peek through the peephole and see who was there.

At first Mr. Whirlwind tapped very slowly and very lightly, and then he tapped a little faster, and then faster, and faster still, and at last he was tapping so rapidly and so hard that when Mrs. Lovepenny moved aside the brass plate to peek out, he poked her right in the eye. And Mrs. Lovepenny screamed and fainted.

Mr. Whirlwind was terrified and ran away so fast he couldn't stop until he was far beyond the edge of the city. It was very late in the evening when he got home to his shop again, the shoes still under his arm.

The next morning he was sitting at his workbench, sadly counting nails, when Mrs. Lovepenny's housemaid appeared at the door.

"Good morning, only it isn't," said Mr. Whirlwind in a doleful voice.

"To be sure, it isn't," replied the maid. "My mistress was attacked by robbers yesterday, and they would have killed her if the doors hadn't been locked!"

Pretending to be excited, Mr. Whirlwind exclaimed, "My awl and nails! What happened?"

"Oh, there were three robbers!" said the maid. "One of them tried to cut out Mrs. Lovepenny's eye with a big knife!"

"My nails and awl!" said Mr. Whirlwind, seeming to believe every word of the girl's fantastic story. "Nobody's safe these days. It's terrible." And he began to nod his head gravely back and forth and back and forth.

At first he nodded his head very slowly, then he nodded faster, and then faster, and faster still, until he was nodding his head backward and forward so rapidly and violently that his neck stretched and his own head hit him first in his stomach and then in his back. And every time he struck his stomach, he grunted, and every time he struck his own back, he groaned. Finally he had to seize his head in his two hands to hold it still, and he had a difficult time trying to catch it, but at length he did and gave it a shake and a push down on his neck.

The maid's eyes were popping out of her own head with astonishment, but she was even more amazed when Mr. Whirlwind, having gotten control of his head, handed her the shoes for Mrs. Lovepenny.

"But these are new shoes, and the ones I gave you were old and patched!" cried the maid.

Mr. Whirlwind started to nod again and stopped himself. "I know, but I'm a good cobbler," he said modestly. "I can repair shoes that are in the worst possible shape and make them look like new. I know my business, you see."

"Goodness, I should say you do," she said in an awed voice, and took the shoes as carefully as if they were made of blown glass, and went out of the shop.

Mr. Whirlwind, as soon as she was out of hearing, began to laugh. He laughed and laughed because he had tricked her, and he felt very merry for the rest of the morning.

But that afternoon, back came the maid dragging a laundry basket.

"What have you there?" asked Mr. Whirlwind.

"Shoes," said the girl.

And shoes they were—thirty pairs of them, in the most awful condition imaginable. They were ragged, without heels, without soles, ripped and torn, and moldy from having been so long in Mrs. Lovepenny's closets. When he saw so many shoes, in such a state that no shoemaker could possibly repair them, his face fell so hard that his chin bumped the workbench.

"I won't even try to repair such shoes!" shouted Mr. Whirlwind angrily. "Such shoes! Such shoes, such shoes, such shoes, s-shoes, shoes, shoes, s-shoes, s-shoes, shs-shzzzz," and he sounded like an irritated steam engine.

The frightened maid ran out of the shop and ran all the way home. And she told Mrs. Lovepenny she wouldn't go to Mr. Whirlwind's shop again because he was a magician and wicked.

But Mrs. Lovepenny said, "Pshaw! He can make new shoes out of old ones!" But she couldn't make the girl return to the shop, so she had to go herself.

She put on her best Sunday dress, put on her best hat

with a big white feather, and set out, thinking that when the shoemaker saw what an elegant lady she was, he would be glad to repair her shoes. And she swished into the dim little shop.

For a long time, Mr. Whirlwind, who was very emotional and very tenderhearted, had wanted to get married, but he had never seen any lady who made his pulse gallop. The instant Mrs. Lovepenny set her foot inside his shop, he gulped and shivered and fell head over heels in love. Being a man of action, down on his knees went Mr. Whirlwind and asked her to marry him.

Mrs. Lovepenny, who hadn't had a chance to say a word about the shoes, was furious. "Do you think I'd marry a common shoemaker?" she snapped, and flounced out of the shop and hurried home, white with anger.

But when she had cooled off, she regretted that she hadn't prevailed upon Mr. Whirlwind to repair her shoes. She tried to think of a way to persuade him, and finally she had a wonderful idea.

The following day she sent him this letter by a messenger.

> My dear Mr. Whirlwind—
>   If you will repair all the shoes for me, I will become your wife.
>
>   Mrs. Lovepenny.

And she sent two pink roses with the letter, to make it more alluring.

In the meantime, Mr. Whirlwind sat in his shop, not even bothering to count nails, and he was profoundly sad. He sighed heavily, and tears rolled down his cheeks. He was sure that if he were not a cobbler, Mrs. Lovepenny would marry him. And he wondered what to do about it. At length he decided to sell his equipment and his shop and to become something else—a lawyer or a banker or a doctor or something.

He wiped his tears away and blew his nose and felt cheerful again. He put on his good suit and was just about to start out to sell his equipment when the messenger arrived with Mrs. Lovepenny's letter and the two pink roses.

Mr. Whirlwind was so overjoyed that he flung his arms about the surprised messenger and hugged him and kissed him. At first the messenger was quite pleased: he had never been hugged and kissed before for delivering a letter. But when Mr. Whirlwind nearly cracked his ribs, he became anxious, and he tripped Mr. Whirlwind and they both fell on the floor in a heap. The messenger untangled himself and ran out of the shop.

Mr. Whirlwind limped to his bench and sat down, sniffing the roses. He rubbed his knee and sniffed. "Oh, dear, there I've gone and been a whirlwind again," he thought remorsefully. He read Mrs. Lovepenny's letter a second time. He could never in this world repair the thirty pairs of shoes, and he had no money with which to buy thirty new pairs. He didn't know what to do.

At last he had an idea. He hurried to another shoe-maker, told him the story, and asked him to lend him thirty pairs of shoes. "As soon as I'm married to Mrs.

Lovepenny," said Mr. Whirlwind. "I'll pay you twice over for them."

The shoemaker agreed, and they picked out the shoes.

Late that afternoon, Mr. Whirlwind called upon Mrs. Lovepenny. "Here are the shoes, my dear," he said, beaming.

Mrs. Lovepenny was astonished. "How could you fix so many shoes in so short a time?" she asked.

"Oh, it's nothing. I make thirty pairs of shoes a day," lied Mr. Whirlwind, not even blinking. And he knelt down and again asked Mrs. Lovepenny to marry him.

"Wait just a minute," she said, and went into the next room. She sat down at her desk. If Mr. Whirlwind could fix thirty pairs of shoes in one day, in one year, which has three hundred and sixty-five days, he could fix

$$\begin{array}{r} 365 \\ \times 30 \\ \hline \end{array}$$

And that was as far as she got, for she didn't know much about multiplying. But she was sure it would be hundreds of pairs.

She hurried back and told Mr. Whirlwind that she would become his wife, and Mr. Whirlwind was terribly happy.

They gave each other a ring, and then they decided to go for a walk on the promenade. Mr. Whirlwind asked her to wait while he went home and changed his clothes.

He put on his striped trousers, his frock coat, his stovepipe hat, and took his large silk umbrella and set out again. At a flower shop he bought two large bunches of pink roses, one for Mrs. Lovepenny and one for himself.

Mrs. Lovepenny was waiting for him, dressed in her best dress and wearing the hat with the white feather.

Smiling and very proud of each other, they set out hand in hand, each carrying a bunch of roses. Everybody gazed at them admiringly, and they were very happy.

Mr. Whirlwind reminded himself that he must be careful not to get the speeding fever. Then he thought that when he had married Mrs. Lovepenny, he would be a rich man, and he let his mind wander pleasantly into the future. Little by little he began to increase his pace without knowing it.

"Please don't walk so fast!" cried Mrs. Lovepenny, panting. "I can't get my breath! I'm all out of it!" The stout widow's face was as pink as her bunch of roses. "Please, Mr. Whirlwind!"

But Mr. Whirlwind was going too fast even to slow down, much as he wanted to. He walked faster, and then faster, and faster still, overtaking and passing the horses and the cabs and the trolley cars, tearing along like the wind.

Mrs. Lovepenny, still holding on to Mr. Whirlwind's hand, stumbled and fell, but Mr. Whirlwind could not stop. She screamed and screamed, but he dragged her along over the cobblestones, not knowing where he was going, but having to get there. Finally some people in the crowd managed to block Mr. Whirlwind's flight; he bumped head on into them and stopped and said, "Oh, I beg your pardon!"

Mrs. Lovepenny had fainted, her best dress was torn and dirty, her face was dirty, and her best hat with its lovely white feather was lost. Bruised and shaken, she was taken home in a cab. Her servants put her to bed and called the doctor, who said she must stay in bed for three months. And that was the end of the romance between Mrs. Lovepenny and Mr. Whirlwind. Indeed, at the very whisper of his name, she went into hysterics.

The shoemaker who had lent the thirty pairs of shoes demanded that Mr. Whirlwind pay him twice over, according to their contract. But Mr. Whirlwind had no money, as usual. So he was thrown into debtor's prison.

And there he sat in his small dark cell, with no nails to count, brooding and brooding and wishing the devil would take his speeding fever. Mr. Whirlwind's kind face became longer and longer, and as he rocked back and forth in his great unhappiness, he bumped his chin again and again against the hard stone floor.

SAINT STANISLAW AND THE WOLF

Long ago in Poland, when animals could talk, there lived in a small hut in a deep forest a very holy man, Saint Stanislaw. So gentle was he, and so filled with compassion for all the creatures of earth, that the wild beasts of the forest, from the lion and the bear down to the puff-tailed rabbit and the pert-tailed squirrel, often stopped to talk with him. The Saint always listened to them with patience and sympathy, and always he gave them excellent advice. All of the wild creatures regarded him as their constant friend and they loved him very much.

One sunny morning as he was walking through the woods, listening to the birds and saying his prayers, a big gray wolf came up to him.

"Good morning, Saint Stanislaw," said the wolf, licking his hand.

"Good morning, gray brother," said the Saint. "Isn't this a lovely morning?"

"Yes, it is, I suppose," said the wolf in a mournful voice.

"You sound sorrowful," said Saint Stanislaw. "What's the trouble?"

"It isn't really trouble," answered the wolf, "but I can't stop thinking about it."

"About what?"

"Food," said the wolf. "I've tasted many kinds of meat in my lifetime—lamb and goat and sheep, and when I was old enough and strong enough, I had stag and horse. But I've never tasted human flesh, and the jackal says it's tender and sweet."

"The jackal is wrong," said Saint Stanislaw. "Human flesh is bitter and tough. Don't ever think of touching it."

The wolf shook his gray head. "I'm sure you're mistaken, great Saint. Why would my cousin, the jackal, say it was sweet if it weren't? He says it's delicious."

"You ought to know why. Your cousin is wily and he thinks he can distract you from hunting the lamb and the deer. Pay no attention to him." And Saint Stanislaw rubbed the wolf behind his ears.

"That feels good," said the wolf. "But please let me taste human flesh just this once."

"You'll be sorry," warned the Saint.

"I don't care a cobweb," said the wolf. "I just want to satisfy my curiosity for once in my life."

Finally the Saint said, "All right, I'll permit you to devour a human being, but on these conditions: you may not eat a little boy with a book under his arm going to school, and you may not eat an old man whose beard and hair are white like mine. The only human you may eat is a blacksmith. Remember that!"

"I'll remember, great Saint," said the wolf, and licking his chops, he loped away through the woods. At the edge of the road he sat down to wait for the blacksmith.

He looked up and down and listened, and he saw that someone was coming down the road. He sniffed the air greedily and called out, "Who are you?"

It was a child with a book under his arm, and he answered, "Can't you see that I'm a little boy with a spelling book who has to go to school?"

"Hurry up, then," said the wolf, "or you'll be late. A schoolboy is good for nothing." And he sat back on his haunches to wait, but he was growing pretty hungry.

He looked up and down and listened, and he saw that

someone was coming down the road. He stretched out his muzzle eagerly and called, "Who are you?"

It was an old man with white hair and a white beard like the great Saint's, and he answered, "I am a very old man, and I am going to the next village to pray in the church."

"God be with you, then," said the wolf, "and take you to the church safely. I'm waiting for someone else."

He looked up and down and listened, and he saw that someone was coming down the road. He sharpened his teeth and called out, "Who are you?"

It was a bold young blacksmith, wearing a leather jerkin, who came whistling along the road. "Don't you see that I'm a blacksmith? But what are you sitting here for?"

The wolf grinned. "I'm waiting to eat you up, blacksmith."

"Why?" asked the young man.

"Because I'm hungry," said the wolf, "and Saint Stanislaw said that I might devour a blacksmith."

"Then before I die, friend wolf, let me wash myself in the pond beyond the bushes. My face is black with soot, and my arms and hair are powdered with ashes from the forge."

"Go ahead and wash yourself," said the wolf, "but please hurry because I am very hungry. And don't try to run away, because if you do, I'll catch you and tear you to pieces."

"I have no doubt of it," said the blacksmith with a wry smile. "I'll be as quick as I can."

He pushed through the bushes to the pond, quickly cut a stout cudgel and hid it under his jacket. Then noisily he splashed his big hands in the water and raised them over and over to his smudged face until he had washed it clean. Then he hastened back to the road.

"Friend wolf," he said, "I am ready, but I'm dripping wet. Will you allow me to dry my face and hands on your long gray brush?"

"I'm very uncomfortable when my fur is wet," said the wolf a trifle peevishly. "However, since I'm going to eat you right away, you might as well dry yourself for once on the fur of my tail." And the wolf turned around.

The blacksmith immediately seized the wolf's thick tail and wound it tightly three times around his powerful wrist. Then he pulled out the heavy club and beat the wolf until the creature lay half dead in the road. He tossed the club into the bushes, thrust his hands in his pockets, and went on down the road, whistling merrily.

Some hours later, the poor wolf regained his senses, and dragged himself back to the forest, bruised and aching in every joint. He howled painfully as he limped along, and his mind hurt him as well as his beaten body.

Saint Stanislaw in his small bare hut heard the crying of the injured wolf, and he set out at once to find him and help him. He found the wolf sitting on a patch of moss, licking a welt on his left hind haunch and whimpering softly.

"Wolf, what happened?" asked the Saint kindly.

"Oh, great Saint!" sobbed the wolf. "Human flesh is

terribly bitter! It's like gall and wormwood! Ow—I hurt!"

"Is it as bitter as all that?" asked the Saint, repressing a smile.

"You don't know—you can't know, Saint Stanislaw!" said the shivering wolf. "Lamb and venison are good, but the flesh of a blacksmith—"

"What is it like?" asked the Saint. "Come here, and I'll bandage your wounds."

"Oh, never mention it to me again!" begged the wolf, limping to the Saint's side.

The Saint rubbed the wolf behind the ears. "Don't worry, my friend," he said, with a gentle laugh. "I won't."

THE JESTER WHO FOOLED A KING

A very long time ago, when King Jan ruled the kingdom of Poland, there had lived in the royal palace for many years a jester named Matenko.

Before old age had stiffened his joints and dulled his wits, Matenko had been the favorite clown in King Jan's household, delighting the King and the Queen, the lords and the ladies, with his antics and his jokes. But now when he performed, the nobles simply yawned, and finally they complained so much that King Jan sent for Matenko to dismiss him.

The old clown approached the King slowly, not only because his bones ached, but because his heart was filled with sorrow. He bent his purple and pink knee and his respectful but stiff bones cracked loudly, and he wished he could die then and there.

King Jan sighed. "My dear old joker," he said sadly, "for a lifetime you have been a merry clown, but age has caught you at last. Put away your gay clothes now, and become a citizen." The King sighed once more and straightened his crown. "I've bought a little house in the village for you and your wife, Elzunia. I'm sorry to say I can give you only a little money to live on, Matenko, because the last court ball was terribly expensive, and the treasury is nearly empty."

"I understand, Your Majesty," said Matenko, and he managed to bow himself out of the royal chamber without too much creaking. He removed his gay clown's clothes and the absurd cap with donkey ears, and laid aside his brightly colored rattle. Then he offered his arm to his wife, Elzunia, and together they made their way to the village to live out their lives in the small cottage the King had given them.

Before long Matenko and Elzunia were penniless, for the King had given them only a few pieces of gold. And there was nothing for the old couple to do. Matenko would willingly have gone to work, but who would give work to an old man who knew nothing except how to act like a fool? They were very hungry, but they had no money for bread; and all day and all night they thought of their poverty and were filled with despair.

One night Matenko turned to his wife and asked, "Elzunia, dear, are you asleep?"

"No, Matenko," she answered.

"I have an idea," he said. "Tomorrow you will go to the Queen and tell her that I have died. But before you go, rub both your eyes hard with a raw onion."

"Oh," said Elzunia. "I see."

The next morning she appeared before the Queen with her eyes swollen as if she had been crying long and bitterly.

The Queen asked, sincerely troubled, "Dear Elzunia, why are you grieving so?"

Elzunia answered, sobbing, "Most gracious Queen, last night at eleven o'clock my good husband died. How can I continue to live?"

"Oh, you poor woman!" said the Queen in compassion. "I'm terribly sorry. I know how I would feel if anything happened to King Jan. Here, perhaps this will help to give our old jester a decent burial, and you'll have something left to live on." And she handed Elzunia her little blue-embroidered purse containing fifty pieces of gold.

When she reached home, Elzunia, laughing, showed Matenko what the Queen had given her. "It was easy, my love. It's too bad you can't die every day," she said, and gave a quick girlish squeak when Matenko kissed her.

"Now," he said, "it's your turn to die. Tomorrow I'll go to the King and tell him that you have left me desolate." And he kissed his old wife again for luck.

The following day, the old clown twisted his face into an expression of misery and sorrow and set out for the palace. As he bowed before King Jan, he groaned mightily and his shoulders shook with sobs.

"Oh, my poor old joker!" said the King with the utmost compassion. "What misfortune has happened to you?"

Matenko wiped his eyes. "Gracious Majesty, my dear wife entrusted her soul to God only this morning. She is lying dead in our little cottage, and I am all alone in the world and penniless."

"My poor clown," said the King gently, "take this purse of gold and do not grieve so desperately. But I know how I would feel, should anything happen to my Queen."

When Matenko reached the cottage, he poured the money from the purse onto the table and found that the King had given him two hundred pieces of gold.

"My dear wife," said Matenko, putting his arm around her, "the King's sympathy, as you see, is worth more than the Queen's. We have two hundred and fifty pieces of gold, so we won't starve for a little while. But we'd better lie down and pretend we're dead, in case the King and Queen come to find out if we really are."

And with much giggling on the part of Elzunia and much chuckling on the part of Matenko, they put a thick coating of flour on each other's face. Then they lay down on the bare floor of the cottage and covered themselves carefully with a white muslin sheet.

"Stop laughing," said Matenko, trying to compose his features into a semblance of death.

"*You* stop," retorted Elzunia. "You're making me shake off all my flour!"

And there they lay quietly with one candle burning at their heads and one candle burning at their feet.

At the palace, in the meantime, a fine argument was going on, for the Queen declared that the old jester was dead, whereas the King insisted that it was not the clown but his wife who had died. They argued back and forth and got nowhere, and at last the King suggested that they go to the cottage and see for themselves. The Queen agreed, and they summoned the royal coach.

At Matenko's house they found the old jester and his wife lying on the floor under a white shroud, with candles for the dead burning at their heads and their feet. King Jan and his Queen looked at each other, and tears filled their eyes, for they had loved their old clown. They prayed for the departed souls of Matenko and Elzunia, and the Queen wiped her eyes and the King coughed loudly.

As they were about to leave the little house, King Jan said to the Queen, "I wonder which of the two old folks died first."

"In all honesty, my beloved King," replied the jester from the floor, "my wife died first, but I was dead before."

"Oh, you rascals!" The King choked and laughed. "Get up immediately and tell me what this trickery means!"

Matenko was reluctant to tell how poor he and

Elzunia had been, but King Jan understood at once and realized that he was to blame. He gave Matenko another purse of two hundred pieces of gold, but asked him to promise never again to use his wits dishonestly.

And with a chuckle the old clown promised.

China   ✶   ✶   ✶   ✶   ✶

THE GODS KNOW

IN THE TEMPLE COURT THE SACRED HORSE WAS IN A temper. He glared at a thin-faced, ragged little girl who was peering through the bars at him. "That rascal of an attendant has been stealing my bean cake again!" he said furiously. "And I am the Sacred Horse! I don't know what my life is coming to!"

The little girl held a dirty small hand through the bars. "You may have my bread, and perhaps it will keep you from being so hungry."

The Sacred Horse rolled his eyes suspiciously at the very small piece of coarse pone she held out; then he accepted it, and it tasted quite good. Her dark eyes smiled at him. "Well, who are you?" he asked crossly, without even saying thank you.

"I don't know," she answered gravely. "I think I fell from the moon."

The Horse couldn't help laughing. "But who takes care of you?"

"I do."

"How old are you?"

"Nine. I sleep anywhere, in the fields or under the trees or in the temple if it rains. And I get so lonely sometimes, I wish I were dead."

When he saw the tears in her soft eyes, the Sacred Horse swallowed and blinked, himself, and said hastily, "There, my child, don't cry. I've just been thinking how differently you and I feel about this freedom you have. I've been shut up in this temple for fifteen years, and I would love to roam about from place to place and sleep in the fields and under the trees as you do."

The little girl scrubbed her eyes with a grimy fist and stared at him in astonishment. "You would?"

"I certainly would. Here I am imprisoned in this temple court for fools to gaze at, believing that I am sacred."

"But aren't you?"

The Horse shook his head. "Not half as much as you, my dear, who gave me your crust of bread."

"I should think you'd like it," she protested, "having people worship you and offer up their incense in your name.

"Well, I don't," said the Horse emphatically. "I'll admit that my head was turned when I was a young colt, and I was very conceited for a while at the sight of people coming to offer me their prayers and bowing down before me. But I soon outgrew that."

The child nodded wisely. "There isn't much sense in vanity."

The Horse suppressed a smile. "No, there isn't." He sighed. "And then I grew impatient of being a prisoner.

I tried twice to get away, but my jailers caught me. Then I refused to eat and meant to starve myself to death, but after I was good and hungry, that seemed pretty silly. And now this scoundrel has taken to robbing me of my bean cake. "I could kick!" said the Sacred Horse fiercely.

"You still have much more to eat than we poor people. I'd be happy to get in three days what they give you at one feeding."

"Hmm," said the Horse thoughtfully. "You would? Then I'll tell you what let's do—let's change places!"

"What?"

"Oh, I don't mean that you change into a horse and I into a girl," he said, chuckling. "That would be rather impossible. But if you'll come here tonight and let me out, then you may come in and take my place. I'll have the freedom I want so much, and you'll have fun being worshiped and fed by the people."

The little girl was breathless. "But won't they kill me for letting you loose and pretending that I'm sacred?"

"I told you," said the Horse, a trifle exasperated, "you're just as sacred as I am. And they'll simply call it another wonder of the gods when they see you instead of me."

"When do you wish me to come?" she asked, her eyes shining.

"At midnight," said the Horse happily. "Then I can get far beyond Lan T'an before dawn, where people won't know I am the Sacred Horse. Then I shall set out on my adventures."

That night after the moon had risen, and midnight

approached, the little girl hurried to the temple and found the stall of the Sacred Horse.

The Horse was watching for her anxiously. "I was afraid you wouldn't come."

"I promised to come. But what shall I say if the priests and the people ask me any questions?"

The Horse replied, "Say simply, 'The gods know.' Then be silent and look wise. They will be sure that their Sacred Horse has been changed into a goddess. Here is a chest of beautiful silken cloths which are my trappings for state occasions. Drape them around yourself so that your ragged things will not show."

"You are so kind and thoughtful." The little girl drew back the bars and set the Horse free. "Wherever you go, remember you have one friend who will always think of you. And come back if you should grow tired, and I shall comfort you." And she stroked the Horse's neck gently, as high up as she could reach.

He nuzzled her thin cheek in farewell and trotted out through the gateway of the temple court. The child closed the bars of the sacred stall. She wrapped the silken cloths about herself and lay down to sleep, thinking fondly of the Sacred Horse and wishing him happiness on his travels.

A little later she awoke with a start and heard two hoarse voices talking outside the bars of the sacred stall.

"What's a Sacred Horse?" said one roughly. "If he can gallop, that's all we care. This treasure of the Mandarin's is heavy. Sling it on this old nag and we'll get out of this valley before we're captured."

"But what'll happen to us if we're caught on the Sacred Horse?"

"Don't be a coward at this point!" said the first voice angrily. "The Horse can't tell on us, and a little race through the country won't hurt him any." The thief coughed. "Come on, let's get started. Who'll know about it anyhow?"

"The gods know," said a clear sweet voice.

Terror-stricken, the thieves turned and saw a tiny form clad in heavenly raiment and a small fair face with dark eyes that looked into their very souls. They cried out in fear, dropped their plunder and fled into the night.

The little girl laughed gaily at the rumpus she had caused. She opened the bars and pulled and tugged until she had dragged in the heavy bag of the Mandarin's treasure. She opened the bag and spread in the moonlight the silver and golden ornaments, the jade, the precious ivory, and gazed in astonishment at beauty such as she had never dreamed of in her short life. She curled up in the moonlight, feasting her eyes upon these wonders, until once more she fell asleep.

When she awoke, the sun was halfway up the sky and the court was filled with staring people. And in front of the crowd, stood the Mandarin himself, in all his glittering clothes, gazing at the marvel of a child where the Sacred Horse should be. He looked from her to his stolen treasure spread out on the ground, and asked in an awed tone, "Where did you come from, my child?"

"The gods know," she answered gravely.

"But where is the Sacred Horse?"

"The gods know," she replied once more.

The Mandarin's guard of soldiers grew pale, and many of the people fell on their knees, murmuring, "A goddess! She is a goddess!"

The Mandarin waved his jeweled hand toward his treasure. "These were stolen from my palace last night. How did they come here?"

"The gods know," she said again, looking full into his eyes.

"Truly the gods know all," the Mandarin cried, "and this is a miracle they have wrought." And at once he and his followers sank to their knees and pressed their foreheads to the earth before the little girl in the stall of the Sacred Horse.

The people hailed her as the little Goddess of the Bereft and came to pray to her that what had been stolen from them and what they had lost might be returned. They built a great palace for her and came every day to worship her. But the little girl did not forget the Horse and wished that he were there to share her splendor, although she hoped that he was having a fine time adventuring in freedom about the world.

So ten years passed and the little girl grew to womanhood; yet for all her riches and the reverence given her by men, she was lonely and unhappy, for she had no friend.

One night as she was strolling alone about her moonlit inner garden, a servant came to her and kowtowed. "Most gracious goddess," he said, "a strange thing has been happening at the outer gate. An hour ago there

was a rattling at the gate, and when the porter opened it he found an old white horse, riderless, trying to enter. He drove the horse away, but the knocking began again. The more he beats it, the more the horse comes back."

"Let the horse enter," said the girl. "Not even an animal shall be denied an audience."

When the servant returned, he led by the mane an old white horse with drooping head and faltering pace. The girl dismissed the servant and turned to the weary horse.

"Sacred Horse, you have come back!" she cried. "And to you I owe all this homage and splendor!"

"Yes, I have returned," he answered in a disheartened voice. "I have come to beg of you a corner of your stables, where I may die near the one mistress whom I adore."

She gazed at him with pity. "But did you not enjoy the freedom you desired so much?"

"No," he said, gazing at her sadly, "for liberty is nothing without friendship, and friendship is nothing without love. When I ruled in the temple, I was master of men, for they believed me sacred; but in the world where I was free, every man became master. And in neither life did I have friendship. You alone as a little girl were my friend; and now I have returned to ask your protection and to die."

The girl threw her arms about the neck of the Horse and once more stroked him; she laid her head against his neck while tears of compassion fell from her dark eyes.

"Is it possible," asked the Horse hesitantly, "that you, too, are unhappy?"

"The gods know," she answered.

As she spoke, her being was pierced with a wondrous thrill, and lifting her head, she saw that the Horse had vanished and that her arms were about the neck of a young and handsome prince.

"Oh, my beloved," he murmured, holding her close in his arms, "did I not say that liberty is nothing without friendship, and friendship nothing without love?"

"The gods know," she repeated.

"Yes," he said, in a voice shaken with profound and holy passion, "the gods know!"

THE BLUE ROSE

Long ago there lived in China a wise Emperor who had one daughter. His son had begotten a son, so the Emperor was unworried about the succession to his throne. But he was growing old and wished to see his daughter married to a man worthy of her.

His daughter was famed far and wide for her beauty. Her long, slanting eyes were brown as brook water sparkling over sunlit pebbles, her laughter was like a silver bell in her slender throat, and her feet were the smallest in all the world. Furthermore, she was as wise as she was beautiful, and she chanted the songs of the great poets better than any scholar in China, young or old, who might roll the three silver balls in his fingers.

As soon as it was heard that the Emperor wished a

husband for his daughter, a hundred and fifty suitors presented themselves at the palace. The Lord Chamberlain met them in the outer courtyard and told them that the only man who might marry the Emperor's daughter must find and bring back the blue rose. The puzzled suitors asked each other what the blue rose might be and where it might be found. None of them knew, and fifty of them then and there gave up all thought of winning the Emperor's daughter, for they thought the idea of a blue rose absurd as well as impossible.

Of the hundred suitors, after some thought and effort, all abandoned the quest but three men.

One was a rich merchant who went to the largest shop in the city and said, "I want a blue rose, the largest possible."

But the shopkeeper, with kowtows and apologies, explained that he had never heard of blue roses, although he had pink, white, and yellow roses.

The merchant said he must have a blue rose and commanded the shopkeeper to find him one, no matter how difficult it might be to obtain. The shopkeeper promised to do his very best.

Another suitor was an extremely courageous warrior. Riding his stallion, and taking with him a hundred archers and a thousand horsemen, he came into the land of the King of the Five Rivers, the richest king in the world and the possessor of the rarest treasures. The warrior demanded the blue rose, threatening the King with dire doom if he refused to surrender it.

But the King of the Five Rivers, who could not bear

warriors and abhorred fuss, physical violence, and fidgets, looked around at his own bodyguard, who were armed with fans and sunshades. He arose on his royal cushions, tinkled a little silver bell, and said to his servant, "Bring me the blue rose."

The servant returned, bearing on a silken cushion a great blue sapphire carved to represent a full-blown rose with all its petals.

With brief military thanks, the warrior took the sapphire, and went at once to the Emperor's palace, declaring that he had found the blue rose. He was ushered into the Emperor's presence, where he told his story.

The Emperor summoned his daughter and said, "This courageous warrior claims he has brought you the blue rose. Has he accomplished the quest?"

The Princess took the beautiful thing into her narrow hands. After a moment she said, "This is not a rose. It is a blue sapphire, and I have no need of precious stones." She returned it to the warrior with gracious thanks. And the warrior went off to his wars, very much put out.

The merchant heard of the warrior's failure, and he hurried to the shopkeeper, demanding the blue rose. "If you have not found it," he said, "I shall have you put to death, for I am related by marriage to all the chief officials in the kingdom!"

The terrified shopkeeper begged, "Give me three days, sir, and I shall find it without fail."

The merchant granted the three days. The shopkeeper shivered and shook for two days, for he well knew there was no such thing as a blue rose. On the third day he went to his wife and told her about it.

But his wife, who had a certain amount of cleverness, said, "Nonsense! We'll make a blue rose. Go to the chemist for a strong dye to turn a white rose into a blue one!" And she frowned at the shopkeeper.

He hustled to the chemist, who gave him a bottle of red dye and told him to dip the stalk of a white rose into the liquid. The shopkeeper did so, and the white rose turned blue. He took it to the merchant, who hastened with it to the Emperor's palace.

The Emperor summoned his daughter and said. "This wealthy merchant claims he has brought you the blue rose. Has he accomplished the quest?"

The Princess took the flower into her narrow hands. After a moment she said, "This is a white rose, and its stalk has been dipped in a poisonous dye which turned it blue. If a butterfly or a hummingbird were to settle on it, it would die of the fatal fumes. Merchant, take the flower back. I have no need of a false blue rose." She gave it back to the merchant with gracious thanks. And the merchant went off to his trading, very much put out.

The Lord Chief Justice, a skilled statesman, sent for the most famous artist in the land and said, "Make me a china cup, milky in color and perfect in shape, and paint on it a blue rose."

The artist worked for three months on the cup and never was there such a beautiful porcelain cup, so perfect in shape, so delicate in texture, with the blue rose on it like a living flower, plucked in heaven and floating on the rare milk-white porcelain.

The Lord Chief Justice, who was a great lover of porcelain, was overcome with admiration and delight when he saw it. He rewarded the artist and hurried to the Emperor's palace.

The Emperor summoned his daughter and said, "This eminent statesman claims he has brought you the blue rose. Has he accomplished the quest?"

The Princess took the cup into her narrow hands. After a moment she said, "This is the most beautiful bowl of china I have ever seen in my life. If you will permit me to keep it, I shall put it safely aside. For it is so beautiful that no other flower is worthy to be put in it but the blue rose."

The Lord Chief Justice thanked the Princess with many finely turned phrases for accepting the bowl, and went back to his statesmanship, very much put out.

Not long afterward a young roving minstrel chanced through the Emperor's kingdom. He had heard nothing of the quest of the blue rose but went humming on his way, playing on his one-stringed lute and singing whatever came into his head. One evening he leaned up against a dark wall and felt a fresh glory in his heart from the loveliness of the sundown and the color of the oncoming violet twilight. He began to sing a brief song over and over to the monotonous tune of his lute, listening meanwhile to the tree frogs and the wash of the river.

Beside the willow trees I stood
And watched the evening as it came
Across the river: in my heart
I never knew my own love's name.

But from the tangled grass there rose
A bird who over water flew
And in the river's silver tide
I saw a tender flash of blue.

As he sang it the third time, he heard a faint rustle on the wall behind him; looking up, he saw a slender figure white against the twilight, who beckoned to him. Along the wall he found a gate, and there someone was waiting, and he was drawn gently within and led into the shadow of a dark cedar tree. In the growing night, and under the light of the stars, the minstrel and the Princess whispered a thousand things to one another; and the hours fled in silver mist until the east began to lighten. The Princess said that she must go.

"This morning," said the minstrel, "I shall come to the palace and ask the Emperor for your hand."

"Alas!" said the Princess. "My father has made a foolish condition that only he who finds the blue rose may wed me."

The minstrel smiled and touched her hand gently. "That is simple. I shall find it."

In the morning the minstrel went to the palace, and on his way he plucked a white rose from a wayside garden.

The Emperor summoned his daughter and said,

"This penniless singer has brought you what he claims to be the blue rose. Has he accomplished his quest?"

The Princess took the common rose into her narrow hands. Unhesitating, she said, "Yes. This is without doubt the blue rose."

The Lord Chief Justice and all of the court protested the rose was an ordinary white rose and not a blue one.

"I know the rose is blue," said the Princess quietly. And with kindness she added, "All of you are perhaps color-blind."

The Emperor decided that if the Princess thought the rose was blue, it was blue, for it was well known that her perception was more acute than that of anyone in the kingdom, including the wizards, astrologers, scholars, and prophets.

The Princess and the minstrel were married, and they lived happily forever after in a secluded house by the sea, with a garden full of white roses. And the Emperor, knowing that his daughter was happy, and liking the songs his son-in-law sang, died in peace.

YU-KONG AND THE DEMON

The thirteenth Emperor of China, a wise and good sovereign, was famous for his bodyguard. These men were the pick of the empire and noted for their size and strength.

Each year, at a time of a full moon, the Emperor held an athletic contest, open to all, that he might choose the best archers, the strongest swordsmen, the swiftest runners, the greatest wrestlers. But one year he proclaimed that the best all-round athlete that year should be made Captain of the Bodyguard, the highest honor in the Middle Flowery Kingdom.

Thousands of spectators crowded to the games, the Emperor sat in the royal box, and hundreds of skilled athletes took part in the competitions. But to the amazement of all, a slim boy named Yu-kong won each event. No one could defeat him in running, leaping, wrestling, javelin throwing, and wielding the sword.

The final event of the contest was a grand tourney for archers. The people were feverish with excitement, and even the Emperor felt his royal pulses beating at an unusual rate. A hundred of the finest and cleverest bowmen of the world were present that day, and among them stood Yu-kong, the stripling.

The contest narrowed down to three men; two were champions of the empire, and the third was Yu-kong. The spectators were wild with enthusiasm for the boy.

The two champions preceded the youth, and their aim was so true that neither failed to strike the *moon*, or center of the target. Then, fingering his bowstring with an easy grace, Yu-kong stepped confidently forward.

He let his shafts fly in such quick succession that it seemed as if all four had left his bow before the first had pierced the target. But the twelve arrows of the three archers were all within the *moon*, and the contest was declared even.

The Emperor caused a target to be suspended from the limb of a tall tree, in such a fashion that it would sway back and forth in the breeze. One shot was to be fired by each contestant, and on these alone would depend the decision of the Emperor.

When the first of the champions stepped forward, only a slight breeze was stirring, so that the heavy mark swung very slowly. His arrow pierced the second circle. The shaft of the second champion struck just within the border of the *moon.*

But as Yu-kong stepped forward, a brisk wind sprang up, swaying the tree and making the target swing and twist wildly about.

The first bowman offered to let Yu-kong wait until the wind had lessened. But Yu-kong thanked him and said he would rather lose than not abide by the rules agreed upon.

The boy aimed carefully, and in spite of his handicap, his shaft struck the *moon* in the very center. The spectators shouted for joy, and the Emperor named Yu-kong champion of the Middle Flowery Kingdom.

But the second archer, E-shen, called aloud for justice.

The Emperor looked down at him in surprise. "What would you have?"

E-shen frowned. "Your Majesty, this boy has been lucky all through the games. He could not have made that last shot at the target, had it not been for a fortunate breeze. Furthermore, he is too young to be made captain over the rest of us who have seen years of hard service under Your Majesty's command."

An angry mutter arose from the crowd, and the Emperor himself was disturbed. But Yu-kong stepped forward.

"Your Majesty," he said humbly, "I am ready to shoot again for this prize. But I know I need more years and training under your wise guidance. Pray give me simply a place in your household."

This pleased the Emperor, who crowned Yu-kong victor, but reserved the office of Captain of the Bodyguard. And there was no one more loved and admired in the Imperial City thereafter than the young athlete.

But E-shen, who was no man but an evil spirit, hated the youth and planned to do him harm. He vanished from the city as an archer and returned in the form of a fortuneteller.

He bided his time until he should be able to destroy Yu-kong. And when the athlete's faithful servant fell ill of a disease at that time unknown in China, and was on the point of death, Yu-kong's companions asked why he did not consult E-shen.

"Because I've never believed in such powers as he claims to possess," Yu-kong replied.

"But he cured the Mandarin's daughter, and has healed more people than all the doctors in the city," a friend said.

"I don't care, I don't trust him," answered Yu-kong. "He has a bad eye."

But finally, because of the love he bore his dying servant, Yu-kong went to E-shen's quarters.

Overjoyed, E-shen bowed low, "Honored sir, so you scorned my powers! But your servant—"

"What do you know about me and my servant?" asked Yu-kong.

"That is my business," said E-shen. "Your servant will be dead before you reach home, and you will die also before the first of the next moon, unless you submit to my wishes."

"What do I care for you and your threats!" cried Yu-kong angrily. "May the curses of the gods rest upon your false head!"

On his return home, he found that his servant was dead. And there were only two days before the first of the moon, two days more of life, if what the fortune-teller had said were true.

The next day Yu-kong visited every armorer in the city, and at night went home with the strongest, sharpest sword he could buy. He went to bed early for the rest which he would need on the morrow, slept late, arose, and ate well. Throughout the day he mingled with his friends, laughing and talking with them as if nothing were about to happen. But at nightfall he retired to his room.

Suddenly there was noise like the sound of a swiftly rising storm, and a giant ogre burst into his presence, shouting vengeance against him. Without a moment's hesitation, Yu-kong leaped to his feet to fight. With one quick step forward, he gave a terrific thrust with his sword, and the horrible monster fell to the floor. Looking down at his opponent, Yu-kong began to laugh, for the body was only a paper bogie with a grinning, frightful head.

There came a second noise like an explosion. A second monster, more frightful than the first, leaped through the casement, a sword in his hand. This demon was a master of the blade and made his sword fly about Yu-kong's head. Calmly and coolly, Yu-kong waited for an opening, and when the monster was off guard for a breath, the athlete sprang forward with a thrust that pierced his breast.

Again Yu-kong laughed when he found this second monster to be made of potter's clay. But he knew that the demon, E-shen, had escaped from this figure also and would return to the attack. And Yu-kong thought, "Though all the demons of darkness attack me, I shall battle them single-handed, and try to prove worthy of my father and my Emperor!"

Then a roll of thunder shook the building. Sulphur fumes poured in the window, and before Yu-kong appeared a form hideous enough to unnerve an army. The monster had seven grinning heads and seven arms. In each arm he carried a sword that dripped with blood, and leaping about the room, he slashed the air until it seemed as if every inch of space had been cut and recut a thousand times. But Yu-kong was so quick, his body so limber and steely, that he escaped the sword thrusts and suddenly pierced the very heart of his enemy. It was E-shen's own black heart that Yu-kong reached at last, and with a terrible roar, the monster fell lifeless and sulphur fumes filled the room in dense clouds.

As he rushed to the window to get air, Yu-kong saw in the court below a great crowd of people, who, seeing him uninjured, shouted with joy. Yu-kong bowed modestly in thanks and gratitude. At that moment a messenger arrived bearing a message from the Emperor, appointing Yu-kong, the unconquered, the winner of a hundred contests, Captain of the Bodyguard of the Emperor of the Middle Flowery Kingdom.

Norway 🖋 🖋 🖋 🖋 🖋

THE SQUIRE'S BRIDE

THERE ONCE LIVED IN NORWAY A SQUIRE WHO owned a large farm. He had plenty of silver in his chests and gold in the bank, but he was very lonely, for his wife had been dead for a long time.

One day he saw the daughter of a neighboring farmer working in the hayfield, and he liked her very much. Because her father owed him money, the squire thought that the daughter would marry him at once. So he told her he had been thinking of getting married again.

The girl laughed. "One may think of many things," she said, and kept on raking hay.

"Well, I thought you might become my wife," he said.

She laughed at the old fellow again. "No, thank you! I'm not likely to marry you!"

The squire was all the more determined to capture her, but she only ridiculed him until he flew into a rage and sent for her father. "Look here, I want to marry your daughter," he said, "and if you'll get her consent,

I'll cancel your debt to me and give you the piece of land close to your meadow into the bargain."

"I'll bring her to her senses," said the father. "She's very young yet and doesn't know a good thing when she sees it."

But he coaxed and scolded the girl in vain. She would not marry the old squire, she said, if he sat buried in gold up to his ears.

The squire waited day after day, until he became so angry and impatient that he told the father he'd wait no longer. The father had to let the squire prepare for the wedding, and agreed that when the parson and guests had arrived, the squire should send for the girl as if she were wanted for work on the farm. When she reached the squire's house, she would be married at once before she had time to refuse again.

The squire began brewing and baking and preparing for a fine wedding. When the guests had assembled, he called one of his farm boys and told him to run down to his neighbor and ask him to send what he had promised. "And if you're not back in a hurry," he said, shaking his fist, "I'll give you a good beating!"

The boy ran off as if he had been shot at. At the neighbor's house, he said, "My master sent me to ask for that you promised him, and there is no time to be lost!"

"Of course," said the father. "Run down into the meadow and take her with you!"

The boy ran down into the meadow where he found

the daughter raking hay. "I am to fetch what your father has promised my master," he panted.

"Ho," said the girl. "Is that what they're up to? Well, I suppose it's that little bay mare of ours. She's tethered on the other side of the field—go take her."

The boy raced to the field, jumped on the mare's back, and rode home at a gallop.

"Did you bring her back?" asked the squire.

"She's waiting down at the door," said the boy.

"Take her up to the room my mother had," ordered the squire.

"But, master, how can I manage that?" asked the boy.

"Do as I tell you!" snapped the squire, whose impatience was making him cranky. "If you can't manage her alone, get the men to help you."

The boy knew there was no use in arguing, so he got all the farm tenants to help him. Some pulled at the mare's head and others pushed from behind, and at last they managed to get her upstairs and into the bedroom. There lay all the wedding finery spread out on the bed.

The boy went back to the squire. "That's done, master, but it was a terrible job."

"Never mind," said the squire. "Now send the women up to dress her."

"But, master, she—" began the lad.

"Don't answer back!" said the squire. "Tell them they must dress her and not to forget the wreath on her head!"

The boy raced down to the kitchen. "Oh, lasses," he cried, "you must go upstairs and dress up the bay mare as a bride! I guess the master wants to make the guests laugh!"

The women dressed the bay mare in the fine wedding petticoats and the dress with ruffles, and put the wreath over her flattened ears.

"She is ready, master," they called and could scarcely contain their merriment.

"Bring her down!" shouted the squire. "I'll receive her at the door to the parlor!"

Then there was a terrible clatter and racket on the stairway, for the bride wore hooves, not silken shoes. When the door was opened and the squire's bride entered the parlor, the guests burst into peals of laughter. They held their sides and roared, and the squire became as red as a cock's comb. He had enough of that bride then and there and never again did he bother the neighbor's daughter, and he never went courting again as long as he lived.

THE GOLDEN BIRD

Once in a Norwegian king's garden there stood an apple tree; and on that tree every year there grew a golden apple. But when the time came to pluck the apple, it disappeared, and no one knew who stole it.

The King had three sons, and one day he told them that he who would bring him the apple or capture the thief, would inherit the kingdom, no matter whether he was the eldest or the second or the youngest son.

So the eldest son went out and sat down under the

apple tree to watch for the thief. The evening had fallen and the dark was coming on when a golden bird came flying, and the light from it was blinding. The Prince was so dazzled by the gleaming bird that he was terrified and ran indoors as fast as he could.

The next morning the apple was gone. The Prince vowed, however, that he would find the golden bird and recover the golden apple, for with daylight his courage had returned and he was ashamed at having been frightened by a little bird. The King gave him money and fine clothes, and the Prince set out in high spirits. But when he had gone a little way, he became hungry. So he sat down by the roadside, opened his scrip, and began to eat.

A fox came out of the woods and sat down and looked at him. "Do give me a bite to eat," he said.

"I'll give you some powder and shot!" said the Prince crossly. "I want all my food myself, for nobody knows how far or how long I shall have to travel. Go away!"

"Very well," said the fox, and he padded off into the woods again.

When the Prince had finished eating and rested a while, he started off again. He came to a big city and in that city there was a tavern where there was always joy and never any sorrow. He entered in, and there was such dancing and drinking and merrymaking that he forgot his father and the golden bird and his journey and the whole kingdom.

The following year, when the golden apple began to ripen, the second Prince went out into the garden and sat down under the apple tree to watch for the thief.

One night, all of a sudden, the golden bird came flying, shining like the sun, and the Prince was so frightened that he ran indoors as fast as he could.

In the morning the apple was gone. The Prince, his courage returned, swore he would find the golden bird and recover the golden apple. The King give him money and fine raiment, and the Prince set out. When he had gone a distance, he became hungry, so he sat down by the roadside and opened his scrip.

A fox came out of the woods and sat down and looked at him. "Do give me a little to eat," he said.

"I'll give you some powder and shot!" said the Prince. "I want all my food myself, for I don't know how far or how long I shall have to travel."

"Very well," said the fox, and he went back into the woods.

When the Prince had finished his meal and rested a while, he set out again. He came to the same city and the same tavern where there was always joy and never any sorrow; and he entered in. And there was his brother, and there was so much dancing and drinking and merry-making that the second Prince also forgot his father and the golden bird, his journey, and the whole kingdom.

The third year, the time approached for the apple to ripen again, and the youngest son went out into the garden to watch for the thief. He took a companion to help him up into the apple tree, and he took a keg of beer and a pack of cards to pass the time so that he wouldn't fall asleep. Suddenly they saw the golden bird, and its light was as bright as the sun. Quickly the Prince climbed up into the tree and at the same moment the golden bird swooped down and stole the apple, but the Prince tried to seize the bird and caught a feather out of its tail before it flew away.

He hurried into the palace, to the King's bedroom, and as he entered with the golden feather, the room became as light as day. "My father," he said, "I wish to go and search for my brothers, and search also for the golden bird, for now I would know it anywhere."

"I don't want to lose you, too," answered the King. "You must let me consider this awhile."

But the Prince begged so earnestly that at last the King said that he might go, and gave him money and fine raiment and his blessing.

When he had journeyed for a while, the youngest Prince became hungry, so he sat down by the roadside and opened his scrip.

A fox came out of the woods and sat down close to him and looked at him. "Do give me a little to eat," said the fox.

"Hello, red brother," said the Prince. "I shall want food myself, for I must travel long and far, but I have enough to give you a little."

"Thank you," said the fox, accepting a piece of meat. "Now tell me where you are going."

The Prince explained about the golden apple and the golden bird and the disappearance of his two brothers.

"I will help you," said the fox, "if you will take my advice."

The Prince said that he would, and they set out together. They came to the same city and the same tavern where there was always joy, but no sorrow.

"I shall have to stay outside here," said the fox, "for the dogs are a nuisance, but your brothers are in the tavern, and if you enter there, you will not get any further, either."

The Prince promised that he would not enter, and he took the fox's paw in his hand and shook it, and each went his way. But when the Prince came near the tavern, he heard the music and the merriment and he felt he must go in. When he met his brothers, there was great rejoicing, and he forgot the fox and the journey, the golden bird, and his father. But when he had been there for a space, the fox ventured into the city and came to the tavern and signaled the Prince that it was high time to be going on. So the youngest Prince left the tavern, and he and the fox journeyed on.

When they had traveled a while they saw a great mountain far away.

The fox said, "Three hundred miles in back of that mountain there is a gold linden tree with golden leaves, and in that tree sits the golden bird."

And they journeyed there together.

"Here are some feathers," said the fox. "Wave them in your hands to attract the bird, and it will fly down and alight on your hand. But you must not touch the linden tree, for if you brush even the smallest twig, the troll who lives there will come out and kill you at once!"

"I promise not to touch it," said the Prince.

But when the bird flew down and perched on his

finger, he knew he must have a twig of the tree, it was so beautiful. So he took a tiny little twig, but the troll came roaring out.

"Who is stealing my tree and my bird?" yelled the troll, and he spurted sparks of fire.

"Thieves believe that all men steal, but only those get hanged who do not steal properly," answered the youngest Prince.

The troll was about to kill him, but the Prince begged for his life so eloquently that the troll relented.

"Young man," said the troll, "if you can bring me back the horse which my nearest neighbor has stolen from me, I'll allow you to keep your life."

"Where shall I find the horse?" asked the Prince.

"My neighbor lives three hundred miles in back of that big blue mountain against the horizon," said the troll.

"I'll do my best," said the Prince, and went to find the fox.

But the fox was in a rather bad temper. "Now you've gotten yourself into trouble!" he said. "Why didn't you listen to me and leave the tree alone?"

They set off for the big blue mountain on the horizon, and at last they reached the neighboring troll's house.

"Now listen to me," said the fox. "When you reach the stable, you'll find gold and silver bridles hanging on the wall. Don't touch them, or the troll will come and kill you at once; you must take the ugliest and shabbiest bridle you see."

The Prince promised that he would; but when he

came into the stable and saw the wonderful bridles, he thought it would be nonsense not to take a fine one, so he took the brightest he could find. The troll came roaring out and he was so angry that sparks flew from him.

"Who is stealing my horse and my bridle?" he howled.

"Thieves believe that all men steal, but only those get hanged who do not steal properly," said the Prince.

"I'll kill you right this minute!" shouted the troll.

But the Prince begged for his life so eloquently that the troll relented.

"All right, if you'll bring me back the fair maiden my nearest neighbor has stolen from me, I'll spare you," said the troll.

"Where does he live?" asked the Prince.

"He lives three hundred miles in back of that big blue mountain against the horizon there," said the troll.

The Prince said that he would do his best, and went to find the fox.

But the fox was very angry. "Now you've done it again!" he said crossly. "I'm not going with you any further."

"Oh, please come with me!" begged the Prince. "I promise to do everything you tell me in the future!"

"Well, all right, but see that you do!" said the fox.

So they set off again and came to the place where the fair maiden was.

"Look here," said the fox, "I have your promise, but I don't dare let you go in after all; this time I'll go myself." The fox went in and took the girl away from the troll, and they returned the way they had come.

When they reached the troll who had the horse, they took the horse and the brightest bridle; and when they reached the troll who had the linden tree and the golden bird, they took the tree and the bird and started off with them.

They came to a field of rye, and the fox said, "I hear a roaring noise. You'd better go on ahead—I'll stay here a while and catch up with you later."

Then he plaited himself a gown of rye straw which made him look like a preacher. Suddenly the three trolls came thundering up, trying to overtake the Prince.

"Have you seen anyone passing here with a fair maiden, a horse with a golden bridle, a golden bird, and a golden linden tree?" they called to the fox.

The fox stopped preaching and answered, "Well, I heard from my grandmother's grandmother that someone like that passed this way, but that was a hundred years ago when my grandmother's grandmother baked halfpenny cakes and gave back the halfpenny."

The three trolls burst out laughing and they laughed so hard they had to hang on to each other. "If we've slept too long, we might as well go home and sleep some more," they said, and went back the way they had come.

The fox threw away his rye straw dress and made haste after the youngest Prince. When they reached the city where the tavern and the brothers were, he said, "I dare not go through the city because of the dogs, but do you take care that your brothers do not catch you."

But when the Prince reached the tavern, he stopped in to speak to his brothers. But they seized the maiden, the horse, the bird, and the linden tree, and they put him in a barrel and threw him into the sea. Then they set off for the King's palace.

But the maiden would not speak, and she grew pale and unhappy; the horse became so thin it could hardly hold together; the bird became silent, its plumage dulled and shone no more; and the linden tree withered.

Meanwhile the fox was waiting outside the city for the youngest Prince and the maiden. He went hither and thither, searching for them and could not find them. At length he went down to the seashore and there he saw a drifting barrel. He shouted, "Why are you drifting about there, you empty barrel?"

And the Prince in the barrel cried, "It is I!"

Quickly the fox swam out into the water and towed the barrel to land; then he gnawed the hoops and when he had removed some of them from the barrel, he told the Prince, "Kick as hard as you can!"

The Prince kicked and kicked until the staves fell apart, and he jumped out of the barrel. Then he and the fox hastened to the King's palace; at once the maiden regained her beauty and began to talk, the horse became fat and sleek, the light shone from the golden bird and it began to sing, and the linden tree blossomed and its golden leaves gleamed. And the maiden cried to the King. "He is the one who has saved us!" And she told the King how the two brothers had stolen her, after the youngest Prince had rescued her from the trolls. The King ordered the two brothers put each in a spiked barrel and rolled down a steep mountain.

The linden tree was planted in the garden, and preparations were made for the wedding of the Princess, for such the maiden really was, and the youngest Prince.

And the fox asked the Prince to put him on the block and chop his head off. The Prince cried out that he couldn't and wouldn't do that to his old friend, but the fox was insistent. Finally the Prince agreed, and sorrowfully he did so. Immediately the fox became a handsome Prince, and he was the brother of the Princess whom they had rescued from the trolls.

The wedding was celebrated with great pomp and joy; and each year thereafter, the golden bird plucked the golden apple from the apple tree and brought it to the Princess and sang her a golden song.

Russia ❧ ❧ ❧ ❧ ❧

THE FLYING SHIP

ONCE IN BLESSED RUSSIA THERE LIVED A MAN AND a woman who had three sons. Two of the boys were clever, but the third was a fool. The parents loved the first two and gave them the best of everything, but they scorned the third boy, beating him often and giving him the scraps from the table. The boy did not complain, but he grew up shy and silent and his parents were sure that he had become more stupid than ever.

There was sent to the village a proclamation from the Tsar which read:

Whoever builds a ship that can fly, to him will I give my daughter, the Tsarevna, to wife.

On hearing this, the elder brothers determined to go out into the world and seek their fortunes and find a flying ship. The mother prepared their clothes for the journey and gave them meat and a flask of wine; she and their father blessed them and the youths set out in high spirits.

Then the fool wished to go away also, but his mother

laughed at him. "Where would you go, you fool?" she asked. "The wolves would eat you up, and probably get indigestion!"

But the boy said, "I will go! I will go!"

When his mother saw that she could do nothing with him, she gave him a crust of dry bread and a flask of water and drove him out of the house.

The boy traveled and traveled, and at last he met an old man. They greeted each other politely, and the old man asked the boy where he was going.

"Did you not hear," said the fool, "that the Tsar has promised to give his daughter to him who shall make a flying ship?"

"Can you make a flying ship?"

"No, I can't," answered the fool, "but I think someone will make it for me somewhere."

"Where is that somewhere?" asked the old man.

"God knows," replied the fool sadly.

"Let us sit down and rest a bit," the old man said. "Take out what you have in your knapsack and let us eat."

"It is only a crust of bread and some water, and I am ashamed to offer it to you," said the boy.

"Never mind, take it out! What God has given is good enough to be eaten." The old man seated himself on the grass and waited.

Reluctantly the boy opened his knapsack and could not believe his eyes, for instead of the crust there were white rolls, many different kinds of meat, and a flask of wine, and he offered everything to the old man. So they ate together and drank together, and the boy felt much happier.

Then the old man said to him, "Go into the woods and at the first tree you come to, cross yourself three times, strike the tree with your ax, then fall face downward on the earth and do not move until you are awakened. Then you will see the flying ship ready for you. Sit in it and fly wherever you like, but gather up everything you meet on your way."

The boy blessed the old man and said goodby and went to the woods. He went up to the first tree, crossed himself three times, struck the tree with his ax, fell with his face to the ground, and went to sleep. He was awakened by an invisible hand on his shoulder, and he sat up and there before him was the ship with wings. The fool climbed in and sat down and the ship flew up into the air. It flew and it flew, until, on the road below, the fool saw a man lying with his ear to the earth.

"Good day!" he called. "What are you doing?"

"Good day," answered the man. "I'm listening to what is going on in the world."

"Take a seat here in the ship beside me," invited the boy.

The man climbed in, and they flew on. They flew and they flew, until they saw a man hopping along on one leg, with the other leg tied tightly to his ear.

"Good day," called the boy. "What are you hopping on one leg for?"

"Good day," answered the man. "If I untied my other

leg, I would step halfway around the world at a single stride."

"Won't you climb into the ship with us?" invited the boy.

The man sat down in the ship, and they flew on. They flew and they flew, until they saw a man standing with a gun and taking aim, but at what they could not tell.

"Good day," called the boy. "What are you aiming at? I can't see a single bird."

"Good day," replied the man. "I'm shooting at short range, at a bird seven leagues away. I can hit a bird or an animal at one hundred leagues."

"Won't you sit down with us in the ship?" invited the fool. "That is certainly what I call shooting."

The man climbed into the ship, and they flew on. They flew and they flew, until they saw a man carrying on his back a whole sackful of bread.

"Good day," called the boy. "Where are you going?"

"Good day," answered the man. "I'm going to get some bread for my dinner."

"But you have a whole sackful on your back already!"

"This! Why, I can eat this in a single mouthful!" the man said.

"Won't you come and fly with us?" invited the fool.

The man sat down in the ship, and they flew on. They flew and they flew, until they saw a man walking around a lake.

"Good day," called the boy. "What are you looking for?"

"Good day," replied the man. "I'm very thirsty but I can't find any water."

"There's a whole lake in front of you," said the boy. "Why don't you drink it?"

"That would be only a mouthful to me," said the man.

"Won't you climb in with us?" invited the boy.

The thirsty man sat down beside the others, and they flew on. They flew and they flew, until they saw a man walking in a forest, carrying a bundle of wood on his shoulders.

"Good day," called the boy. "Why are you carrying wood around in the forest?"

"Good day," replied the man. "This is not ordinary wood."

"What kind of wood is it?" asked the fool.

"If I scattered it," answered the man, "a whole army would spring up."

"Won't you come and fly with us?" invited the boy.

The man climbed into the ship, and they flew on. They flew and they flew, until they saw a man carrying a sack of straw.

"Good day," called the fool. "Whither are you carrying that straw?"

"Good day," answered the man. "I'm carrying it to the village."

"Isn't there any straw in the village then?"

"Yes, of course," said the man. "But this straw is not ordinary straw. If you scatter it on the hottest summer day, the weather will immediately become cold, with frost and snow."

"Won't you climb into the ship with us?" invited the boy.

The man sat down in the ship, and they flew on They flew and they flew, until they came to the Tsar's courtyard. The Tsar was at dinner, and when he looked out of the window he saw the flying ship. Astonished, he sent a servant out to ask who was in the ship; the servant returned and told the Tsar that a simple young peasant was flying it with a crowd of people. The Tsar did not like the idea of giving his daughter to a miserable peasant, so he tried to think how he could get rid of the boy for a whole year. He decided to give the peasant many grievous tasks to do.

"Go and tell that muzhik," said the Tsar, "that I command him to bring me, by the time this imperial meal is over, the living and singing water."

At the very moment when the Tsar was speaking, the first comrade whom the fool had met, the man with his ear to the earth, heard what the Tsar said and told it to the boy.

"Oh, what shall I do?" cried the fool. "If I searched all my life I could never find such water!"

"Don't worry," said the man with his foot behind his ear. "I'll fetch it for you."

The servant came and told the Tsar's command, and the fool replied, "Tell him I'll bring it."

The swift-footed comrade untied his other leg from his ear and ran off, and in no time he drew from the end

of the world some of the living and singing water. "I must hurry and return, but I'll have a nap first," he said to himself, and he sat down under a watermill and went to sleep. The Tsar's dinner was drawing to a close, and the boy and the comrades in the ship grew uneasy. The first comrade put his ear to the earth and reported that the swift one was asleep under a watermill.

The comrade with the gun took careful aim, shot into the mill, and awakened the swift-footed man with the noise of his shots. He jumped up and in a minute he was back at the ship with the water. The fool sent the living and singing water in to the Tsar, who had not yet risen from the table.

The Tsar was annoyed. He sent his servant out to the fool with the command that he and his friends must eat at one meal twenty roast oxen and twenty large measures of baked bread.

The first comrade heard and told this to the boy.

The boy was aghast. "I can't eat even one whole loaf at a meal!" he said. "What shall I do?"

"Don't worry," said the hungry comrade. "That will be little enough for me."

When the servant came with the command, the boy said, "Let us have it and we'll eat it."

The servants brought twenty roasted bullocks and twenty measures of baked bread, and the hungry man ate everything and complained about there being so little.

The Tsar then commanded that the peasant boy drink

forty barrels of wine, each barrel containing forty buckets.

The fool was terrified. "Why, I couldn't drink a single bucket!"

"Don't be afraid," said the thirsty man. "I'll drink it all."

The servants poured out the forty barrels of wine; the thirsty comrade drank the whole lot at one swallow, and complained, "The Tsar is stingy with his wine—I could drink that much again."

Then the Tsar commanded the boy to prepare for his wedding, and to go to the bathroom to bathe. But the bathroom was of cast iron, and the Tsar ordered it to be heated frightfully hot, so that the fool might be suffocated in an instant. The servants heated the bath red-hot, but when the fool went to wash himself, behind him came the comrade with the straw. When they were both locked in the bathroom, the comrade scattered his straw, and it became so cold that the fool was scarcely able to wash himself properly, the water in the bath froze so hard. The boy climbed up on the stove to keep warm and went to sleep.

When the servants opened the bath in the morning, the fool was alive, leaning on his elbow on the stove and singing songs to his comrade.

The Tsar was furious, for he did not know how to get rid of the boy. Finally he commanded the boy to produce a whole army, and at once.

The boy was in despair.

"You're a fine one, to forget me!" said the comrade with the wood.

The servant came and said, "If you would wed the Tsarevna, you must have a whole army here by morning."

"I shall," said the boy. "But tell the Tsar that after this, if he still refuses me his daughter, I shall conquer his whole empire and take the Tsarevna by force."

That night the comrade with the bundle of wood went out into the fields and began scattering the faggots in all directions. And immediately a great army sprang up, both on horse and on foot. And he led the army to the fool, who commanded the soldiers to line up in the courtyard. But there were so many of them that they stretched out into the country, as far as the eye could see.

When the Tsar beheld the mighty army arrayed against him, he was terrified in turn. Hurriedly he sent the fool precious jewels and rich clothing, and told his servants to lead him into the court that he might marry the Tsarevna.

The boy, clothed in costly raiment, became very handsome, and his shyness disappeared and he possessed both wit and sense. He was led in to the Tsar's court, fell promptly in love with the beautiful Tsarevna, and was married to her at once. His comrades cheered loudly, and bade him farewell, and went away. And the peasant boy and the Tsarevna were in love with each other for the rest of their long and happy lives.

THE HARP THAT HARPED WITHOUT
A HARPER

Far behind the blue sea and far behind the fiery
chasm in the emptiness, in the midst of the green meadows, stood a tall city, and in the city ruled Tsar Wise-
Head with his Tsaritza. To their great joy, a lovely little
daughter was born to them. They named her Neotsyenaya, or Not-To-Be-Priced. And the next year they
had another little daughter, just as lovely, and they
called her Beztsyenaya, or Without-Price.

On the occasion of each birth, the Tsar, in his happiness, gave his generals and high officials three hundred
and three buckets of mead to toast him in, and a great
feast. And he regaled his whole realm with ale for three
days. Whoever wished to drink, might drink as much as
he liked, so long as he toasted the Tsar and the Tsarina
and the new Tsarevna. And because the people loved
the Tsar and the Tsarina, everyone was very merry
throughout the kingdom.

After the celebrations, the Tsar began to worry about
how to bring up his little daughters. They were fed only
with golden spoons, they were laid to sleep on eider-
down, they were covered with sable coverlets. Three very
special nurses watched constantly over the little girls,
so that the sun never touched them, the dew never fell
on them, and the wandering wind never dared even to
breathe upon them.

For the further protection of his daughters, the Tsar
had seventy-seven other nurses to attend them, and

seventy-seven guards. And the baby girls were healthy and pink-cheeked and grew more beautiful as the days went by.

When the young Tsarevnas grew up into young ladies, suitors thronged the court, but the Tsar was in no hurry to marry off his charming daughters. He knew that a destined wooer cannot be avoided even on a swift horse, whereas a wooer who is not destined can be held fast by iron chains.

One day while he was thinking about his beloved children he heard a great noise and wailing in the courtyard. The three special nurses were weeping, the seventy-seven other nurses were howling, and the seventy-seven guards were shouting at the top of their lungs.

The Tsar rushed out into the courtyard and asked, "What in the world is the matter?"

The three special nurses, the seventy-seven other nurses, and the seventy-seven guards, all fell on their knees and cried out, "We must be guilty! The Tsarevnas have been carried off by a whirlwind!"

"Come now," said the Tsar. "One of you must tell me exactly what has happened, and the rest of you stop yelling."

So the first special nurse, who had silver hair now and more sense than the rest, tried to speak calmly. It seemed that the two young Tsarevnas had gone out to walk in the Tsar's own garden, to pick a sweet pea and smell it, to pluck a poppy and gaze at its black heart, to nibble at a ripening apple. Abruptly a black cloud rose above them—where it came from nobody knew—and blew dust into the eyes of the nurses and the guards, and by the time they could rub their eyes clear and see again, the two Tsarevnas had vanished completely.

The Tsar was half crazed with anger and anxiety. He promised the three nurses and the seventy-seven nurses and the seventy-seven guards a dire punishment, but he was so frantic he forgot to have his threat carried out. And they understood, for they were devoted to the young Tsarevnas and did not blame the Tsar for blaming them for the disappearance of his daughters.

The Tsar could neither eat nor drink nor sleep. There were no more banquets at the court, no more music, no more merriment. The Tsarina grieved even more than the Tsar did, but because she loved him she was silent and kept her sorrow to herself. The Tsar felt that grief, like a crow, sat beside him croaking of evil. So passed two years.

And another child was born to the Tsar and the Tsarina, and this time it was a little boy. The Tsar was overjoyed, and he called his son Tsarevich Ivan. He placed beside the child old-men nurses, foster fathers, wise teachers, and brave nobles.

The boy Ivan grew and grew and became both stately and beautiful, both dreamy and considerate. And the Tsar was worried.

For Ivan seemed to have neither heroic courage nor knightly skill. He would not tear off the heads of his enemies, or break their arms and legs. He would not play with Damascan steel; he would not touch swords of tempered metal under any conditions. He talked and laughed with soldiers as if they were nobles; and he talked with nobles as if they were ordinary people. Battalions of warriors meant nothing to him. His only joy was to play on the harp that needed no harper.

Ivan played so that strong men forgot everything else as they listened. The instant he placed his fingers on the strings, they sang with such a marvelous voice that all men wept in delight. Beautiful were the Tsarevich Ivan's songs, but they did not refill the Tsar's treasury, nor defend the kingdom, nor conquer the inevitable enemy.

One day the Tsar called his son before him.

Ivan bowed and kissed his father's hand. "My father, what do you wish of me?"

"My dear son," said the Tsar, "you are both good and handsome, and I am well pleased with you. But there is one thing which grieves me. You have neither the valor of a warrior nor the skill of a hero. You care nothing for the clash of steel, and the tempered blade is a thing to which you are indifferent. But I am growing old, and we have violent foes. They will make war on us, despoil our kingdom, kill our people, and capture your mother and myself, for you cannot defend us."

Ivan replied to the Tsar, "Dear father, Tsar Wise-Head, cities are not taken by strength but by thought, and by my own wits shall I conquer our foes. Test my courage, my father, and make trial of my strength. They tell me that I had two young sisters who were very beautiful, and that a whirlwind carried them away. Summon your heroes, your warriors and your nobles, your peasants and your princes, and command them to find my sisters, the Tsarevnas. Let them go forth with their Damascan blades, their lances and their darts; and if any one of them finds my sisters, give him my Tsardom and command me to serve him as a scullion and a jester. But if they cannot render you this service, then I will do so, and you will find that my wit is sharper than tempered steel, and my wisdom stronger than all their lances together."

The Tsar rejoiced at Ivan's words and called up his boyars, his voivods, his heroes, and said to them, "Is there any one among you, my warriors and my generals, brave enough to go and search for my lost daughters? If so, to him will I give to choose which of my daughters he wishes to be his wife, and with her he shall have half my Tsardom."

But the warriors, the generals, the heroes, hid one behind the other and none spoke.

Then Ivan bowed low before his father. "My father, if no one dares to render you this very small service, give me your blessing on my journey. I will go to seek my sisters."

"My blessing go with you," said the Tsar. "Take silver and gold and precious stones, and if you need soldiers, take a hundred thousand horse and a hundred thousand foot."

But the Tsarevich Ivan answered with a smile,

"Thank you, my father, but I need neither silver nor gold, neither horse nor foot, neither sword nor lance. I will take with me my harp that plays without a harper, and nothing else. And you, my Tsar, wait for me for three years, and if I do not return in the fourth year, choose my successor."

His father blessed him, Ivan commended himself to God, took his harp under his arm, and went on his way as his eyes led him.

As he journeyed, he played songs upon his harp, and he journeyed near and far, high and low. At nightfall he lay down in the sweet grass and slept beneath the great roof of stars; when dawn came, he arose and traveled onward. At last he came to a vast forest, and deep among the trees he heard a crashing and thundering as if someone were smashing them all. "I shall go on," said Ivan to himself. "A man must die once though no man can die twice." And he followed the sound until he came to a place where two wood demons were fighting.

One was beating the other with an uprooted oak, and the other was attacking his comrade with an enormous pine tree, and the two of them were in a devilish rage.

Ivan drew near to them and began to play a dance on his harp. The demons stopped fighting at once and began to dance wildly. They danced and they danced and they danced until they danced themselves off their legs and rolled on the ground.

The Tsarevich Ivan laughed. "What are you quarreling about?" he asked. "Here you are, perfectly good wood demons, and yet you make fools of yourselves as if you were common people. What is your argument?"

"Why shouldn't we fight?" said one of the wood demons. "We were on our way and we found something. And I said, 'It's mine!' but he said, 'It's mine!'—and we tried to divide it and we couldn't divide it. So we're fighting."

"What was it you found?" asked Ivan.

"We found a little bread-and-salt tablecloth," said the second demon.

"And self-moving boots," said the first demon.

"And a little invisible cap," said the second. "If you want to eat and drink, just spread out the tablecloth and twelve young men and twelve maidens will bring you mead to drink and sweetmeats."

"And you have only to put on the self-walking boots," said the second demon, "and you can go seven versts at one stride, you can even go fourteen versts in one stride, and no bird can fly level with you and no wind can overtake you."

"And if you are in danger," said the second demon, "put on the little invisible cap, and you will vanish completely."

"So you see why we quarrel," said the first demon.

"What nonsense!" said Ivan. "Will you agree to what I say if I divide what you've found?"

"I'll agree," said the first demon.

"And I'll agree," said the second.

"All right," said the Tsarevich Ivan. "You both run

toward that small path over there, and whoever reaches it first shall have the tablecloth, the boots, and the invisible cap."

"You're a sensible youth," said the first demon.

"You hold the treasures," said the second, "and we'll do the running."

And off the two demons raced at full tilt, disappearing in the forest. Quickly the Tsarevich Ivan put the self-moving boots on his feet, the invisible cap on his head, the little tablecloth under his arm, and strode off. The wood demons came tearing back, but could not find him; and Ivan, striding with great strides in his boots, looked back and laughed when he saw the demons running around in the forest, searching for him and wringing their hands.

Ivan strode and he strode until he came to the open plains. There three roads stretched before him, and at the crossroads stood a wretched little hut turning around and around on hen's legs. Ivan called out to it, "Wretched little hut, turn your back to the forest and your front to me!"

The hut stood still and he entered it, and there sat Baba-Yaga bony-leg, the witch of witches.

"Fie, fie, fie!" cried Baba-Yaga. "Here is a Russian soul right before my eyes! Where are you going, young man?"

"Granny," said Ivan, "you ought to feed me before you ask questions."

Baba-Yaga sprang up, heated her little stove, and fed

the Tsarevich Ivan. Then she asked again, "Where are you going and why, young man?"

Ivan smiled at the witch of witches. "I'm seeking my sisters, the Tsarevna Neotsyenaya and the Tsarevna Beztsyenaya. Tell me, Granny, where shall I find them and how shall I get there?"

"I know where Neotsyenaya lives," answered Baba-Yaga. "She lives in the white stone palace of her old husband, the Monster of the Forest, and you will have to take the middle road to reach her. The road is hard and long, and even if you do get there, it will do you no good, for the Forest Monster will eat you."

Ivan chuckled. "Well, Granny, I expect I shall choke him, for a Russian man is a bony mouthful. Goodby and thank you for your bread and salt." And he strode off and took the middle road.

Soon he saw the white stone palace of the Forest Monster gleaming across the plain. He hurried up to it, and there on the gate sat a small devil who shouted, "No admittance! No admittance!"

"Open the gate, my small friend," said Ivan, "and I'll give you some vodka!"

The small devil took the vodka and drank it, but he refused to open the gate. So Ivan decided to climb over the wall. He climbed up, but the top of the wall was strung with wires, and when his foot touched one, a hundred bells began to ring. But he jumped down, and out on the balcony rushed his sister, Neotsyenaya.

"Is it you, my dear brother Ivan?" she cried.

"It is I," he answered, and kissed his sister.

"I must hide you from the Monster of the Forest," she said, "for he will be here shortly."

They were still talking when there sounded the roar of a whirlwind, the palace shook, and the Monster of the Forest appeared. But Ivan hurriedly put on his cap and became invisible.

"Where is your guest who climbed over the wall?" thundered the Forest Monster.

"I have no guest," replied Neotsyenaya.

"I heard the bells!" roared the Forest Monster

"The sparrows have been flying over the wall, and they must have struck the wires with their wings," said the Tsarevna.

"Sparrows!" said the Monster. "I smell a Russian soul here! And I am hungry—I'll eat him up!"

Ivan took off his invisible cap, bowed to the Monster, and asked, "Why do you want to eat me? I'm too bony. But let me give you a breakfast such as you've never eaten!" And he spread out his little bread-and-salt table-cloth. The twelve young men and the twelve maidens appeared and offered the Forest Monster as much as he could eat and drink. He ate and ate and ate, then he drank and drank and drank, then he ate again, until he couldn't stir but fell asleep where he sat.

"I must say goodby now, my dearest sister," said Ivan. "But tell me—where does our sister, Beztsyenaya, live?"

Neotsyenaya sighed. "You must seek her along the great sea Ocean. She lives in the whirlpool of the Ocean with her old husband, the Monster of the Sea. But the way there is hard, and he will doubtless devour you."

Ivan laughed. "He may chew me, but he will find me bony to swallow. Farewell, my sister."

He strode onward until he came to the great sea Ocean. On the shore was a Russian fishing boat; the shrouds and gear were of linden bast, the sails of fine hair mats, and the boat itself was sewed fast with birch bark. The sailors were getting ready to put to sea, to sail to the Rock-Salt Island, and Ivan asked them to take him along.

"I can't pay you for my passage," he said, "but I'll tell you stories so that you'll never notice how long the voyage is."

The mariners agreed, and Ivan stepped into the boat, and they sailed away upon the great sea Ocean. They sailed past the Rock-Salt Island; Ivan told them stories, and they sailed and sailed. Abruptly a tempest blew up, the ship shook, and the sailors were terrified. They cried out that they must pay tribute to the Monster of the Sea and they cast lots. The lot fell upon the Tsarevich Ivan.

He took his little tablecloth, his self-moving boots, his invisible cap, and the harp that harped without a harper, and the sailors lifted him and swung him out into the great whirlpool of Ocean. The sea grew calm, the boat sailed on, and Ivan went like a rock to the bottom of the sea, into the marvelous flowery halls of the Monster. There he saw the Sea Monster sitting on his throne with the Tsarevna Beztsyenaya beside him.

"Dear brother, is it you?" she asked.

"It is I," said Ivan.

"Ho," said the Sea Monster, "it is a long time since

I have eaten. Welcome, young man! Come here so that I may eat you!"

"I am much too bony," said Ivan. "Furthermore, I am the brother of the Tsarevna Beztsyenaya, and in our family it is considered very impolite to eat each other up."

But the Sea Monster howled, "Are you trying to force your rules upon other people? Speaking of bad manners, this is too much!"

Ivan knew he would have to do something quickly, so he began to play on his harp that harped without a harper. He played a sad song, and the Sea Monster's face began to pucker up; he sighed, he moaned, and finally he wept. Then Ivan played the song "Let the merry drinking bowl go round the little table!" and the Sea Monster skipped up and down, stamped his feet, snapped his fingers, rolled his eyes, and made such funny faces that all the fishes nearly died laughing.

The Monster of the Sea had such a good time that he decided not to eat Ivan after all. "Stay with us," he said. "Won't you be our guest? Come and sit down at our table!"

Ivan and Beztsyenaya and the Sea Monster ate and drank and made merry. A whale danced a waltz in front of them, the herrings sang glees, the carp performed on one musical instrument after another. After dinner the Sea Monster fell asleep.

And Beztsyenaya said, "My beloved brother, I am glad to see you. But if the Monster awakes in a bad humor, he will eat you."

"Dear sister," said Ivan, "tell me how I may save you from the Monster of the Sea and our sister, Neotsye-naya, from the Monster of the Forest."

"It will be very difficult," she answered. "Behind the great sea Ocean lies a large Tsardom, ruled not by a Tsar but by the Tsar-Maiden. If you can get into her garden, then she will become your wife, and she alone can free us. But she has a heavy guard on the shore with guns and lances, and on each lance is the head of a youth who came to woo her. The youths were strong warriors and kings and kings' sons, but they could not prevail against the guard."

"I am not afraid," said Ivan. "Only tell me how to reach the Tsardom of the Tsar-Maiden."

"I'll give you my sturgeon," said Beztsyenaya. "Sit upon him and he will take you there, and my swift ster-let will swim before you to show you the way."

Ivan said farewell to his sister and sat upon the stur-geon, and off they went, with the sterlet leading the way. They met up with a crowd of crabs, who saluted Ivan with their mustaches and beat the drums with their clippers. When they reached the shore of the Tsar-Maiden's Tsardom, Ivan put on his invisible cap and the sturgeon set him safely on the beach and jumped back into the water. The guards were sharpening their swords and putting keener points on their spears, but they did not see Ivan and he went past them and into the garden.

Twenty white doves flew over his head and alighted beside a pool; they changed into twenty beautiful maidens, and among them walked the Tsar-Maiden, who was more beautiful than all of them together.

"It is hot, my friends," said the Tsar-Maiden. "Let us bathe in the pool. No eye can see us here. The guards on the shore are so strong that not even a fly could pass them."

"Is that so?" said Ivan. "See what a big fly has passed them!" And he took off his invisible cap and bowed to the Tsar-Maiden.

She and her maidens shrieked and ran about.

But Ivan said, "Tsar-Maiden and lovely maidens, fear nothing. I'm not a bear. But if my destined bride is here, then I am her destined bridegroom."

At that the Tsar-Maiden blushed furiously, gave her hand to Ivan, and said, "Welcome, good youth. You have come here as a gentle guest and dear friend, not as a rough wooer. Come into my crystal chambers."

The next day there was a wedding feast and the whole Tsardom rejoiced that their Tsar-Maiden had found a husband after her own heart. When the feasting was over, Ivan spoke to his wife about releasing his sisters from the Monster of the Forest and the Monster of the Sea.

"My beloved husband," she said, "what would I not do for you! I shall command the Monsters to give up your sisters at once."

Ivan wrote to his father, the Tsar, "You see, O noble Tsar, that wit and wisdom can prevail as well as valor and strength. And the harp that harps without a harper is of as good service as a Damascan blade. And now you and my mother come and be my guests, and my wife and my sisters will be here also."

And Ivan lived a long and joyous life, and his wife delighted to hear him play on the harp that harped without a harper.

Greece ✒ ✒ ✒ ✒ ✒

DEMETER AND PERSEPHONE
(Ancient Greece)

HIGH UP IN THE MOUNTAINS IN THE ISLAND OF Sicily there was once a lovely valley called the valley of Enna. Seldom did even the goats climb so high over the steep slippery paths, but those who did knew what soft sweet grass grew there. Very occasionally sheep and sometimes swine made their way upward, and nuzzled rare flowers.

There was no other mountain valley anywhere like this one. It was never visited by any of the winds except Zephuros, who was always gentle and soft. Forever was the grass green and forever were the flowers in bloom, and there were cool streams of sparkling water among the trees.

The valley of Enna was the home of one of the wisest of goddesses, Demeter, the Earth Mother. She was the goddess of all that grows out of the earth; she knew the secret of young wheat and filling fruit, and she watched over the lambs in the field and young children. The flowers, the springs of water, and the apple root were hers.

One day Persephone, the little daughter of Demeter, was playing in the meadows of Enna, her hair flying like yellow gold and her cheeks as pink as apple blossoms. She, and the daughters of the valley nymphs, who were children of her own age, had taken off their sandals and were running in the soft grass in their bare feet, laughing and giggling as the grass tickled their toes.

"Come on," cried Persephone gaily. "Let's pick flowers!"

The children shouted and began to gather the flowers that grew so thickly in the valley of Enna—hyacinths and violets, lilies and purple irises. Suddenly Persephone saw a flower which made her forget everything else. It appeared to be a strange new kind of narcissus; it was gigantic and its one stalk held at least a hundred blossoms. And its fragrance was powerful enough to fill the whole island and drifted far out at sea.

Persephone called her playmates to come and see this wonderful flower, but when she turned around she noticed for the first time that she was alone. She had wandered from one flower to another until she had left the other children behind.

Running forward to pluck this marvelous blossom, she found its stalk was spotted like a snake, and feared it might be poisonous; still, it was too beautiful to be left alone in the meadow, and she tried to pluck it. But she could not break the stalk, so she tried to pull the whole plant up by the roots.

Suddenly the black soil about the stalk loosened, and the little girl heard a rumbling underground. All at once the earth opened, a great black cavern appeared, and from its depths sprang four magnificent black horses drawing a golden chariot. In the chariot sat a King with a crown on his head, but his face was the saddest and gloomiest ever seen by mortal. Persephone stared in astonishment.

When the sad-faced King saw the child standing by the flower, too frightened to run away, he reined in his horses for an instant, leaned forward, and snatched up Persephone from the ground. He placed her in the chariot at his side, whipped up his horses and drove off at a furious speed.

Persephone, still holding tightly to her flowers, screamed for her mother.

Only Helios, the sun-god, saw the dark-faced King steal Persephone, and Hecate, who sat in her near-by cave, heard the scream and the sound of wheels. No one else suspected what had happened.

Demeter was across the sea in another country, attending to the gathering of the harvests. But she heard Persephone's scream, and like a sea bird when it hears the distressed cry of its young, came rushing home across the water.

The valley echoed and rang with the sound of her calling, but no little girl answered to the name of Persephone. The strange flower had disappeared; a few wild roses lay scattered on the grass and near them were prints of a child's feet. Demeter was certain that they were the traces of Persephone's little bare feet, but she could not follow them, because a herd of swine had wandered that way and left a confusion of hoofprints behind them.

Nor could Demeter learn anything of her daughter from the nymphs. She sent out her own messenger, the great white crane who brings the rain; but although he flew swiftly and far on his powerful wings, he brought back no news of Persephone.

When it grew dark, Demeter lighted two torches at the flaming summit of Mount Ætna; and she wandered up and down for nine days and nine nights. On the tenth night, near dawn, she met Hecate, who was carrying a light in her hand, as if she, too, were searching for something. Hecate told Demeter how she had heard the scream and the sound of wheels but had seen nothing; and she went with Demeter to ask Helios, the sun-god, whether he had seen what happened that day.

Helios was sitting in his chariot, ready to ride across the sky. He held his fiery horses in for a moment while he told Demeter that Hades, the King of the underworld, had stolen her daughter and taken her away to live with him in his dark palace.

When Demeter heard this, she knew that Persephone was lost to her, and she kept away from the other gods and hid herself in the dark places of the earth. She kept away from mortals, too, for wherever she went she saw mothers with their children about them, and she could not bear the sight of their happiness. So she wandered alone over the earth, grieving for her lost Persephone.

As she mourned, she neglected the little seeds that lay in the brown earth. The seeds could not sprout and grow, and consequently there was no grain to be ground into flour for bread and the people became hungry. All growing things missed the care of Demeter: the grass turned sere and withered away, the trees in the olive orchards dropped their leaves, and the little birds all flew away to a distant country. Even the sheep that fed among the water springs in the valley of Enna grew thin and pitiful-looking.

Zeus saw that without Demeter, the Great Mother, there could be no life on the earth, for in time all men and animals would perish for lack of food. So he told Iris to set up her rainbow bridge in the sky and hasten down to the dark cave where Demeter was mourning for Persephone; he charged Iris to persuade Demeter to forget her grief and return to the fields where she was desperately needed.

Iris found Demeter sitting in a corner of the cave, wrapped in dark blue draperies that made her almost invisible in the shadows. The coming of Iris set beautiful colors dancing everywhere, but Demeter did not smile.

Then Zeus sent the gods, one after another, down to the cave, but none of them could comfort the Earth Mother or persuade her to go forth once more.

Zeus than dispatched Hermes down into Hades' kingdom to persuade the dark-faced King to allow Persephone to return to her mother. When Hermes told his errand to Hades, Persephone jumped from her throne with such eagerness to behold her mother again that

Hades consented. He ordered the golden chariot and the black horses to be brought forth, but before she jumped into the chariot, he asked her if she would not eat one of the pomegranates that grew in his garden.

Persephone tasted the fruit, taking just four seeds. Then the black horses carried Hermes and the child to the cave where Demeter sat mourning.

Demeter clasped her little daughter with great joy, but she asked anxiously, "My child, have you eaten anything since you have been underground?"

"Only four pomegranate seeds," answered Persephone.

And Demeter despaired and appealed to Zeus. He said that Persephone might spend eight months of the year with her mother, but would have to pass the other four, one for each pomegranate seed, in the underworld with Hades.

So Demeter returned to her beautiful valley of Enna. And the little brown seeds sprouted and grew, the brown grass became green, the grapevines and olive trees put forth new leaves, and all the little birds came back under the leadership of the crane of Demeter.

But when the time came for Persephone to go back to Hades, Demeter withdrew and sat among the shadows of the cave, as she had done before. And all nature slept for a while. But the peasants were not afraid now, for they knew that Persephone would surely return, and that Demeter. the Earth Mother, would once again care for her children.

THE LION, THE TIGER, AND THE EAGLE
(Modern Greece)

Once on a time there was a King who had three sons and three daughters. When the time came for the King to die, he said to his sons, "My sons, I am now dying, but I charge you first to get your sisters married, and afterwards to marry, yourselves. As for you," he said to the youngest son, "I have a fairy for you shut up in the crystal chamber, and when your sisters are married, see that you get married, too."

After counseling them further, he died. A few days later, the Queen died, too, so the six children were left orphans.

A short time passed, and there came a lion who knocked at the palace door.

"Who is there?" asked the King's children.

"I am the lion," came the answer, "and I am here to take your eldest sister to wife."

"How far off is your dwelling?" they asked.

"For such as myself, five days' journey, and for such as you, five years," said he.

"Five years!" they cried. "We will not let our sister go. If she should ever fall ill, how would we get to see her?"

But the youngest brother took the eldest sister by the hand and led her to the lion. "Go where your fortune takes you," he said.

So when they had made love to one another, the lion took her and fled. And all but the youngest brother sor-

· 120 ·

rowed for her. But he thought of his father's counsel and kept silent.

The next day the tiger knocked at the door.

"What do you want?" they asked.

"I have come to take your second sister to wed," he replied.

"How far off is your dwelling?" they asked fearfully.

"For such as I, ten days, for such as you, ten years," he replied.

"Ten years!" they cried. "We will not let our sister go!"

But the youngest brother took the second sister by the hand and led her to the tiger. And the tiger hastened away with her.

The next day the eagle came and knocked on the door.

"Who is there?" they asked.

"I am the eagle," he said, "and I have come to wed your youngest sister."

"How far off is your dwelling?" they asked.

"For such as I, fifteen days, but for such as you, fifteen years," he answered.

"We will not let our sister go!" cried the elder brother and the second brother. "One sister we have let go five years' journey away, another ten, and shall we let this one go a fifteen years' journey? We will not!"

But the youngest brother took the youngest sister by the hand and led her to the eagle.

When the maidens were married, the young men were married also, first the eldest, then the second. At last the youngest opened the crystal chamber to take out the fairy.

But the fairy immediately escaped and called to him, "If you want me, make an iron staff and iron shoes, and come

To the Illinees, the Billinees, the Alamalacusians,
Unto the marble mountains, and unto the crystal
meadows.

So the youngest brother made the iron staff and the iron shoes and went to find the fairy. When he had gone five years' journey, he came to his elder sister's house and sat down outside in the courtyard on a stone seat. Then a maidservant came out to fill her pail with water, and he asked her for a drink from the pail. At first she refused him, but finally she listened to his entreaties, and gave him the pail. While he drank the water, he dropped his ring into the pail. The servant brought the water to her mistress, and the elder sister perceived at once that her brother was outside.

"To whom have you given water?" she asked.

"To nobody," replied the servant.

"Don't be afraid," said her mistress. "Tell me who the man was."

"He is a traveler, and he is sitting on the stone seat outside," said the servant. "He besought me for water, and I gave him a drink."

"Go and bid him come in," said the eldest sister.

When he entered, they embraced each other, and his sister asked him. "How did you come here?"

He told her all that had happened to him, and as they were talking, they heard the lion returning home.

"Let me hide you," she said to the youngest brother, "for he might eat you." And she gave him a pat and he was turned into a broom, and she put him against the door.

When the lion entered, he said, "I smell kingly blood!"

"Kingly the ways that you walk!" replied the King's daughter. "Hence the smell of kingly blood in your nose!"

While they were eating, she asked the lion, "If my eldest brother were to come, what would you do to him?"

"I would rip him up," said the lion.

"And if the second one were to come?"

"I would turn him into mincemeat!"

"And if the youngest came?"

"I would kiss him on his eyes," said the lion.

"He has come," said the King's daughter.

"And you hide him from me?" said the lion.

Then she took the broom and gave it a pat and it became her youngest brother.

The lion embraced him, kissed him, and asked him why he had come.

So the youngest brother told all that had befallen him, and asked the lion if he knew where were the

Illinees, the Billinees, the Alamalacusians,
The mountains made of marble, and the meadows all of
    crystal.

"I'm sorry, but I don't know them myself," replied the lion. "But tomorrow I'll summon all the beasts, and perhaps one of them may know."

On the morrow he summoned all the beasts, but none of them knew. So the youngest brother set out again to find the crystal fairy. After another five years' journey, he came to the home of his second sister, and he sat again in the courtyard on a stone seat. When the maid-servant came to fetch water, he begged her for a drink from her pail.

As he drank, he dropped his ring in the pail, and when his sister saw the ring she sent the servant to call him in.

When they had embraced each other, she asked him why he had come. And while he was telling her all that had happened to him, they heard the tiger coming home. She gave him a pat and turned him into a dustbox, so that the tiger might not eat him.

"I smell kingly blood!" roared the tiger as soon as he entered.

"Kingly are the ways that you walk!" said the second sister, "hence the smell of king's blood in your nose." And as they were eating, she asked the tiger, "What would you do if my eldest brother were to come?"

"I'd rip him up!" said the tiger.

"What if the second one came?"

"I'd make mincemeat of him!"

"What if the youngest one came?"

"I would treat him as a brother," said the tiger.

"He has come," she said, "and I was afraid you would eat him, so I hid him."

"Bring him forth," said the tiger.

So she gave the dustbox a pat, and there was the younger brother smiling at the tiger. The tiger embraced him and kissed him and asked why he had come.

The youngest brother told his story and asked the tiger if he knew of the Illinees, the Billinees, the Alamalacusians.

"I don't know them," answered the tiger, "but tomorrow I'll call together all the beasts, and some of them may know."

So in the morning he summoned the beasts, but none of them knew.

The youngest brother set off again, and after another five years' journey, he came to the home of his youngest sister. Again he sat on the stone seat before his sister's house, again he begged a drink from the maidservant and threw his ring in the pail. When the youngest sister saw the ring and knew that her brother was outside, she had him come in. When he entered, they embraced and kissed each other and she asked why he had come. And he told her all that had befallen him.

When the eagle came in and welcomed him and asked why he had come, the youngest brother told his story again and asked the eagle if he knew of the Illinees, Billinees, the Alamalacusians.

"I regret that I know them not," answered the eagle, "But tomorrow I'll gather together all the birds, and perhaps one of them may know."

On the morrow he called all the birds together and asked them, but not one of them knew. "However," said one, "there is a lame she-hawk absent, and perhaps she may know."

Then the lame she-hawk came, and she did know. Then the eagle said to her, "Take this Prince to

The Illinees, the Billinees, the Alamalacusians,
Unto the marble mountains, and unto the crystal
meadows!"

"I will," said the lame she-hawk.

And when she had led the youngest brother there, the iron shoes were full of holes and the iron staff was worn thin. And there the fairy awaited him among the other fairies, and she embraced him and kissed him, and he took his bride home to the King's palace and they were married amid much happiness.

Czechoslovakia ❧ ❧ ❧ ❧

THE DEVIL'S LITTLE BROTHER-IN-LAW

MANY YEARS AGO THERE LIVED IN CZECHOSLO-vakia a boy named Peter. When his father, a rich farmer, died, his stepmother robbed him of his inheritance and drove him out into the world.

"I never want to see your face again!" she shouted. "Be off with you!"

"But where shall I go?" asked Peter.

"Go to the Devil, for all I care!" his stepmother cried angrily, and slammed the door in his face.

Sadly Peter took to the road, looking back over his shoulder at the farm he loved. But he was a strong boy, unafraid of work, and he felt sure he could make his way in the world. He trudged to the next village and stopped at a large farmhouse. The farmer was standing in his doorway, eating bread and butter.

Peter touched his hat and said, "Let everyone praise Lord Jesus!"

"Until the Day of Judgment," answered the farmer and swallowed his bread. Then he asked harshly, "What are you after?"

"I'm looking for work. Do you need a laborer on your farm? I know farming well."

"You?" sneered the farmer. "With those fine clothes? Go to the Devil!" And he slammed his door in Peter's face.

Peter tramped on to the next village and knocked at the door of the bailiff's house. The bailiff's wife, a kindly woman, answered his knock.

She spoke in a gentle voice to Peter. "The master is playing cards with a couple of his friends. I'll go and ask if he has any work for you. Wait here, boy." And she left the door open.

Peter heard her speak to someone, and a rough voice shouted, "No! How many times must I tell you not to interrupt me when I'm busy? Tell the rascal to go to the Devil!"

Weary and heavy-hearted, Peter turned away without waiting for the bailiff's wife to return. He wandered off on a woods-path, and when he had gone some distance among the green trees he sat down on a stone and put his chin in his hands. There didn't seem to be any place for him in all the world, and he felt like crying, but big boys don't cry. If he knew the way to hell, he thought, he would certainly go to the Devil.

At that moment a handsome man, dressed in green, strolled past.

Peter touched his hat politely and said, in greeting, "Let everyone praise Lord Jesus."

But the man did not return his greeting. Then he looked back and paused in the path. "Why do you look so discouraged, my boy?" he asked.

"Because," answered Peter, "wherever I ask for work, people tell me to go to the Devil. If I knew how to get to hell, I'd take their advice and go. The Devil must surely be kinder than people are."

The man smiled strangely. "Wouldn't you be afraid of the Devil if you saw him?"

"No," said Peter. "He can't be any worse than my stepmother or the farmer or the bailiff. I'm positive of that."

Suddenly the man turned black. "Here I am!" he said. "I'm the Devil!"

Unafraid, Peter looked him calmly up and down. "So you're the Devil!" he said in an even tone.

"I am. And if you'd like to enter my service, fine. I can use a fearless, industrious boy like you. The work is light and the hours are good, and if you do as I tell you, you'll have a pleasant time."

"I'd like to work for you," said Peter.

"Good. I'll keep you in my service for seven years, and after that time, I'll give you a gift and set you free. Agreed?"

"Agreed," said Peter, and he and the Devil shook hands on the bargain.

Then the Devil put his arm around Peter, and before he knew it Peter was in hell. The Devil gave him a leather apron and took him into a room where there were three enormous caldrons.

"It's your job to keep the fires always burning under these caldrons," the Devil explained. "Keep four logs under the first, eight logs under the second, and twelve logs under the third caldron. And remember, Peter, you are never to peep inside the caldrons!"

"I'll remember," Peter promised, and set to work very happily.

Time passed quickly, and Peter enjoyed his life in hell. In fact, he was so well treated that it seemed rather that he was in heaven. He had plenty of excellent food and drink, no one scolded him, and he had the young apprentice devils for merry companions. They were always telling funny stories and playing pranks on each other, and Peter found them the best of friends. He kept the correct number of logs on the three fires and never once did he peep into the three caldrons. The Devil was thoroughly satisfied with his services.

But finally Peter began to grow homesick for earth. He longed to see the green grass and walk in the woods and talk to village folk again. So he asked the Devil how much longer he would have to serve, for he had lost track of time.

"Your seven years are up tomorrow," the Devil said.

The following day while Peter was piling fresh logs under the caldrons, the Devil came into the room. "Peter, you are free today," he said. "You've served me well and faithfully, and I shall reward you. Money would be too heavy for you to carry back to the world, so I am going to give you this magic bag. Whenever you open it and say, 'Bag, I need some ducats,' the bag will always have as much money as you need. And good luck to you, Peter. I've grown rather fond of you, you know. But I

don't think you'll have much fun at first, for people will think you're a devil. You're pretty black, for you haven't taken a bath for seven years and you haven't cut your hair or your nails."

"That's right," said Peter. "I'd forgotten I haven't washed since I've been here. I certainly must take a bath and get a haircut."

"No, Peter," the Devil said. "One bath won't do it. Water won't wash off our kind of black. But I won't tell you what to do just yet. You go up into the world as you are, and if people ask you who you are, tell them you're the Devil's little brother-in-law. And if you ever need me, call me."

So Peter said goodby to all the little black apprentices who were very sorry to see him go. And the Devil lifted him on his back, whisked him up to earth and put him down in the woods on the exact spot where they had met seven years previously. The Devil said goodby and vanished, and Peter, with the magic bag in his pocket, tramped to the nearest village.

But when the children playing in the road saw him, they screamed and ran home, crying, "The Devil! The Devil is coming!"

Mothers and fathers rushed out of the houses to see what the trouble was, but when they caught sight of Peter, they dashed inside again, barred the doors and windows, and prayed God to protect them.

Peter was a little worried, but he went on to the tavern. As he came up the road, he saw the landlord and his wife standing in the doorway, smelling the sunlight.

He walked toward them slowly, wondering if he were really as black as people seemed to think.

But when they looked at him, they cried out and in their haste to get inside the tavern, tripped over each other and fell down. Peter had to laugh. He stepped over them, went inside the tavern, and sat down.

"Landlord," he called, "bring me a drink, please!" And he was still chuckling.

The landlord and his wife untangled themselves and came into the tavern, shaking with fear. The wife scuttled to the back quarters of the tavern, while the landlord, pale and trembling, hurried to the cellar to draw a big pitcher of beer.

"Yirik," called the landlord to his little herdboy who was working in the stable.

The herdboy came running at the urgency in his master's voice. "What is it, master?"

"Take this beer into the house quickly," said the landlord. "There's a strange man waiting for it, but don't be afraid—he won't harm you."

Yirik started into the tavern, the pitcher of beer in his hand, but when he caught sight of Peter, he dropped the pitcher and raced for the stable.

The landlord, bulky in the stable doorway, stopped the boy's terrified bolting by the simple expedient of getting his stout stomach in the way. With a grunt, he seized Yirik by the back of his shirt. "Where are you going?" he yelled. "You didn't give the gentleman his beer! And you broke the pitcher, too! Both of them will come out of your wages! Draw another pitcher at once and put it before the gentleman!" And he gave Yirik an extra shake toward the cellar.

Yirik was mightily afraid of Peter, but he was more afraid of the landlord whom he served for his keep and three dollars a year. With shaking hands he drew another pitcher of beer and forced himself to enter the tavern.

"Good day, boy," called Peter in a kind voice. "Don't be afraid—I won't harm you. I'm not the Devil, you know."

Yirik shivered but held firmly to the pitcher.

"I'm only the Devil's little brother-in-law," said Peter with a smile.

Yirik placed the beer in front of Peter and stood there, not daring to raise his eyes and look upon the Devil's little brother-in-law.

"Who are you?" asked Peter. "This is excellent beer. I didn't realize that I was so thirsty."

"I'm an orphan," answered Yirik, still afraid to look up.

"How did you come to be working here?"

"I had to find work," Yirik answered and found he could look this stranger straight in the eyes. "I'm not afraid of work."

"Nor I," said Peter. "But from all I've seen, you're not being treated any too well."

Yirik gazed directly at Peter and found he was unafraid. "I don't mind work," he said modestly. And he forgot that Peter looked like a devil and found he was talking to him as if he were an old friend.

Moved by Yirik's story, which reminded him of his own, Peter pulled out his magic bag and filled Yirik's cap with golden ducats. The orphan boy was dazzled at first, and then he began to jump up and down with joy. He hugged Peter and ran out to the stable to show the landlord the gift which the stranger had given him. He showed the villagers, too, his capful of ducats.

"And he's not the Devil!" cried Yirik. "He's only the Devil's little brother-in-law!"

Since Peter had no horns, the landlord, thinking of ducats, became courageous all of a sudden and hastened into the tavern with a pitcher of foaming beer which he set before Peter with a flourish. "Dear master," he begged, "pray give me a few golden ducats, such as you gave that young imp, my servant!"

But Peter, drinking the beer, only laughed at him. "I think, though," said Peter, "that I shall stay the night here. I want a good room and a comfortable bed."

"Anything," said the landlord. "Anything at all."

But just as Peter was falling asleep, somebody shook his shoulder, and he opened his eyes to see the Devil standing by his bed.

"Hurry!" the Devil whispered. "Get up and go to the shed quickly! The landlord is going to murder the orphan boy for his money!"

Peter jumped out of bed and rushed out of the tavern to the shed where Yirik slept. As he flung open the door, he saw the landlord bending over the sleeping boy with a dagger.

"Murderer!" cried Peter. "You go off to hell with me this minute, to stew forever in burning oil!"

The landlord fainted dead away with fear, and Peter dragged him into the tavern and dumped him on the floor. When he regained his senses, the landlord, shaking with terror, begged for mercy and promised Peter all he possessed if only he might have another chance.

Peter scowled and the landlord trembled like a leaf in a gale. "I won't want your possessions," said Peter. "But you must treat Yirik as if he were your own son. You must be kind to him and send him to school."

"I promise, I promise!" gasped the landlord.

"Get up," said Peter. "The instant you forget your promise and treat him with cruelty, I'll carry you off to hell! Remember!"

"I'll remember!" quavered the landlord.

And he did. From that night on, he was a different person. He sent Yirik to school, he fed him well, and was as kind to the boy as he knew how to be. He gave up his evil ways and became honest and forthright.

Peter found the tavern very comfortable to live in, so he stayed on there, going for long walks in the woods whenever he felt like it. Tales of him and his golden ducats began to spread throughout the country. One day a messenger came to him from the Prince of the land, demanding his presence at the castle. But Peter replied that if the Prince wished to see him, he could come to the tavern. And the messenger. looking a trifle pale, hurried off.

When Peter asked the landlord why the Prince could

possibly want to see him, the landlord explained that the Prince probably wanted to borrow some money, "He has two wicked extravagant daughters," said the landlord, "and he can't do a thing with them. They spend the money of the country as if it were sand, and the people are about to rise up against him because of it. Those two are the daughters of his first marriage, but he has a third daughter, the child of his second wife. Her name is Angelina."

"Hmm," said Peter thoughtfully, reaching for his beer.

"And she's as good as an angel and probably more beautiful," said the landlord, "God bless her. I've never seen an angel, but I can't imagine any angel lovelier than our Princess Linka. As for the other two, may they go to the Devil!" Suddenly remembering to whom he was talking, he gulped and slapped his hand over his mouth. "Oh, my goodness!" said the landlord.

But Peter laughed. "Don't mind me, landlord. I'm not the Devil. I'm only the Devil's little brother-in-law."

"Even so," said the landlord, "I can't say I see much difference." And with his heart still thudding heavily in his chest, he hurried off to draw another pitcher of beer for Peter, while Peter grinned at his stout back.

On a bright afternoon shortly afterward, when Peter was just about to start out for a walk in the woods, the Prince came riding down to the tavern.

"Oh, bother!" said Peter, but he waited to see what the Prince wanted.

The Prince shuddered when he looked at Peter, but

politely he invited him to visit the castle at any time Peter might feel like it. Then he asked to borrow a large sum of money.

"I'll give you all the money you need," said Peter, "if you'll permit me to marry one of your daughters."

"Which one?" asked the Prince.

"It doesn't matter particularly," Peter answered. "Any one of them." He gave the Prince some money, and accepted the Prince's invitation to come to the castle the next day to meet his future bride.

When he reached home, the Prince told his daughters that he had met the Devil's little brother-in-law, and that he wouldn't be such a bad-looking fellow if only he washed his face and had his hair trimmed and his nails cut.

Then the Prince talked to them in a serious tone about the state of the treasury and warned them that he must raise a large sum of money very soon, or there would be an uprising among the people. And he told them that one of them must marry Peter, for he saw no other way to obtain the money and keep the peace of the country.

The two elder princesses laughed and jeered. Both of them declared that they wouldn't marry a black creature like Peter, even if the country went to wrack and ruin.

"In that case, I don't know what I shall do," said the Prince in despair.

But Linka, the youngest, put her hand on her father's arm. "Father, I'll marry him, if it means your happiness and the peace of our country," she said.

"Little sister-in-law of the Devil!" mocked the elder sisters. "If you were to marry the Devil himself, that would be worth something, for you'd be Princess Lucifer. But to be only his sister-in-law—ho! ho!—our little Linka is a fool!"

The following day Peter appeared at the castle, and when the elder sisters saw how black he was, they were overjoyed that they had refused to marry him. But when Linka saw him, she fainted. And Peter felt very badly. When she came to herself, the Prince led her to Peter and put her hand into Peter's. She was trembling with terror and her small hand was icy.

But Peter whispered to her, "Don't be afraid, little Princess. I know I look horrible, but I won't always be so awful. And if you will marry me, I shall always love you deeply."

The gentle sound of his voice comforted her, but every time she looked at him, she shook with fear. Peter gave the Prince a great sum of money and hurried off, promising to return in eight days for the wedding.

He went into the wood where he had first met the Devil, and called him by name.

The Devil appeared at once. "Can I help you, little brother-in-law?"

"Yes," said Peter. "I want to look like myself again, so I won't frighten the Princess Linka half to death whenever she looks at me."

"Come along then," said the Devil. "Leap on my back."

Peter obeyed, and they flew over mountains and forests and strange countries until at length they came down in a thick forest beside a clear spring.

"Wash in this water, little brother-in-law," said the Devil, "and you will be a handsome young man."

Peter flung off his clothes and jumped into the pool, and when he emerged his skin was as clean and fresh as a child's. Again they flew off but this time they went to a great city. There Peter purchased marvelous clothes, jewels, coaches, and horses. He hired servants and dressed them in splendid livery, and set out for his bride with a retinue worthy of a prince.

In the meantime, Princess Linka sat pale and quivering in her room, while her elder sisters ridiculed her and made jokes about her black lover. Then from the window they saw a long line of gleaming coaches with outriders in wonderful livery. When the coaches stopped at the castle gate a beautiful young man descended and hurried into the castle. He made his way directly to Linka's chamber and took her cold hand.

"Linka," said Peter, "look at me. You won't be afraid now."

She looked at him and she thought that he was the most splendid youth in the world. She fell in love with him immediately.

Her two elder sisters at the window glared at her with envy and astonishment. Suddenly they were clutched from behind, and there was the Devil, laughing at them.

"I'm Prince Lucifer himself," he said, "so in marrying me, you won't be losing rank!" And he chuckled. "See, Peter, you really are my brother-in-law! You're marrying one sister, and I'm taking the other two!" And he picked up the two wicked sisters and all three of them disap-peared out of the window.

And Peter and Linka were married, and they never saw their brother-in-law, the Devil, again for all of their long and happy lives.

India 🖋 🖋 🖋 🖋 🖋 🖋

THE UNFORGIVING MONKEY

THERE ONCE LIVED A KING NAMED MOON, WHO kept a pack of monkeys for his son's amusement. He also had a herd of rams for the Prince to play with.

One ram was extremely greedy, and he would run into the kitchen at any hour of the day or night and gobble everything in sight. The cooks would beat him with the broomstick or anything else they could snatch up, but he learned nothing and his appetite seemed to increase instead of lessen.

When the chief of the monkeys observed this, he thought, "This quarrel between the ram and the cooks will mean the death of the monkeys! The ram is a glutton, and when the cooks are angry they hit him with anything that may be handy. Suppose they snatched up a firebrand and beat him with it! His wool would catch fire. And if he ran, burning, into the stable near by, the thatch would blaze and the horses would be scorched. And since the standard work on veterinary science pre scribes monkey fat to relieve burns on horses, we are about to be destroyed!"

He assembled the monkeys and told them his conclusion and added, "Let us leave the house and take to the woods before we are all dead!"

But the monkeys laughed at him, and one of the young boy monkeys jeered, "Ho! You're old and your mind is slipping! We certainly don't intend to give up all the dainties which the Prince gives us with his own hands, in order to live on the puckery sour fruits out there in the forest!"

The chief monkey made a face. "You are fools," he said. "This life may be sweet now, but before long it will turn to poison. I don't intend to witness the death of my friends and family, so I'm off to the forest this minute!"

One day after the chief monkey had departed, the ram bounced into the kitchen and started gnawing a roast. The cook, enraged, finding nothing else handy, picked up a firebrand, half consumed and still blazing, and struck the ram with it. On fire, the ram plunged, bleating wildly, into the stable. There he rolled until flames started up on all sides, some of the horses died while others, half burned to death, snapped their halters and whinnied loudly with pain.

The King named Moon hastily assembled his veterinary surgeons and demanded that they prescribe some method of giving the horses relief from their pain.

The veterinary surgeons replied, "O King, the master of our craft prescribed for this emergency as follows:

Let monkey fat be freely used;
Like dark before the dawn,
The pain that horses feel from burns
Will very soon be gone.

Pray use monkey fat at once, before the poor horses perish."

So the King ordered the slaughter of the monkeys, and every single one was killed.

The chief monkey did not behold the outrage, but he heard the story of the destruction of the monkeys as it passed through the forest, and he did not take it with good grace.

As he was wandering about the forest one day, feeling thirsty, he came to a lake where lovely clusters of lotuses blossomed. He noticed footprints leading into the lake, but none coming out, and he knew there must be some sort of fiend in the water. So he stayed at a safe distance and drank through a hollow lotus stalk.

No sooner had he finished drinking when a man-eating fiend with a pearl necklace around his neck arose from the water. "Monkey," he said, "I eat everyone who enters this water; and you are very shrewd to drink through a lotus stalk. I have taken a liking to you. Name your heart's desire."

The chief monkey asked promptly, "How many people can you eat at one time?"

"Oh, hundreds," said the fiend, smacking his lips. "Hundreds, thousands, hundreds of thousands, if they enter the water. Outside of the water, a jackal can conquer me."

"Well," said the monkey, "a certain King named Moon is my mortal enemy. If you'll lend me that pearl necklace I'll arouse his greed with a story and will make him and his whole retinue enter your lake."

"Fine," said the fiend, and he gave the monkey the necklace.

When people saw the monkey wandering over the trees and the palace roof with a pearl necklace around his throat, they asked, "Where have you been all this time, chief? And where did you get that marvelous pearl necklace?"

The chief monkey replied, "In the forest there is a cunningly hidden lake, created by the god of wealth. If anyone bathes there at sunrise on Sunday, the god comes out with a pearl necklace like this around his neck and gives it to the bather."

The King, hearing this tale from one of his courtiers, summoned the monkey and asked for the truth.

"O King," answered the monkey, "you have visible proof of the truth in this pearl necklace around my throat. If you, too, could find use for a necklace, send somebody with me and I'll show him the lake."

But the King said, "I'll come myself, with my retinue, so that we may acquire many pearl necklaces."

"O King," said the monkey happily, "your idea is excellent!"

So the King and his retinue set out, greedy for pearl necklaces. And the King had the monkey ride with him in his palanquin and showed him honor as they traveled.

They reached the lake at dawn, and the monkey said, "O King, all of your attendants must rush into the lake together at sunrise. You, however, must enter with me, for I will pick the place I found before and show you plenty of pearl necklaces."

All the King's attendants ran into the lake just as the sun arose, and they were immediately eaten by the fiend.

Then, as he waited, the King said to the monkey, "Tell me, chief, why don't my attendants return?"

The monkey hurried to climb a tree before he answered. Then he called down, "You wicked King, your attendants have been eaten by a fiend that lives in the lake. My anger at you, caused by the death of my household, has now ended. I did not make you enter the water, because I recalled that you were the King. Go back to your palace now. You plotted the death of my family and friends, and I of yours."

The King, grief-stricken, hurried home, and when he had gone, the fiend, pleased with his feast, arose from the water. He called to the monkey, who was sitting contentedly in the tree:

> *Very good, my monkey—O!*
> *You've won a friend and hurt a foe!*
> *You've kept the pearls without a flaw*
> *By drinking water through a straw!*

THE MAGIC LAMP

There once lived a poor widow who had an only son, and the boy was well-mannered and handsome One day a merchant from a distant country came to her house and said, "I am your husband's elder brother."

But the widow replied, "My husband died many years ago."

The merchant mourned the loss of his younger brother, and stayed several days in the widow's house. At the end of that time, he said, "The boy and I will go in search of the golden flowers. Prepare food for our journey."

The widow did so; and in the morning her son and her brother-in-law set out.

When they had gone many miles, the boy was exhausted and said, "Uncle, I can't go any further."

The merchant scolded him for being a weakling and walked on as fast as he could.

After a while the boy said again, "I am so tired, I can't go any further."

But his uncle turned back and gave him a beating. Pressed by fear, the boy struggled to walk rapidly along the road. Finally they climbed a hill, and the uncle made the boy gather a large pile of firewood. They had no fire with them, but the uncle made the boy blow with his mouth as if he were kindling a fire. He blew until he was worn out, and then asked, "What sense is there in blowing when there is no fire?"

"Blow," said the merchant, "or I'll beat you again."

Once again he blew and he blew, and then he paused and said, "There is no fire. How can it possibly burn?"

The merchant struck him severely, and the boy tried harder. Finally the pile of firewood burst into flame. When the pile of wood had burned down, an iron trap door appeared among the ashes, and the uncle ordered the boy to open it. The boy pulled, but was unable to life the heavy door.

"It will not open," he said.

"Pull harder," said the uncle.

The boy pulled with all his strength, but the door refused to move. "It will not open," he said.

His uncle struck him violently. "Open that door!" he shouted.

The boy tugged and tugged and at last the door was raised, and the boy saw a light burning in a vault and beside the lamp was a great quantity of golden flowers.

"Go down there," said the merchant, "and as you enter, don't touch any of the golden flowers, but put out the lamp. Then pile on that gold tray as many of the gold flowers as you can, and bring them up to me."

The boy did as he was told, and on reaching the door asked his uncle to take the gold flowers so that he could climb out.

"Climb out the best way you can!" growled the merchant.

"How can I," asked the boy, "when my hands are full?"

At that, the merchant shut the iron trap door on him, and went away.

Imprisoned in the dark vault, the boy wept in despair; and being without food, in a few days he became very weak. Taking the lamp in his hand, he sat down in a corner and unwittingly began to rub it. A ring which he was wearing came into contact with the lamp, and at once a fairy came out of it and asked, "What do you wish of me?"

Astonished, the boy said, "Please open the iron door and let me out."

The fairy did so, and the boy hastened home to his mother, taking the lamp with him. "Mother," he said, "I'm terribly hungry."

"My poor son," she answered, "there is nothing in the house to give you."

The boy said, "I'll clean this lamp and sell it, and buy some food with the money." He began to scrub the lamp, and his ring touched it.

The fairy came forth and asked, "What do you wish?"

"Cooked rice and uncooked rice, if you please," said the boy.

The fairy immediately brought him a tremendous quantity of both kinds of rice, and he and his mother had a fine supper.

A while after this, some merchants brought horses for sale, and the boy, seeing them, wished he could buy one. But he had no money, so he pressed his ring against his lamp, and said to the fairy, "Please bring me a horse." At once the fairy presented him with a herd of horses.

When the boy had grown up into a young man, he chanced one day to see the Rajah's daughter being carried to the ghat to bathe. He watched her palkee with the attendants passing; then he hurried to his mother and said, "I'm going to see the Princess."

His mother tried to persuade him not to go. But he argued that she must give him permission. Finally she said that he might go.

He went to the ghat and hid and watched secretly as the Princess was bathing, and he fell in love with her. When he returned home, he said to his mother, "Mother, I have seen the Princess, and I am in love with her. Please go and tell the Rajah that your son loves his daughter and asks her hand in marriage."

His mother answered, "But we are poor people, and the Rajah will never in this world consent."

But the young man kept urging her to go, until she was at last weary of his talking. So she went to the palace and gained an audience with the Rajah, and told him that her son loved his daughter and begged that the Princess might be given to him in marriage.

The Rajah replied that if her son would give him an immense sum of money, more than the Rajah himself possessed, he would give his daughter to the young man. The mother went home and told her son. "Of course he doesn't wish the Princess to marry a poor boy like you," she said.

But the young man rubbed his ring on the lamp, and the fairy gave him a much larger sum than the Rajah had asked for. He took the money to the Rajah, who was amazed at so much wealth.

After a suitable time the mother went to the Rajah to request him to keep his promise. But the Rajah, hoping to evade fulfilling his promise, demanded that a palace befitting her rank and station be prepared for his daughter.

The young man rubbed his ring on the lamp, and the fairy, overnight, built a beautiful castle where before there had not been even a hut. The Rajah could not now refuse his daughter's hand, although the Dewan tried to dissuade him. The Princess fell in love with the young man on sight, and they were married with great joy.

Some time after the marriage, the Rajah and the young man went to the forest to hunt. While they were away, the wicked uncle who had shut the boy in the vault of the golden flowers appeared at the castle gate. He carried a new lamp which he offered to the Princess in exchange for any old lamp she might have around. She exchanged her husband's old lamp for a new one, not knowing what she did. The merchant at once rubbed his ring on the magic lamp and commanded the fairy, "Carry the castle, as it stands, with the Princess in it, to my own country."

When the Rajah and the young man returned from the hunt, they were greatly distressed to find that the castle and the Princess had vanished.

"Aha," said the Dewan. "Didn't I tell you some calamity would follow your giving your daughter to this unknown person?"

Grieved and angry, the Rajah said to the young man, "I give you thirteen days to find my daughter! If you fail, I shall have you executed on the fourteenth morning!"

The young man searched frantically everywhere, but he could not find his beloved wife. The thirteenth day arrived, and he resigned himself to his fate, thinking, "I shall go and rest, for tomorrow morning I shall be killed." And he climbed to the top of a high hill and lay down to sleep upon a rock. While he slept, he accidentally rubbed his ring upon the rock, and a fairy appeared and awakened him, asking, "What do you wish of me?"

"Oh," said the young man, "I have lost my wife and my palace, and if you know where they are, please take me to them!"

At once the fairy took him to the gate of his castle in the merchant's country. Taking the form of a dog, the young man entered the palace. The Princess knew him immediately, and embraced him, and told him that the merchant was out on business. "He has taken the lamp with him," she said, "and he wears it on a chain around his neck."

"What shall we do?" asked the young husband.

"I'll put poison in his food this evening," said the Princess.

When the merchant returned and called for his supper, the Princess set the poisoned rice before him. He ate it greedily and promptly died. The young husband then took his lamp and rubbed it.

"Take my castle with the Princess and myself in it, and set it down where it stood before in the Rajah's country," he asked the fairy, and instantly the castle was back where it had stood before.

When the fourteenth day dawned, the Rajah was delighted at finding his daughter returned. He divided his kingdom with the young man, and they ruled the country peacefully and happily for many years.

United States of America 🖋 🖋

JOHNNY APPLESEED

THE AUTUMN STARS STOOD AT MIDNIGHT OVER THE Ohio wilderness when Johnny Appleseed rose up on his elbows. He glanced around the Indian encampment and saw that the council fire had burned down to a few smoldering embers. Johnny's friends, the warriors, were asleep on the leafy ground, and no one heard him as he reached for his mush pan, his hoe, and his sack of appleseeds.

Barefooted, he slipped noiselessly out of the clearing and into the dark woods. He must warn the white settlers that the Indians would attack their lonely cabins at daybreak! Johnny hid his hoe and his sack in a hollow log and set off at a run through the deep forest, his mush pan slapped on his wind-tangled head like a helmet. He carried no weapon, for though wolves and bears and bobcats roamed the woods, he believed that they were all God's creatures and had as much right to live as he.

Racing tirelessly in his ragged shirt and tattered

breeches, Johnny came out of the woods into the clearing where William Hunter's cabin stood.

He pounded heavily on the plank door, shouting, "Bill! Bill Hunter! Wake up!"

He heard the wooden bar being lifted from the slots inside; the door opened a crack. "Who is it? Oh, Johnny! What's the trouble?"

Johnny said quickly, "The savage will come at break of day! I am he who sows while others reap!" He saw swift fear in Bill's eyes.

"Thank you, Johnny!" The lantern Bill held in his hand flickered in a sudden gust of wind. Behind him, Mrs. Hunter's white face appeared. "Indians, Clara," he said.

Johnny Appleseed lifted his mush pan to Mrs. Hunter. "I must warn the others," he said and jogged off through the clearing to the woods.

Two days later, he was back in the Indian camp, attending to the warriors' wounds and brewing them catnip tea.

"Great Medicine Man," the Chief said, "in seven sunrises we shall attack the little garrison at Mansfield. The British will give us firewater and shooting irons! Will you start us another garden of these healing herbs?"

"I'll plant it this afternoon," Johnny answered, wondering how in the world he could run sixty miles through the wilderness to get reinforcements for the garrison. This war of 1812 was perilous for the stubborn settlers in Ohio, and the soldiers in the scattered garrisons were few. If the soldiers at Mansfield were wiped out, the neighboring pioneers would have no soldiers at all to defend them against the warring savages. Johnny sighed and gave the Chief a birch-bark bowlful of catnip tea.

That afternoon he hoed and planted another patch of herbs for the Indians. And that night when they were asleep, he started out once more, jogging and running instinctively through the black, trackless woods. A wind was up and it smelled of rain.

As he leaped fallen trees and skirted swamps, he thought of his father's farm on the outskirts of Boston Town. There he had been born in 1775, when the slanted orchard behind his father's house was cloudy white with apple blossoms. His grandmother, he'd been told, had washed and clothed him, his father and mother had admired him and called him Jonathan, and he had been tucked under a homespun blanket in the Chapman cherry cradle. And he had grown as all lads grow, running the earth in woven breeches and a butternut shirt which he was forever tearing on trees and boulders.

Johnny chuckled remembering how he and the neighboring boys had whittled wooden guns and fought the American Revolution up and down the dusty roads, over the orchard hill and through blackberry brambles and juniper thickets, bruising their shins on rocks and the bark of trees. The war had ended when he was eight; and he had become a dreamer, wandering off into the hills and woods where he'd stayed for days with his Bible, reading aloud to the red-brushed foxes, the shy spotted fawns, the impudent chipmunks, and the merry-eared rabbits.

Johnny Appleseed sniffed the wet smell of the wind and hurried on. A surf of cloud was covering the stars. He must get to the fort within two more nights, storm or no storm, to give the soldiers time to ride to the aid of the Mansfield garrison. Otherwise, the garrison would be massacred, and so would the helpless settlers.

As he ran, he recalled how the Thirteen Colonies had become the Thirteen States. The pioneer wagons had begun to roll westward to the new lands beyond the Alleghenies. And Jonathan Chapman, wiry and lean and young in his buckskin shirt, had heard the creak and the clunk of the wagons drawing him toward the far frontiers.

He had traded the brown bread and gingerbread fragrance of New England supper smoke for the wild wood smell of ponecake baked on scattered open fires under the settlers' stars. He'd set his heart and his toes toward the westward plodding wagons; and he'd brought with him, by canoe and horse and his own tough back, the sacks of the small brown pointed seeds whereby he'd sown the lonely sundown wilderness with apple.

He had planted his seeds in nine young states, he'd run ahead of the westward wagons, leaving young orchards for unborn children, leaving the sweetness of apple blossoms for straight-backed mothers with steady eyes. He'd traded a deerskin pouch of appleseeds for a promise of tended orchards and a coffee-sack shirt or a pair of discarded breeches. The settlers had nicknamed him Johnny Appleseed, and he liked that name.

There was a slow surge in the tops of the trees and

then silence. Johnny could hear the rain coming through the darkness and then it struck him, but he only lifted his face to the chill sluice of the rain and ran on, slapping his mush pan more firmly on his head. At daybreak he paused to gulp from a rainy spring and to gather a handful of wet blueberries. He didn't stop to sleep, but raced on through the drenched woods, side-stepping rattlers and porcupines.

On the third evening, soaked to the skin and exhausted, he panted through the gate of the log fort and gasped his message to the captain. When he heard the horses galloping out toward Mansfield, Johnny lay down on the rough floor before the captain's fireplace and fell asleep.

He arose early the next morning. A month ago, he had promised Cy James, a new settler from Rhode Island, to help him with his house-raising, farther north up the Ohio River. Johnny jogged back through the forest to collect his sack of appleseeds and his hoe and hatchet. Cy would want an apple orchard on his land, too. He made up songs as he went along, about the apple trees he had planted by Ohio water, Ontario water, Wabash water. He sang at the top of his lungs to the hawks circling over the woods. The rabbits twitched their whiskers at him out of the thickets. And the drifting deer paused to flick their ears and look at him with dark, astonished eyes. Johnny laughed at them and sang all the songs he could think of, hurrying among the pines and the hemlocks and the buckeyes.

His coffee-sack shirt flapped behind him, and he

shouted cheerfully to the warm October air, "I need new pants before winter comes on! And nobody knows where I'll get them from! Ahead of the westward plodding wagons, I've sown my beautiful apple trees!"

A bluejay flew before him, crying hoarsely, and Johnny tilted his mush pan jauntily on his head, singing happily:

> *I'm Jonathan Chapman from Boston Town,*
> *And the sun comes up and the sun goes down!*
> *Once I was young in a buckskin shirt,*
> *And that red squirrel is trying to flirt!*
> *Oh, I'll swap you a deerskin pouch of seeds*
> *For a pair of pants for my winter's needs!*
> *Hi-up, gray wolf, have you by chance*
> *An extra pair of furry pants?*

On his way back up the river to help Cy James, Johnny stopped overnight with Mark O'Brien, and Mark gave him a pair of sky-blue breeches and a pair of yellow breeches. Johnny presented Mark's four children with some toys he'd been carrying around since his last journey to Pittsburgh; he planted an herb garden for Mrs. O'Brien and started an apple nursery on Mark's river slope. Then he borrowed shears and thread from Mrs. O'Brien, and he cut off and sewed together one blue leg and one yellow leg of the trousers. The children laughed with delight when Johnny, in his new pied breeches, swaggered off toward the James clearing.

Twenty men, with their wives and children, were already there when he arrived, and the foundations of the house were laid. While the women prepared the noon-day meal and the young ones played games, Johnny and the settlers sawed and notched and lifted the logs into place.

"Give me a hoist on this log, Johnny," Cy James called.

"Sure," said Johnny, seizing his end of the log.

"Say, Johnny!" yelled Ed Cooper. "There's a hornet crawling up your blue pant leg!"

"Let her crawl," answered Johnny, grunting as he lifted the log into place. The hornet was stinging him furiously, and his feelings were hurt because after all he hadn't done anything to harm her. But he patted her down his leg and out, while his friends laughed.

"Mrs. Hornet," he said quietly, "you go on home and attend to your children. I'm kind of busy today."

The men doubled up with laughter.

"Johnny, you're the limit!" Cy said.

"Remember that rattlesnake you wouldn't kill?" Ed asked. "I don't know why it didn't bite you. It's a wonder you didn't go to Kingdom Come years ago!"

"Pshaw!" said Johnny. "That snake had as much right to live as I have. But Jake killed it."

"And a good thing, too," said Ed with a shudder. "The way you go stepping over snakes in your bare feet is enough to give a man the creeps."

Johnny Appleseed smiled and lifted the end of another log. "God's creatures," he said. "Same as flies. Or hornets. Or birds or catamounts. I can't hurt them."

One evening the following winter, Johnny was caught

in the woods far from any settler's cabin. He decided to spend the night in a large hollow log, so he smacked his mush pan firmly on his head and got down on his knees in the snow. But as he crawled into the log, a she-bear at the other end growled softly. Johnny backed out, lifted his mush pan and bowed. "I beg your furry pardon, my lady," he said. Then he curled up in a near-by snowdrift and went to sleep under the glittering stars.

When Johnny Appleseed died, in 1847, he had spent fifty years in the wilderness; and his apple trees slanted their elbows over the hills, veered to the wind by the low-banked rivers, and shook petals on lonely window sills.

THE CREATION OF MAN
(An Indian Legend)

When the Coyote had finished making the world and the inferior creatures, he called a council of the creatures to deliberate on the creation of Man. They sat down in an open space in the forest, ranging themselves in a circle, with the Lion at the head. On his right sat the Grizzly Bear, next the Cinnamon Bear, and so on around, according to rank, ending with the little Mouse, who sat at the Lion's left.

The Lion spoke first, and he declared that he would like to see Man created with a tremendous voice like his own, wherewith he could frighten all animals.

"Furthermore," said the Lion, "Man ought to be well covered with hair, have terrible fangs, and strong, sharp talons in his paws. I don't really care what color he is, but I should think a nice tawny shade like mine—"

The Grizzly Bear interrupted. "That's ridiculous! Why should Man have a voice like yours? You're always roaring with it and scaring away the very prey you want to capture! *I* think Man ought to have mighty strength, and move about silently but very swiftly if necessary, and be able to grip his prey without making any noise!"

"To my way of thinking," said the Buck, "Man would look very foolish unless he had a magnificent pair of antlers on his head to fight with. I also think," said the Buck, "that it's very absurd to roar so loudly, and I'd pay less attention to Man's throat than to his ears and eyes. I'd have his ears like a spider's web, and his eyes like fire."

The Mountain Sheep protested that he never could see what sense there was in such antlers, branching every which way only to be caught in the thickets. "Give Man horns like mine," said the Mountain Sheep, "mostly rolled up; they would be like a stone on each side of his head, giving his head weight and enabling him to butt a great deal harder!"

Then it was the Coyote's turn to speak, and he declared that all these were the most stupid speeches he had ever heard in his life, and that he could hardly keep awake while listening to such a pack of nitwits and nincompoops. Every single one of them wanted to make Man like himself! They might just as well take one of their own cubs and call it Man! "As for me," said the Coyote, "I know I'm not the best animal that can be made, and I can make one better than myself or any other. Of course Man will have to be like myself in having four legs, five fingers, and a head with eyes and ears and a nose." The Coyote became so excited, he began to pace up and down. "It's well enough to have a voice like the Lion's," he said, "but Man doesn't need to roar all the time with it."

"Get back in your place in the circle!" said the Lion loudly. "Stop fidgeting—you make me nervous!"

The Coyote sat down. "The Grizzly Bear," he continued, "has some good points, one of which is the shape of his feet, which allows him to stand erect easily, and therefore I am in favor of making Man's feet nearly like the Grizzly's. Also," said the Coyote, "the Grizzly is lucky in having no tail, for I have learned from my own sad experience that a tail is only a harbor for fleas."

The Grizzly Bear nodded and looked smug.

"Now the Buck's eyes and ears are pretty good," said the Coyote, "perhaps better than mine."

The Buck shook his antlers from side to side and gave a little whistling sigh. He opened his mouth as if to speak, but thought better of it.

"And there's the Fish," said the Coyote, "which is naked all year around, and I've always envied it, for hair is a burden most of the year. Consequently, I'm in favor of a man without hair on his body. And his claws ought to be as long as the Eagle's, so that he can hold things in them."

"Humph!" said the Mountain Sheep, out of turn.

The Coyote glared at him. "But taking it all in all,"

he said, "you must acknowledge that there is no animal besides myself who has had wit enough to supply the Man, and I would be much obliged, therefore, to make Man like myself, and also cunning and crafty." And he lifted his nose in the air and looked very important.

The Beaver stood up and said he'd never heard such nonsense and twaddle in all his born days. "No tail, indeed! I'd make Man with a broad, flat tail, so he can haul mud and sand on it!"

"All you animals have lost your senses!" said the Owl grumpily. "Not one of you has wanted to give Man wings! Now I don't see of what use anybody on earth can be to himself without wings!"

"Stuff and nonsense and fiddle-de-dee!" said the Mole. "You're crazy to talk about wings, for a Man with wings would be certain to bump his head against the sky! Aside from that, a Man with wings and eyes both would get his eyes burned out from flying too near the sun. But without eyes he could burrow in the cool soft earth and be happy. That's my opinion!"

Finally, the little Mouse squeaked out, "I'd make a Man with eyes, so he could see what he was eating. But as for burrowing in the ground, that's silly!"

So all the animals disagreed among themselves, and the council broke up in a terrific row. The Coyote flew at the Beaver and nipped a piece out of his cheek: the Owl jumped on top of the Coyote's head and began lifting his scalp; the Lion and the Cinnamon Bear began a boxing match; and there was a high old time.

When they grew tired of fighting, every animal set to

work to make a Man according to his own ideas; and taking a lump of earth, each one began molding it like himself. But the Coyote started to make a Man such as he had described in the council. It was so late when they fell to work that evening came on before anyone had finished his model. They all lay down and yawned and went to sleep. But the cunning Coyote stayed awake and worked eagerly on his model all night. While all the other animals were sound asleep he poured water on their models and spoiled them.

Early in the morning, he finished his model and gave it life, long before the others awoke to make new models. When they opened their eyes and yawned and sprang up, there stood Man. And the Coyote was laughing at them.

Thus it was that Man was made by the Coyote.

PAUL BUNYAN

There ain't never been no loggin' before nor since like Paul Bunyan done.

When he was born down east in Maine, Paul must've been a pretty husky baby and smart, too. When he was only three weeks old he kicked around so much in his sleep, he knocked down four square miles of standin' timber, and the government says to his folks, they'd have to move him away from there.

So his pa and ma, they lashed some timbers together and made a floatin' cradle and anchored it off Eastport, but every time Paul rocked shorewards in his cradle it made a swell that come near drownin' out all the villages on the coast of Maine. The government said that wouldn't do, they'd have to take Paul somewheres else, but when they went to get him, he was asleep in his cradle and couldn't be budged. So they had to send for the British Navy and it took nine hours of bombardin' to wake him up. Then when Paul stepped out of his cradle and rocked it, it made such a swell there was a seventy-five-foot tide in the Bay of Fundy and a lot of villages was swept away and seven of the invincible British warships was swamped to the bottom of the sea. Finally Paul got out of his cradle and that kept Nova Scotia from bein' a island, but the tides in the Bay of Fundy is high as they ever was.

The King of England sent over and confiscated the timbers in Paul's cradle and built himself seven new warships to take the place of the ones that had sunk.

They say Paul cut his teeth on a peavey and drove logs down the Kennebec in his first pair of pants. He went to work for his uncle up in Ontario while he was still just a kid, and on account of he was so big but not clumsy, they used to give him jobs nobody else in camp could do. He was quicker and stronger than anybody else, and one job they handed him was day breaker. The cook used to send him up in the Blue Mountains with an ax to break day, and Paul could get his job done and get back to camp and call the men to breakfast before the daylight got there. Another job he had was blowing the dinner horn for the cook. When Paul'd toot, the noise was so loud the men could ride in out of the woods on the echo. And some of the old loggers tell how Paul could blow out the bunkhouse light and get into his bunk before it was dark.

He must've been a great kid, and he was a great logger, that's sure. There never was nobody like him.

When he was loggin' on the Big Onion in Michigan, Paul's camp was so big, nobody could count the men, so Paul says, "Well, count the cattle, then. I know there's about five men for every yoke of cattle." The government wanted a report or somethin', so Paul had to say how many men he had workin' for him. Well, they tried to count the cattle, but they couldn't, so Paul tells 'em to count the yokes. "Pile 'em up and measure 'em and figure from that," Paul says, "and don't bother me—I got loggin' to do."

So the chief clerk and the straw boss, they piled up the yokes and measured 'em and found out there was exactly 370 cords. But Paul had invented the three-shift system, so there was always one shift in camp, one goin' out to work, and one in the woods, and by measurin' the yokes that way, you couldn't naturally get only one-third of 'em at a time. So Paul said, "Oh, just tell the government this is a rough estimate or somethin'. Me and Babe's got to be goin'."

Babe was Paul's Blue Ox, and Paul wouldn't have been able to do all the loggin' he done without Babe. Babe measured forty-two ax handles and a tobacco box between the eyes and weighed accordin', and he used up a log chain once a month on account of he hauled so hard he stretched the chain out into a solid bar and it wouldn't be any good. Babe was so long in the body that Paul had to carry a pair of field glasses around with him so he could see what Babe was doin' with his hind feet.

Every time they shod Babe they had to open up a new iron mine on Lake Superior, and he could haul a whole section of timber with him at a time, the entire 640 acres at one drag and walk down to the landin' with it and dump it in. Babe's color was a pretty deep blue, but he didn't always used to be that color, though. He was white when he was a calf, but he turned blue standin' out in the field for six days the first winter of the Blue Snow and he never got white again.

Babe nearly got stumped once on a job, and that was when Paul was loggin' down on the Saint Croix in Wisconsin. Ordinarily, anythin' that had two ends to it, Babe could walk off with like nothin', but when Paul used him to pull the crooks out of eighteen miles of loggin' road, that come near bein' more than the Ox could handle.

That road doubled back on itself sixteen times and made four figure 8's, nine 3's, four S's, and one each of every other letter in the alphabet, all in eighteen miles. The teamsters met themselves comin' back so many times, it begun to get on their nerves and there was pretty near a crazy-house in camp there, so Paul made up his mind to straighten it out.

He hitched the Blue Ox to the end of the road and then he went up and spoke somethin' low to Babe, and Babe laid hold, and that road come near breakin' the Ox in two.

"Come on, Babe!" says Paul. "Co-ome on, Babe!"

And Babe lays hold and pulls till his hind legs laid almost straight out behind him and his belly was almost down touchin' the ground. But Babe done it.

The way Babe ate was a caution. Four ton of grain wasn't nothin' at a single meal, and as for hay—well it took two men just to pick the balin' wire out of his teeth after he ate. Paul had another man cuttin' the wire up for nails to use in puttin' on the cookhouse roof. Babe was crazy about hotcakes, and the men used to feed him the hotcakes baked on the big griddle Paul had made. The steel that went into that griddle of Paul's would've made 260 breakin' ploughs.

The Frenchmen who worked for Paul used to like their pea soup, and Paul had a hard time gettin' enough for 'em until he got the pea soup spring. How that happened was: One afternoon one of the tote-teamsters was comin' along the road from town with a load of peas for the camp. It was March and the road was slippery. There was a hot spring alongside the road and the steam from it made the road slipperier than ever, and just as the teamster was comin' by that slippery place, the sled slid off the icy road and the whole business went plunk into the spring, load, teamster, cattle and all—that is, the teamster managed to keep himself out and most part of the cattle, their hind legs was in, but the load of peas went clean to the bottom.

Just about then Paul come along and he knew right off what to do. "Unyoke the cattle," he says, "and get out of the way and hand me that ax and peavey you got there."

Then he butchers the cattle and cuts the meat up in hunks and pushes the whole outfit back in the spring again.

"Let it cook a couple of hours," says Paul, "and then tell the men to come up for their pea soup. It'll taste fine, flavored with oxtail that way."

Paul had a wife about the size to match him. It took thirteen Hudson's Bay blankets to make her a skirt, and the sail of a full-rigged ship to make a waist for her. For shoes, she'd just step into an extra big moose hide with each foot and the shoemaker would sew it up around her ankle.

When Paul had a macaroni farm down in Wisconsin, his wife, Carrie, split most of the rails for fencin' it in. But she kicked about that, said she wasn't no ox, and made Paul hire three French Canadians to help her. The Canadians agreed to split 900 rails a day, but Mrs. Paul split 4,756 the first day they went to work. She was goin' pretty fast and they'd lost sight of her, but the last rail she split, her ax stuck and she yelled for one of the Canucks to come and get it out for her. He finally got it out all right, but then he noticed there wasn't no head on the ax, only the handle, and he went to look for it and found it in the first rail she'd split, so there she'd been splittin' all day without no head on her ax.

She didn't go out to the camp much, but when she did, Paul had to ship in a few hundred dozen chickens for her entertainment, on account of she was pretty fond of chicken. And she was all-fired proud of her set of false teeth.

One time when she was out to the camp on a Saturday, she was down by the river watchin' a boom of logs the men was workin' on, and she wanted to go out on one of the logs to see if she could do it, just for fun. And while she was out there on the end of the log, she sneezed, and both her jaws of false teeth went splash into the water.

Well, she screamed and yelled and carried on, and she never expected to see them false teeth again, and they was made for her special by the Krupp's Iron Works in Germany, and she didn't know if she could ever get 'em replaced. About that time, Paul come along and she was screamin', "Oh, my teeth! My teeth!"

Paul stood there lookin' down into the water at the teeth an' scratchin' his head, and he goes away and comes back with a piece of cable and a chicken drumstick. And Paul he hitches the drumstick to the piece of cable and goes out on the log and lowers the cable into the water right in front of the teeth, and when them teeth see that drumstick they just naturally snaps right onto it. And Paul hauled 'em up so then Mrs. Paul was all fixed again.

Well, Paul he logged in Minnesota and out in North Dakota, but one day he got a hankerin' to go west. He took Babe and he started out. He happened to have his snowshoes on that mornin', because he was kind of slow in layin' 'em off in the spring, and he had on his mackinaw, too, but he didn't think about it at first.

Of course it kept gettin' hotter and hotter and his snowshoes was gettin' heavier and heavier in the dust, but he didn't want to stop for nothin' because he wanted to get in Seattle for supper that night. But his south snowshoe warped in the sun more than his north snowshoe, and instead of makin' a straight line from Fargo to Seattle the way he meant to, he swung around in a big half circle, so by six o'clock, when he thought he was in Seattle, he'd landed up in San Francisco instead, and it was nearly ten o'clock that night when he finally got to Seattle.

On the way he'd dragged his peavey behind him to ease his shoulder, and the scratch he made with his peavey is now the Grand Canyon.

Well, Paul set up a new camp in the Northwest, and when he was loggin' in Oregon, he built up Mount Hood for a kind of lookout place from where he could watch his different camps.

Babe's downfall was hotcakes. Paul was loggin' in Vancouver, and one mornin' Babe got into camp just as the cook was cookin' the last stove-top-full of hotcakes There was only about 400 men in camp, it was a small camp, and there wasn't such an awful lot of hotcakes on hand, only four platters stacked four foot high. Well, Babe busts into camp and smells them hotcakes, and he lays the storeroom back of the kitchen out flat, jumps over it, and makes straight for the stove and the platters of hotcakes. He swallows what's on the platters in a swallow and a half, and then he goes for the ones on the stove, and what does he do but swallow the hotcakes, stove, fire, cook, hotcake turner and all in one swallow.

Trouble was, the cook had just filled the stove up with

good dry spruce wood and it had just started to goin'
good, and it burned Babe's insides out before anybody
had time to do anythin' but stand and gawk. Paul was
awful broke up, because he was terrible fond of Babe.

So Paul went off to Alaska to try loggin' up there and
that's the last anybody's heard of him, so he's probably
up there tryin' to get along the best he can without
Babe, the Blue Ox.

HOW BR'ER WASP GOT HIS SMALL WAIST

At one time Br'er Wasp was very different from the
way he is now. He liked company and he liked to talk
and joke and make a fool of himself. He was one person
who had to laugh.

One day when he was walking he met up with Br'er
Mosquito. Br'er Mosquito and his family were very
small but they took themselves very seriously. They
talked big about their crops and their land; and Br'er
Mosquito and his father talked the loudest and called
their little patch of ground a plantation. At the time
when Br'er Wasp was walking down the path there had
been a heavy frost the week before, and everybody was
digging potatoes.

Br'er Wasp came up to Br'er Mosquito's potato field
and asked him how his and his father's crop was getting
along.

"We're doing fine, Br'er Wasp," said Br'er Mosquito.
"We have the biggest crop that ever was seen in the
world."

"Are the potatoes large?" asked Br'er Wasp.

Br'er Mosquito snickered. "You've never seen such potatoes in your life!"

Br'er Wasp asked, "How big are they, Br'er Mosquito?"

"Huh," said Br'er Mosquito puffing up his chest before he bent down and pulled his little breeches tight around his little leg. "The best part of my father's and my crop is bigger than the biggest part of my leg."

Br'er Wasp looked at Br'er Mosquito's little leg and he thought about those big potatoes. He tried to mind his manners but he burst out laughing right in Br'er Mosquito's face. He laughed and he laughed until his sides hurt him and his stomach hurt him and the tears ran out of his eyes. Whenever he tried to stop laughing, he looked again at Br'er Mosquito's toothpick leg, and he laughed harder than ever. His sides hurt him so much that he held them in with both hands and rocked himself to and fro and pushed in hard.

Br'er Mosquito stared at him. "What's the matter with you, Br'er Wasp?"

But Br'er Wasp couldn't answer more than to say, between gasps, "How big those enormous potatoes must be, if you say they are as big as that!" And he went on laughing all the way home, squeezing his sides.

Finally he got home and started to laugh some more and to tell his family about Br'er Mosquito. He was just beginning to catch his breath when his wife got a good look at him.

"Br'er Wasp!" she shouted. "What's the matter with your stomach?"

He looked down to see what his wife was talking about and saw that he had no stomach and scarcely any waist. He stopped laughing immediately. After another astounded look, Br'er Wasp saw what all his pushing in and squeezing and laughing had done to him. He was almost in two! He was afraid to so much as sneeze.

Then Br'er Wasp began to think of the people he had been laughing at all his life and he knew that now they were going to laugh at him. That's why he became so short of patience, because ever since that day he has always expected someone to laugh at him.

And the worst of it is—he can't laugh anymore himself, for if he does he is going to bust himself spang in two!

Netherlands ❧ ❧ ❧ ❧

THE LEGEND OF THE GOLDEN HELMET

IN DAYS LONG PAST, WHEN FORESTS COVERED THE Netherlands and wolves and bears haunted the wilderness, there were no churches in Frisia. The people worshiped many pagan gods; and there was one called Fosite, God of Justice, whom the people particularly venerated. They thought the leaves of his sacred tree cured diseases, and under his tree they often laid their sick and wounded.

These wild people of Frisia ate acorns and berries and wore the skins of animals. There came among them once, from the Christian lands of the south, a singer with his harp. He played such beautiful music and sang such sweet songs before the King of Frisia that the King's daughter listened with unspeakable delight, and tears, first of sorrow and then of joy, fell from her lovely eyes.

The King's daughter was the pride of her father because of her gentle temper and willing spirit, and all the people boasted of her beauty. Because her father worshiped Fosite, the God of Justice, and his daughter was always so just to her playmates, he named her Fostedina, which meant "Darling of Fosite," or "Lady of Justice."

The songs of the singer from the south were different from the songs of the gleemen and harpers in the King's court. Instead of being about fighting and battles, or the hunting of wolves and bears, or the chase of stags, the songs were of healing the sick and helping the weak. Instead of telling of fighting and killing Danes, or of the bloody deeds of the battle god, Wodan, the singer from the south told of gentle folk. He sang of the loving Father in Heaven, who sent his beloved Son, our Lord Jesus Christ, to live on earth and die that men might be saved. He sang of love and hope, of kindness to the poor and suffering. He told the story of the Crown of Thorns and the Cross, and how in His hour of death and shame, Christ forgave His enemies. And when he played upon his harp, the music was now soft and low, now sad, now moving the heart.

But the Frisian warriors were angered. "What, forgive an enemy? Forgive the Danes? Is he mad?" they shouted. "Let us kill this singer from the south!" And they beat their swords on their shields until the clangor was deafening, and the great hall rang with the sound as if the warriors were off to battle. The pagan priests urged the fighting men to kill the singer from the south. But Fostedina, rushing forward to save the harper, covered him with her long golden hair.

Majestically the King arose from his throne. "You may not kill him! This man is our guest. I invited him here and he shall be safe!"

Sullen and with bitter hatred in their hearts, the warriors and the priests left the hall, swearing vengeance. They would never forgive their enemies, the Danes! For the day before a party of Christian Danes had come to Frisia, unarmed, to tell the Frisians about Christ. It was cold in the forest at night, and the Danes unwittingly had cut off some dead branches of the tree sacred to Fosite, the God of Justice, and had built a fire with them. A spy had seen them, and the Christian Danes had been taken prisoners in the forest. In punishment, they were to be given to hungry bears and wolves to be torn to pieces.

Fostedina, who had been deeply moved by the songs of the singer about faith in the one God and His love for His creatures, resolved to set the captives free. At midnight she called a trustworthy servant, and with a horn lantern, she went out secretly to the prison where the Danes lay waiting to be thrown into the pit with the bears and wolves. Unbolting the door, she commanded them, in the name of their God and hers, to make haste and return to their native land. While the bears and wolves, smelling human flesh, growled and howled in the darkness, the Danes slipped away and escaped, but the King's daughter was caught by the guard as she returned to the castle.

The next morning when the news of the escape reached the people, they were wild at being cheated of their bloody sport, and they mobbed the palace, demanding of the King his daughter's punishment. The King was helpless and agreed that she should be summoned before the council of priests. While the white-bearded priest of Wodan spoke, and the wolves howled, the beautiful girl stood brave and steadfast. In vain the priests threatened her and invoked the curses of the pagan gods upon her. Fostedina said that she would suffer as her Lord did, rather than deny Him.

"Let your words be your sentence!" shouted the high priest. "You shall wear a crown of thorns! Tomorrow you shall stand in the market place from sunrise to sunset, with a crown of sharp thorns pressed down upon your brow!"

Fostedina refused to beg for mercy, in spite of her father's pleas. The following morning she dressed herself in white garments made from the skins of does and unbound her golden hair. With a firm, unfaltering step she walked to the center of the market place.

"Bring the crown of thorns for the blasphemer of Fosite!" called the high priest.

It was brought to him; the King's daughter knelt before him, and the angry old man pressed the sharp thorns slowly and brutally down upon the girl's brow. Quickly blood trickled and spread over her golden hair and her face, but giving no sign of pain Fostedina stood up and gazed at the yelling crowd. All day long the crowd howled around her in honor of their gods, but she stood silent and patient, praying inwardly to God to pardon and forgive the people.

As the years passed, a great change came over Frisia. The scars of the thorns on Fostedina's brow had softened the people's hearts, and thousands of them listened to the words of the missionaries and turned to God. Fostedina became Queen of the land; idols were destroyed and churches were built bearing a shining cross on their steeples. Trees once sacred to the pagan gods were cut down, and where the forest had been, cows grazed in green meadows, and flowers blossomed where wolves had once roamed and hunted.

A Christian Prince from the south was in love with Fostedina and had come to wed her. On the marriage morning, a procession of lovely maidens, dressed in white, came to the palace. One of them carried a golden crown, made like a helmet, and fashioned to conceal the scars on Fostedina's brow. And the King's daughter was married with a golden helmet on her head.

Today, if you go into Frisia of the lovely lakes, you may see young girls wearing gold helmets like Fostedina's. There is a golden rosette at each ear, and a pretty lace cap over the gold. It is the ancient headdress of Free Frisia.

And when Queen Wilhelmina visited her Frisians in the old land of the north so much beloved by her forefathers, she, too, wore the golden helmet.

GREEN GRASS ON THE WALL

Long ago, in the town of Kampen, in the Province of Overijssel, which is noted for its many jokes and its many jokesters, there lived a lot of clever people. In those days, a wall surrounded the town to keep out the enemy, should an enemy dare poke his nose around that territory.

On a fine Sunday afternoon, Willem, one of the most distinguished inhabitants of Kampen, took his little son by the hand and went out for a walk. On the way, Willem met two friends, and they all walked along together.

By and by, they came to the city wall, and Willem, glancing up, discovered, high up on the wall, fresh green grass growing between the stones.

"Look, my friends!" he exclaimed, pointing upward. "Isn't it a sin to waste all that good fresh grass?"

"Yes, my goodness!" cried one friend. "It surely must not be allowed to go to waste." This friend was known throughout the Province of Overijssel as a penny pincher, and it was said that if possible he would skin a stone.

"But what shall we do about it?" asked the other friend anxiously, for he could not bear the idea of waste either.

Willem pretended to think a minute and then, with a perfectly straight face, he declared, "We must let a cow graze there."

"Of course, that's it!" said his friends.

And they called to the people of Kampen, who came racing and chasing to the spot. Everyone agreed that Willem, the intelligent inhabitant, was right, dead right.

Everyone except Willem began to work at once. A beam was placed on top of the wall, and in the end of the beam was fastened a pulley. Someone ran and brought a cow from somebody else's meadow. They put the cow's head through a noose tied in a strong rope, and drew the other end of the rope through the pulley.

They shouted, "Heave! Ho!"—and up went the cow. All of the men—except Willem, of course—hauled and pulled, and the first thing they knew, the cow was half-way up the wall. And then she stuck out her tongue.

"Look! Look! The cow has a wonderful appetite for green grass!" cried the clever people of Kampen. "It isn't every day she gets anything as nice as that fresh green grass growing in the wall!"

When finally, with much toiling and moiling, the clever folk had pulled the cow to the top of the wall, they found she was strangled.

The poor cow never ate grass or anything else again.

THREE HUNDRED AND SIXTY-FIVE CHILDREN

Once upon a time in the city now called The Hague but then called the City of the Count's Wood, a most remarkable thing occurred which surprised the world. At that time, Floris, Count of Holland, had a daughter named Machtelt. He married her to the Count of Henneberg, and the Lady Machtelt went to live with her bridegroom in his castle far from the City of the Count's Wood.

Industrious and proud was Machtelt. She kept her maidens busy from morning till night, spinning, weaving, cleaning, cooking, and heaven knows what else. Her own spinning wheel hummed busily; she watched her household like a hawk so that nothing should be lost or wasted. And her heart was as cold as her cold blue eyes.

One day as she sat spinning furiously and grimly, the porter of Castle Henneberg came to her and said, "My lady, a miserable beggar woman is standing outside of the gate with a crying baby on each arm. All she asks for is a bite of bread."

Machtelt arose impatiently from her wheel. "She is an idle creature, or she would not need to beg! I'll send her away myself."

She hurried down to the outer gate, and there stood a poor woman, holding in each arm a little baby crying bitterly. "Lady," sobbed the unhappy woman, trembling with fear and hunger, "please give me just a bite of stale bread. My babies are dying of hunger!"

"Go to work, you idle thing!" said Machtelt. "Earn your own bread! Why should I give you mine?"

"My husband is dead, Lady," cried the woman, "and my babies are so little that I cannot work!" And she sobbed as if her heart would break.

"What right have you, a beggar, to have two children?" scoffed Machtelt angrily.

But the woman said earnestly, "They are a gift from the Lord, and I love them with all my heart."

"From the Lord!" mocked Machtelt. "It's more likely the Devil sent them! Get away from my gate at once, you good-for-nothing beggar!" And she drove the poor woman with her starving babies away.

But as she stumbled along, the woman lifted her eyes to heaven, and weeping, said, "Lady, if my children came from the Lord, may He send you three hundred and sixty-five children, one for every day in the year!"

Feeling righteous, Machtelt went back to her spinning wheel, but secretly she was troubled. For as her wheel went around, the beggar's curse kept beating in her ears.

Three hundred and sixty-five children!
Three hundred and sixty-five children!
Three hundred and sixty-five children!

At length she could stand her worry no longer, and calling her attendants, she rode away from Castle Henneberg and hastened home to her father in the City of the Count's Wood.

But her father neither would nor could protect her, and the beggar's curse came true. For one bright day there arrived for Machtelt at the City of the Count's Wood, three hundred and sixty-five tiny babies, each as perfect and rosy and sweet (when it wasn't yelling) as any ordinary baby. There were one hundred and eighty-two boys and one hundred and eighty-three girls, and Machtelt was in a frenzy trying to pick them up all at once and trying to think of names for them.

The bishop came running to baptize the babies; and he put them all together in one font and baptized them all at the same time. It saved water. The boys he named Jan, and the girls he called Elizabeth.

So the beggar's curse came true, and Machtelt's nurses had to feed three hundred and sixty-five children, one for each day in the year; and Machtelt herself had to bring them up. And the story goes that it made a good and kind woman out of her, for at last she had so much to do in caring for three hundred and sixty-five charming children that she had no time for a sharp temper or cruelty.

THE MERMAID OF THE MOVING SANDS

Once Westerschouwen Town was a great fishing port; its ships proudly sailed the North Sea and brought home rich cargoes of fish. And on the green Island of Walcheren, the fisherfolk of Westerschouwen grew boastful and cruel, haughty and big-headed; and often they declared, "We are the rulers of the sea! Where in the world are there any fisherfolk like the fisherfolk of Westerschouwen?"

One day when a group of fishermen were out in their boats, one of them pulled up his net, and in it was a lovely Mermaid.

"Oh, let me go, good people!" she begged. "Please let me go free!"

But the fishermen were hard-hearted, bragging men, and they wanted to carry their astonishing prize into port and to show it off to their fellow townspeople. They jeered at the helpless Mermaid and ridiculed her in loud rough voices.

"Oh, pray let me go, fishermen!" she begged in despair. "You shall be amply rewarded!"

"Ho, ho!" laughed the fishermen who had caught her. "How can you reward us?"

At that moment, another voice sounded from the sea,

deeper than hers, but as full of sorrow and shame and despair.

"It is the Merman!" shouted the fishermen with mocking laughter. "There he swims with his child in his arms!"

Like green waves the Merman's hair streamed over his foam-white shoulders; and his face was the color of driftwood that has long been tossed and swirled about in the emerald sea. In his arms he carried his child, its little white head pressed close to his breast. The Mermaid, fast in the net, saw them and held out beseeching arms to her loved ones.

"Oh, give her back to me!" cried the Merman, weeping. "We were so happy, fishermen! What will you do to her? She will perish on land! Give her back to me and to our little child!"

But the fishermen did not answer; they sailed on toward the port. Again and again the Merman rose and gazed in grief toward his dear wife, while she with misty eyes tried to see her beloved through the green waves and white foam.

When the boat reached shore and the fishermen sprang out, there was great shouting; the people rushed from their houses to the beach. The fishermen held the net high and let the women and children stare with gaping mouths at the poor Mermaid. The Merman swam close to the shore and stretched out longing and desperate arms.

"Oh, listen, fisherfolk!" he cried. "Our little house is in the rushes, built of shells which she and I gathered—

blue and white and golden shells which she and I gathered, shell by shell, when we first loved. She is thinking of our little shell house and of our little child. Would you let her die on your dark cruel earth? Oh, have pity!"

But the men and the women howled with laughter, and hurrying to the water tower, they tied the net to it. The Mermaid fainted at last; and the Merman, frantic with despair, swam as close to the tower as he could and watched his lovely wife die. The fisherfolk of Westerschouwen stood laughing and jeering.

"We aren't afraid of you!" called a fisherman.

"How can you hurt us, old Fish Scales?" yelled another.

"You have neither fire to burn us with, nor swords, nor darts, nor axes to attack us with!" cried a woman. "Why should we be afraid of you? Ha, ha!"

The Merman ignored their hoots and laughter, their hard hearts and their taunts. But there was great rage and sorrow in his heart, and at his hand was a weapon of mighty vengeance.

He dove under the sea and swam to the surface again, carrying seaweed and sand. With these he stopped up the channels, blocking them, and filled in the shallow places in the water. Where only a few hours ago had been deep waterways along which the ships sailed, now every waterway was choked with weed and sand. And the Merman sang in a voice like the rising wind:

> *Westerschouwen, Westerschouwen,*
> *You who did not stay your hand,*

But let death carry off my love,
Shall be lost in weed and sand!
Only her tower still shall stand
Above the seas she's dreaming of!

Then the Merman swam slowly away to grieve alone with his little child in the small house built of blue and white and golden shells. And he was never again seen near Westerschouwen.

But slowly and silently, the sand and the seaweed kept moving toward Westerschouwen. It blocked the harbor, and strong ships were held in the throttle hold of the sand. Fishing boats were tangled in the seaweed and could not get free. The storms and winds drove the sand onto the land. Sand flew in clouds over Westerschouwen, blew into houses, piled up in the streets. The fisherfolk, the proud, the cruel, the haughty, fled from their houses and their town, while the sand blew and blew, until the town stood deep in the drifting sandbanks and finally was lost. But the sand did not blow near the water tower where the Mermaid had died. It stood untouched near the green waves that were the color of the Merman's hair.

Mexico ✎ ✎ ✎ ✎ ✎

TEPOZTON

THE GODS, WHO LIVE ABOVE THE CLOUDS ON TOP OF a very high mountain with fire inside it, have jobs to do. They must make the rain fall at the proper time so that the grass and corn and flowers and fruit will grow. They take their great shears, such as men use for clipping sheep, and trim the winds to keep them from becoming too rough. They are forever experimenting with things, and whenever they discover how to do anything useful they teach it to the people. The gods taught the Mexican people how to weave cloth and how to make dishes, how to build houses and dig mines, and how to take rubber out of the trees to make rubber balls so that they could play games.

When they are not busy, the gods ride around in the clouds or turn themselves into different animals to see what it feels like. But most of all they love to play ball. They have big ball games and bet whole mountains on them. When they get out of breath from playing ball, they sit down and smoke out of long clay pipes.

A long time ago, one young god grew restless. He was

tired of watching balls bounce and of riding around in the clouds. He smoked so much he got a headache, but still he wasn't enjoying himself.

"What's the matter with you?" his best friend asked impatiently. "The rest of us are having fun. What's good enough for us should be good enough for you! What more do you want than playing ball and riding around in the clouds and smoking tobacco and blowing smoke rings?"

"I've been thinking," said the tired young god, "that what I would like more than anything else in the world, is a little boy."

"A little boy!" his friend exclaimed. "Have the clouds gone to your head or something? Whoever heard of a god having a little boy? A little boy is nothing but a lot of fuss and trouble, always into mischief and always outgrowing his shirt and pants."

"I know," sighed the unhappy god. "But I still would like to have a little boy. And I think I'll go down to earth and see about it."

"You've got bird wings in your head!" said his friend. "You'll be sorry—you wait and see!"

"No, I won't," said the god, and he slid down the mountain and started walking around on earth.

No one knew who he was, for he was dressed like anybody else; people thought he was just a simple good-looking young man. One day he stopped at a spring for a drink of water, and a beautiful girl came to fill her pitcher at the spring. The god fell in love with her, and she fell in love with him. They went away together, and after a while they had a little boy, and the god was very happy.

But soon he became sad again because he could not stay on earth and play with his baby boy. He had to return to the mountain and help regulate the rain and attend to the crops, for if he didn't the people on earth wouldn't have enough to eat. Even his wife and his own little boy would be hungry. So he kissed the girl, said goodby, and disappeared. And in the place where he had been standing, she saw a small round smooth stone, green as a growing plant. She picked it up, made a hole in it, and hung it around the baby's neck.

Then she took the baby home, but her father and mother were very angry. They wanted to kill the little boy. "Where is his father?" they asked. "A baby without a father has no business being born at all! He must die!"

The girl said, "He is a beautiful baby."

But her father shouted, "I don't care whether he's beautiful or not! He has to die!"

So she walked far out in the fields with the baby, not knowing what to do, for she couldn't bear to hurt him. When it grew dark, she put the baby down gently in the center of a big maguey plant and ran home, crying.

Her father and mother were pleased. "He'll die of hunger and cold," they said with satisfaction. But the girl cried and cried.

The next day she slipped away and went to see what had happened to her baby. The plant had curled up, the big broad leaves had bent over him to keep him warm,

and he was sound asleep. There was a little hole in one of the leaves, and something like milk, warm and sweet, was dripping out of it and falling into the baby's mouth.

The girl played with the baby until it grew late. Then she laid him down in the middle of an anthill and went home crying.

But the next day when she went back she found him covered up with pink rose petals and he was kicking and smiling. Some of the ants were bringing more and more rose petals, while other ants were bringing honey and putting it carefully on the baby's lips. The girl was frightened, for she knew her father and mother would be very angry. So she put the baby in a wooden box, nailed the cover down tightly, and put the box in the river. And the current carried the box downstream and out of sight.

Near the mouth of the river lived a fisherman and his wife who were very happy but who wanted children. The fisherman saw the box in the water, waded in after it, and carried it home to his wife.

When she opened the box and saw the baby, she was overcome with joy. "Oh, at last we have a little boy!" she cried, and at once made him some clothes and some little sandals for his feet. "What shall we call him?"

"He has a green stone, a mountain stone, around his neck," said the fisherman. "Let us call him Tepozton, the Mountain Boy."

The little boy grew up strong and happy with his foster parents. When he was seven years old, the fisherman made him a little bow and some little arrows.

Tepozton was delighted. "Now you won't have to hunt or fish any more, father," he said. "I'll bring home everything we need."

The fisherman laughed indulgently. "What do you expect to bring home for dinner, with that little bow?"

"I can shoot anything," said Tepozton.

"All right," said the fisherman, trying not to smile. "There's a quail over there. Let's see you shoot it."

Tepozton fitted an arrow to his bow and shot, but he shot straight up into the air. And the quail fell dead.

"That's funny," said the fisherman. "There's a wild turkey over there on that tree. Shoot it."

Again Tepozton fitted an arrow to his bow and shot straight up into the air, and the turkey fell out of the tree, quite dead. And the fisherman was amazed.

Thereafter, Tepozton brought home everything that was needed with his little bow and arrows. He went out at six every morning and returned at six in the evening. He walked so much and so far that he wore out his sandals as fast as the fisherman's wife could make them. Once she asked him what he did all day in the mountains.

"Oh, I have many things to attend to," the little boy answered, and she asked no more questions.

But she suspected that the little boy had magic powers and was not an ordinary person, and before long she was sure of it. That was when he had the adventure with the man-eating giant.

There were a great many wild animals in the mountains where he went hunting, but Tepozton was not afraid of them. Very often he would come around a bend in the trail and there would be a wolf directly in front of him. Tepozton would stand still and gaze at the wolf, and the wolf would stare back at him out of burning eyes. And Tepozton would say, "Hello, little brother. Get out of my way, please, for I have many things to attend to." And the wolf would pad quietly off into the woods.

So Tepozton was not afraid at all when he heard about the man-eating giant. Every spring the giant demanded a live human being to eat, as a sort of spring tonic. Every year he chose a different town, and the families in each town took turns in choosing one of them to be eaten by the giant. The people and the giant had made an agreement that if they sent him one of their number he would not go out and kill everybody for miles around. This suited the giant, for he was a lazy fellow as well as a wicked one.

When Tepozton was seven years old, it came the fisherman's turn to feed the giant. He had only his wife and Tepozton and himself; so he decided to go himself. When the soldiers came for him, Tepozton put his little foot down.

"You can't take the fisherman!" said Tepozton. "Take me—I'm young and will taste better." He told the fisherman that nothing could happen to him, and begged to be allowed to go in his place. At last the fisherman consented.

Tepozton built a small fire in the corner of the yard. "Watch this fire," he said to the fisherman and his wife.

"If the smoke is white, I am safe. If it turns gray, I am in danger. But if it becomes black, that means I am dead." And he kissed his foster mother goodby, and kissed the fisherman's leathery cheek, and went off with the soldiers.

As they walked along the road, the little boy picked up small pieces of black glass and put them in his pockets. The glass had been thrown out by the volcano where the gods lived; it was very sharp and a lovely shining black. The people made arrowheads of it. Tepozton filled his pockets full.

When they came to the palace of the man-eating giant, the giant flew into a rage. "Do you expect me to make a decent meal of this little chunk of meat?" he roared. "If I don't have my spring tonic, I'll have indigestion for the rest of the year!"

"He was all there was, Your Majesty," said the frightened soldiers.

Tepozton bowed politely. "I may be little, but I'm tasty, Your Majesty," he said.

"Blast!" said the giant. "All right, cook him, then. But if he isn't good, I'll go out and kill three miles full of people!"

So the soldiers put Tepozton into a big pot full of boiling water and put the lid on. Tepozton didn't make a breath of sound, not even a squeak. And the giant lay down for a nap while his dinner was cooking.

When he woke up he took the lid off the pot to see how his dinner was getting along, but instead of a tender little boy, he saw a great tiger. The tiger opened its mouth and roared so loudly that the giant jumped and put the lid back on quickly. He decided he'd wait a little longer.

When he woke up again, he was hungrier than ever. Carefully he took the lid off, and there was an enormous snake coiled inside the pot and it hissed right in the giant's face. The giant put the lid back quickly and decided to wait a little longer.

The next time he woke up, he was so hungry he didn't care what he ate. He snatched the lid off, and there was the little boy, quite uncooked, laughing at him. The giant was so angry and so hungry that he grabbed Tepozton by the seat of the pants and popped him into his mouth. And the smoke from the fire in the yard of the fisherman's house suddenly turned dark gray.

The fisherman groaned, "I should have gone myself!" and his wife began to cry.

But Tepozton slid down the giant's throat before the giant could chew, and when he reached his stomach, he took a piece of black glass from his pocket. And he cut and cut until he wore out that piece of glass. So he took another piece from his pocket and kept on cutting. Before long, he had made a big hole in the giant's stomach.

The giant held onto his stomach and yelled, "Ow! I've got a terrible bellyache!"

Tepozton went on cutting and cutting, laughing to himself.

"Ow!" howled the giant. "Get a doctor quick! I'm poisoned! That little boy has given me an awful pain!"

Tepozton kept on cutting and cutting, and now the hole was so large that a little daylight was beginning to filter in. Suddenly he cut straight through to the outside, and the giant gave a dreadful yell and died. Tepozton climbed out, safe and laughing, and shook hands with everybody. And the smoke of the fire in the fisherman's yard turned snowy white, and the fisherman and his wife wept together with joy.

After that the people crowned Tepozton king, and he lived in the giant's house, and taught the people many useful things. When he had time, he played ball and rode around in the clouds, and turned into different kinds of animals for the fun of it. But more than anything else, he enjoyed walking around as a poor and ordinary person, helping people.

Some say that now he lives on the mountain with the young god, his father, but others say he lives on earth and keeps an eye on what is going on and helps people. But no one can tell for sure, because he looks just like anybody else.

THE COW THAT CRIED

Florencio had a wife and two children. He was so poor that, in order to feed them, he went every morning to the stockyards and bought the insides of the cattle that were killed for the butchers. The insides were very cheap, and Florencio's wife, Mariposa, cleaned them and boiled them. Then Florencio sold some of them.

and some of them he saved for his wife and the two young ones.

They had a neighbor named Margarita, who came one day to borrow some salt from Mariposa. When she saw Florencio eating the insides of cattle, she asked, "Do you buy those down at the stockyards near the river?"

"Yes, I do," answered Florencio. "They're good and they're cheap, and I must feed my children something."

"Those stockyards are near the cemetery," said Margarita.

"I know they are," said Florencio. "But what has that got to do with anything?"

"A good deal," said Margarita. "Those insides come out of animals that aren't really animals. They're ghosts."

Florencio laughed. "What nonsense you women think up!" he said.

"It's true," said Margarita. "The priest does it. He is a wicked priest."

"You shouldn't talk that way about priests," said Florencio severely. "Don't ever mention it to me again."

Not long afterward Margarita died. "It serves her right for talking nonsense!" said Florencio to Mariposa.

Mariposa didn't feel like arguing with him, so she kept her own counsel. But for a while she didn't feel as hungry as she usually did.

One morning Florencio was waiting at the stockyards, sitting by the gate, when the cattle were driven in. And he heard a curious thing. He heard one bull ask another, "Is this your first time at the stockyards?"

"No, it's my third time," replied the other bull. "How many times have you been here?"

"This is my first time. Does it hurt a lot when they cut off your head?"

"No, not very much. It just bleeds," answered the bull who had been killed three times.

"But when they cut off your neck?"

"That doesn't hurt a bit. Hold stiff, brace yourself, and you won't feel a thing. It's simple," said the bull.

Florencio shook his head and wondered if his ears were playing a trick on him. Then he saw a cow come in. She was a very pretty cow, and there were great tears in her eyes and they rolled down her nose. Florencio had never before seen a cow cry, and it worried him, so he hurried over to her and asked, "What's the matter, cow? Are you sick or have you a pain or something?"

"No, I'm not sick," answered the cow in a choked voice. "I'm crying because I died. I was all alone in the world and there's nobody to cry for me, so I have to do the crying myself. Moo-hoo!"

"Don't be silly—you're not dead at all," said Florencio.

"I am, too!" said the cow. "Don't you know me?"

"No," said Florencio. "Who are you?"

"I'm Margarita. I died because I told you about the wicked priest who changes people into cattle."

"I'm sorry you died, Margarita," said Florencio. "But how can the priest do that?"

"It's very simple," explained the cow. "He and the sacristan go to the cemetery over there at midnight. He says prayers backward and does all sorts of strange things

—black magic. And the graves open and the dead people come out, holding their mats around them. And the priest and the sacristan go around with some white powder in their hands, and they say to the people who really aren't people but ghosts, 'Welick! Welick!' That means, 'Sweet! Sweet!' And all the people take some and turn into cattle. Then the priest and the sacristan drive them to the stockyards and kill them and sell the beef."

Florencio laughed again. "What nonsense you women think up! I don't believe a word of it!"

The cow began to cry again, and she was driven off.

Florencio sat in the sun until the cattle were slaughtered; then he bought the insides as usual.

His wife cleaned them and boiled them; and by and by she came out with a spoonful. "Want to taste them?" she asked.

"I don't believe I care for any," said Florencio, feeling peculiar.

"What's the trouble?" asked his wife. "Did you hear something?"

"It's just women's nonsense," said Florencio. And he told her about the conversation between the bulls and about the cow that cried and said she was Margarita. "I don't believe it," said Florencio. "I'm going to the priest and ask him if it's true."

"Oh, don't! Please don't!" cried Mariposa.

But Florencio, being a man, was stubborn. "I know what I'm doing," he said.

Mariposa was so worried that she followed him to the

church and took the children along, too. Florencio made them wait at the door while he went in alone.

"Well, Florencio," said the priest, "what can I do for you?"

"Good morning, sir," Florencio said. "I just want to ask you a question."

"Go ahead, my son."

"Is it true," asked Florencio bluntly, "that you turn people into cattle? Not people, but just ghosts?"

"Of course not," said the priest. "Who told you that?"

"Margarita."

"Oh, she did, did she?" said the priest, frowning. "And have you told anybody?"

"No, just my wife," said Florencio.

"Hmm," said the priest. "Is that so?"

And that was the last of Florencio. Mariposa and the two children waited at the door of the church, and all they saw was a great bull, black with white spots on his chest and a white tassel on his tail; the bull walked right out of the church and went away, and Mariposa thought that church was a strange place for a bull. But she was worried about Florencio. And after she had waited and waited, she went into the church to look for him, but he wasn't there, and the priest said nobody had been there at all.

So Mariposa and the two children walked sadly home. And Florencio did not come back. Finally she thought he must be dead; everyone told her he must be dead. And people called her the Widow Mariposa.

Now she had to support her two children, and she could think of nothing to do but to help her neighbors grind corn. In this way she managed to feed the children, but they ran about in rags, and she herself wore tatters as well.

One day when she was standing forlornly in a cornfield, suddenly she heard a swishing noise and a young man appeared in front of her. He looked like an ordinary young man, but Mariposa had never before seen an ordinary person appear out of nowhere.

"Don't be sorrowful," said the young man kindly. "You used to weave lovely sashes and ribbons and girdles. Why don't you make some now and sell them, so that you can buy better food and some clothes for your children and yourself?"

"I haven't any wool," said Mariposa.

"I'll give you all the wool you want," said the young man. He reached up and he reached down, and all of a sudden Mariposa's hands were full of yarn of all the colors of the rainbow.

"Oh, thank you!" she cried, guessing at once who he was. "Aren't you Tepozton?"

"Yes, I am. Take good care of your children, and don't cry any more, Mariposa," he said. And he wasn't there any more. But where he had been standing, she saw a beautiful green flower beginning to blossom.

From then on, she made pretty sashes and hair bands and girdles and sold them, and she and the children had plenty to eat and nice clothes. But one day she became ill and could not weave any more. Soon the children were hungry again. Finally Mariposa went to a neighbor's house to grind corn, but she took the corn home to grind so that her neighbor wouldn't see how sick she was.

She worked and worked until she was so tired that she sat down and cried. "Oh, if Florencio were only alive!" she sobbed. The minute she said that, a big black bull ran into the house.

"Close the door, quick!" he bellowed.

Mariposa closed the door.

"Take this rope off my neck and hide it quickly!" said the bull. And all at once he wasn't a bull any more—he was Florencio. "I've just run away from the bull ring," he said, "and they'll be looking for me. You tell them I'm not here. Now that I'm a man, it'll be easier to hide me."

Mariposa rolled him up in a big mat and put him down in the corner.

In a few minutes a crowd came to the door. "Have you seen a big black bull?" they asked.

"Goodness, no," said Mariposa.

But they saw the print of the bull's hooves inside the door and they didn't believe her. They searched the house, in the corners, behind the door, under the bed, and started to look in the mat in which Florencio was rolled up.

"Whoever heard of a bull being rolled up in a mat?" asked Mariposa, and laughed at them, and they went away very disgruntled.

Florencio came out and kissed Mariposa and hugged

his children. He stayed for a long time playing with the little ones and talking to Mariposa. But when the church bells began to ring, Florencio began turning back into a bull once more. Mariposa wept bitterly.

But the bull said, "Don't cry, my dear wife. I can't stay with you because I am under a spell—the priest's black magic. But I can help you at any rate. Stop crying and listen to me closely."

"I'm not crying," said Mariposa, trying to stop.

"Tomorrow there's going to be a big bullfight," said the bull, "and I'll be the third in the ring. Remember, I'm black all over, with white spots on my chest and a white tassel on my tail. I'll pretend to be very fierce and nobody will be able to get near me, and they'll all get tired out. Then you tell the people you're going to be a bullfighter. Take the red cape and dance around me and show them how hard it is to do. You'll win in the end, and there's a prize of a thousand pesos for the best bull-fighter. You and the children will never be hungry again."

"But I'm ill," said Mariposa.

"No, you aren't," said the bull. "Remember, I'm the third bull, black with white spots on my chest and a white tassel at the end of my tail. Goodby, my love." And he raced away, back to the bullring.

The next day the Widow Mariposa felt much better, practically well, in fact, and she put on her best blue shawl and her red petticoat and went to the bullfight. She managed to get a seat down in front, nearest the bullring, so that she could see everything. And she was very much excited.

The first bull that came out into the ring was big and black and had white spots on his back. He had a sad look on his face, but he bellowed ferociously. A man threw a lasso around his feet and toppled him over. And Mariposa knew he wasn't the one.

Then a bigger and blacker bull came out, and he had white spots on his head. He pawed the ground and shook his head from side to side and stuck out his tongue and bellowed loudly, and Mariposa wondered if that could be Florencio. It took three men to throw this bull, and Mariposa knew he was the wrong one, too.

The next bull crashed right through the gate without waiting for it to be opened, and he ran in so fast that Mariposa couldn't tell what color he was. He charged across the ring and stopped in front of Mariposa and bellowed so wildly that the other people were terrified and moved back away from the ring. But Mariposa saw the white spots on his chest and the white tassel at the end of his tail and she saw him wink at her with one merry eye, and she knew it was Florencio.

The first man who came out, pranced up to the bull and cried, "Huh, huh!" but the bull picked him up with the tips of his horns and tossed him into Mariposa's lap.

"This certainly is Florencio," she said to herself.

Another man came running out, but the bull turned on him and scared him so that he ran away and has never been heard of since.

"This is positively Florencio," thought Mariposa, and

she went up to one of the bullfighters and asked to borrow his red cape.

"What do you want it for?" he asked, amused.

"To play the bull," answered the Widow Mariposa.

The man howled with laughter. "Whoever heard of a woman bullfighter? Why don't you use your red petticoat?"

"All right, I will," said Mariposa, and she went to the president of the bullfight and said, "Please, sir, will you let me try that bull?"

The president laughed, too, but he asked, "What will you use for a cape?"

"My red petticoat," said the Widow Mariposa.

"All right," he said, "but the people will laugh at you. And we won't be responsible if the bull kills you, and we won't be responsible for your poor children, either."

But Mariposa said calmly, "If the bull kills me, I'll be dead, that's all."

She jumped in the ring and waved her red petticoat, and the bull came charging up to her. But she wasn't afraid because she knew it was Florencio. The crowd roared with laughter, but in a few minutes they stopped laughing, for she side-stepped the bull's ferocious attacks neatly. The bull roared and ran at her, but she dodged and he roared past. "Huh, huh, huh!" she grunted, like a real bullfighter. At last she took two short spears trimmed with colored paper and waved them at the bull. The bull bellowed and rushed at her, and she stood on tiptoe and jumped clean onto his back and rode him around the ring. Everybody cheered and clapped, the band played loudly, and Mariposa won the prize of a thousand pesos for being the best bullfighter.

After that, everyone called her the Widow Bullfighter.

But she and her children had plenty to eat and fine clothes to wear.

Not long after the bullfight, something happened which broke the spell the wicked priest had put on Florencio. The black magic spell was broken because of a little boy named Chucho.

Chucho lived with his father and mother in a big comfortable cave. They slept on mats, and Chucho's mother cooked over a fire in the middle of the cave; outside of it his father had a corn patch. And there was a palm tree full of cocoanuts growing beside the door, so they drank cocoanut milk and ate the sweet meat. They drew water from a river near by and bathed there, and although they were poor and without a house, they had the comfortable cave and they had a lot of fun together.

Then Chucho's father died. His mother took care of the corn patch and took care of Chucho. But one night when they were asleep a naughty monkey rolled a big rock into the entrance of the cave. In the morning, Chucho's mother pushed and pushed, but she wasn't strong enough to move the rock. Chucho was too little to help any. And up in the tree the mischievous monkey was swinging by his tail and chattering and laughing. Chucho's mother began to cry. And Chucho cried too.

Just then a mule driver happened by and halted his mules by the river. He heard Chucho's mother calling for help, and he came and all he could see was the top of her head. She pushed and he pulled, but the monkey in the palm tree started throwing cocoanuts at him. One cracked him on the head, but he kept tugging. Another hit him on the nose. But finally he rolled the rock away, and Chucho's mother and Chucho climbed on one of the mules and rode to town with the mule driver.

Chucho's mother married the mule driver and he took good care of them and Chucho liked him very much. Often he would take Chucho with him when he journeyed with the mules from town to town. The mules would be laden with packs of things to sell in the markets—cocoanuts, pineapples, corn, pots, or parrots.

When Chucho was seven years old he had learned how to saddle and load the mules and how to talk to them. He was a strong little boy, and he was never afraid. He was destined never to know fear, and that was a good way to be.

One day when he was going to the market for his mother to buy her some brown sugar and some pink yarn, he met Ignacio, a big boy fourteen years old. Ignacio had a job: he rang the bells of the church every morning and every evening.

"Hello, Ignacio," said Chucho. "How's everything with you?"

"Not so good, Chucho," answered Ignacio.

"What's the trouble?"

"Something strange is going on in the church," answered Ignacio. "Last night when I went up the stairs to the top of the church to ring the bells, I heard a moaning sound. Then I heard a screaming sound, like a nahual makes. I ran down fast, but something tried to pull my hair. It scared me purple, I don't mind telling you," Ignacio said, shuddering. "I'm going to the priest right now and tell him I'm resigning my job."

"I'll bet somebody's hiding there," said Chucho.

"It's ghosts," said Ignacio. "And I don't want a job with ghosts in it. Or it might be the priest. People say he turns people into animals and things like that. Anyway, I'm going to resign."

"Why don't you ask him?" said Chuco.

Ignacio shivered again. "Do you think I want to disappear for good? They say if you ask him you disappear. He turns you into a bull or a calf or whatever he wants to. He makes cattle out of dead people. Not I—I wouldn't ask him for anything!"

Chucho thought a minute. "I tell you what—you tell the priest you're sick and that I'm going to ring the bells until you get well. I think there's somebody hiding there, and I'll find out."

Ignacio stared at him. "Aren't you afraid, Chucho? You're only seven. I'm fourteen, and I'm scared to death."

"No, I'm not afraid," said Chucho.

That evening he told his mother he had something to attend to, and he went to the church. It wasn't yet time to ring the bells, and he entered quietly and hid behind the altar.

Very soon he heard moaning and screaming; it sounded as if someone were hurt, but he thought it might be a cat. Then he heard soft footsteps, and he saw

· 211 ·

a man with a big knife and a woman with him. They glanced around guiltily and began to rob the church. They snatched the jewels from the saints, took gold cups from cupboards, seized the silver candlesticks from the altars, and put everything into a big sack. They robbed the poor box and the collection plates.

"Hurry!" whispered the woman. "I hear the priest coming!"

"Don't worry," the man said in a rough voice. "I've settled all that."

The priest came into the church, and the man handed him a sack.

"Here's your share," said the thief. "Gold coins."

"Be quick," said the priest. "It's nearly time for the bells to ring and the people to come and pray, and I'll have to straighten it out here, so no one will suspect anything. The boy who rings the bells might see you—make haste!"

The man with the knife scowled. "We'll hide, and you go up in the bell tower, and when the boy comes to ring the bells, scare him. Then he won't ring the bells and the people won't get to the church so soon, and we'll escape."

"All right, but hurry up because I have a little business of my own to look after—a few cows and things."

Up the stairs to the bell tower went the wicked priest. Chucho slipped out, opened the church door loudly, and came in whistling. It was pretty dark by now, but he went on up the narrow stairway.

As he was climbing, he heard a long moan and then a

scream. He knew it was the priest imitating ghosts and nahuals, so he moaned right back: "Ooooowah, ooowah, ooooo!"

"That's funny," said the priest out loud. Then he moaned and howled. Chucho howled too. "It must be an echo," said the priest in an anxious voice.

Chucho reached the top of the tower and grasped the bell rope. There was a long, long howl right next to him in the dark. He pretended he didn't hear it and stretched higher for the bell rope. The priest howled louder. Chucho seized the bell rope and began to ring. The bells clanged and bonged, and Chucho knew the people would be coming to prayers very shortly.

The priest pulled Chucho's hair. Chucho pretended he didn't feel anything and kept on ringing the bells. Each time the priest pulled his hair, Chucho pulled harder on the bell rope and the bells rang wildly.

The priest got a better grip on Chucho's hair and pulled desperately and screamed in the boy's ear. Chucho pulled the biggest bell up, up, up, as far as it would go, and suddenly turned around and let it loose. It came swinging down and the priest could not get out of the way. The bell hit him with a crash and knocked him out of the bell tower and he fell to the ground and broke. He broke into many pieces and then went up in smoke.

When the people coming to church saw the priest go up in smoke, they said, "So that was it. Too bad!" and entered the church to say their prayers. But there was the man with the big knife, and the woman, and they had the sack of stolen riches. They were trying to escape, but the sack was too heavy, and the people caught them and put them in jail.

Chucho came down from the bell tower, and the people applauded him and called him a hero. But Chucho said, "How can I be a hero if the priest fell down all by himself? I'm a little tired, so I guess I'll go home now."

All the people who had been turned into animals by the priest became people again and returned happily to their homes; and Margarita and all the dead people who had been cattle became dead people again, went back to their graves, rolled themselves up in their mats and lay down to sleep in peace once more.

The people said, "Perhaps Chucho isn't Chucho. Maybe he is Tepozton!"

But whenever anyone said that to Chucho, the little boy laughed. "Oh, no!" he said. "How can I be Tepozton if I am Chucho?"

*F*rance 🖋 🖋 🖋 🖋 🖋

YS AND HER BELLS

THE GHOST OF POOR KING GRALON HAS BEEN wandering over the small paths of Brittany, through the golden mist, for over fifteen hundred years. He is a harmless ghost, lonely, with sad eyes, and sometimes at twilight he speaks to the young girls of Brittany, to try to keep them pure, kind, and happy. For he is still suffering because of the wickedness of his own beautiful daughter, Dahut.

King Gralon lived very long ago, when the people of Brittany had just been converted to Christianity, and not all of them had yet renounced the old wild days of living. The hermit, Guénolé, had no fear of kings, and he spoke severely to Gralon about his daughter, Dahut, who was as willful and proud as she was lovely.

"O King, thy daughter is a curse! Stop her wickedness, have her tried by the judges of thine own court! Else the wrath of God will descend upon thy house and thy kingdom, O King! Remember it is written, 'If thy heart offend thee, cut out thy heart and cast it from thee!' "

Gralon would kneel down before the holy man and pray, but he would not punish his daughter, for she was the light of his life. She was born on the day when his queen died, and Dahut had the same shining braids, the same fathomless eyes. After eighteen years, Dahut was as beautiful as the sea, and Gralon could not believe that her heart was black as the hermit proclaimed. But he worried greatly, for her ways were strange.

She cared nothing for men, except her own father. She despised the young men of the court, of the city, of the world. When she was a little girl, she had secretly betrothed herself to the ocean, for it was the only strong thing she respected and loved. But she wanted men to gaze freely at her beauty, to fall desperately in love with the radiance of her face, and then to fling themselves down from the cliff into the abyss which is still called the Devil's Pit.

And so, one after another, the youths in Gralon's kingdom had gone the same way. Some of them succumbed to Dahut's spell at once; others resisted a longer time. But when she thought a young man might escape her, she gave a ball in the vast hall by the sea, and she would dance and dance and dance with the obstinate boy until he surrendered in his turn to her beauty, and drowned himself at dawn the following day, hoping that the sea would be kinder to him than her cold, fathomless eyes.

When the King protested, Dahut would say in anger, "Father, I never promised anything. Must I be held responsible for the foolishness of weaklings?"

But when she walked about in the streets of the city, the mothers and sweethearts of the drowned boys would close their doors and put a black curtain across their windows.

The capital of Gralon's kingdom was a beautiful city named Ys, and it had a hundred white spires where a hundred bells sang the glory of God louder than the white-foaming sea. Ys was built beside the ocean, just below the level of the water, and an enormous dam had been constructed to protect the city from high tides and storms. The key to the dam was made of pure gold, and only two people knew where it was hidden—Gralon and a poor young man whose father had built the dam.

Gralon had thought it wiser to tell just one person in case he himself died a sudden death. The young man was named Gavin, and he was a faithful, silent youth. Because he was a hunchback, he was not likely to marry, nor, thought the King, likely to attract the attention of Dahut. Gavin had given all his love to Ys and her hundred spires, and he was happy because the safety of Ys and her people depended upon his faith.

Once a year, during a very low tide, the dam was opened so that the people might clean the massive wall, lest the mud and sand and shells and seaweed eat away the stone. They cleaned it quickly and shut the dam before the great tide rushed in, and Gralon would hide the key for another year.

One night in the spring, just before Easter, Dahut lay awake listening to the sea, and she grew mad with the desire to see the waters engulf all things, the city, the people, the stupid men. And suddenly she thought of Gavin, the hunchbacked boy, who had never noticed her beauty, who had passed her in the narrow streets without seeing her, as if he had a vision in his eyes. And the wild idea entered her head that perhaps he knew where the key to the dam was hidden.

The following day she sought him in the little streets that wound around the magnificent churches with their dazzling spires, and she found him at last in a narrow passage which led to the sea. She took a deep breath of the salt wind which made her heart pound, and called to him.

"Gavin! Why dost thou never look at me?"

Then the boy did look at her, but he did not see her radiant face because of the image forever before his eyes; the vision of Ys, with the hundred bells of its hundred spires, stood like a mist between Gavin and Dahut and protected him from danger. "What can I do for thy service, Princess Dahut?" he asked respectfully.

Dahut was abashed and angry. For the first time in her life she saw neither fear nor love in a man's eyes, and she was furious. And slyly taking a chance, she said, "Give me the key to the dam which my father has hidden with thee."

Being a simple boy, Gavin thought that King Gralon had told her the whereabouts of the key, since it was well known that the King could resist none of her demands. And Gavin grew pale, clutched his fingers over his shriveled chest, and cried out, "Never!"

Dahut knew then that the key was hidden against Gavin's faithful heart, and she laughed wildly, while the boy crossed himself. She seized him and began to wrestle with him, and Gavin struggled valiantly and with courage. But she was strong as the wind, slippery as weed, and cool as the green sea water, and she smiled as she fought. As she conquered him and as he was dying, Gavin heard the hundred bells of the hundred spires of Ys ringing in his head and his heart and his soul, and theirs was a great victorious song.

She took the key from the pouch around his neck and pushed the poor misshapen body into the sea with a disdainful foot. She did not want to use the key at once; it was enough to know that she possessed it and that she could open the dam the next time she grew bored with men and bells and life. As she wandered back to the palace, she felt curiously uncomfortable. It was too disgusting to have wrestled with a cripple. And this man had not given in to her magic. The look in his eyes as he died had been strange; she wondered what he had seen that was more beautiful than her own face. Impatiently she began to make plans to ensnare another young man, a handsome one this time.

A few hours after her return to the palace, she was sitting with her father in the great hall, when suddenly the wind seemed to cry, "Death to Dahut! Death to Dahut!" Thinking she was feverish, she opened the window, and she saw at the foot of the cliff a furious crowd screaming, "Death to Dahut!" And in front of the crowd was borne the dead body of Gavin, the hunchback, dripping with water, on a bed of seaweed. "Death to Dahut! Death to Dahut!" chanted the mob, surging against the castle walls.

King Gralon faced the crowd and asked, "What is it, my people? Am I no longer thy King?"

"Death to Dahut!" the crowd cried. "Deliver her up to our justice, O King! Death to Dahut!"

And Gralon remembered the words of the hermit, "If thy heart offend thee, cut out thy heart and cast it from thee!" But he remembered, too, his dead queen, who had left him only Dahut's beauty. And he said, "Take me, my people. If you can prove her guilt, I am ready to pay for her life with my own."

But the mob wanted justice and they loved Gralon. One of the old men spoke, "Have her judged, O King, by thine own court!"

Shivering violently, Dahut flung a white cape about her, and ran to the secret door which led to the huge dam. The tide was at flood, and she could hear it pounding against the massive wall; she could hear, too, the flood of the voices crying, "Death to Dahut!" Swiftly she thrust the golden key in the lock, the heavy door slid open with a roar, the whole ocean stood erect before it thundered down upon Dahut, upon Ys with her spires and her bells, into the streets and upon the helpless people of Ys.

But the King shut the big window and so was safe for a while, since the palace stood high on the cliff and the walls were thick. But his heart was sick, for he knew that Dahut had opened the dam and slain his people,

and he knew that her soul was lost forever. He knew, too, that he had loved her better than God and His law, better than the poor people of his kingdom.

Then Guénolé came for him, leading the King's horse, Morvark, by the bridle. "Mount thy horse and ride, O King!" said the hermit. "For the Lord needs thee elsewhere."

They went out through the big window, and Morvark galloped up the beach, breast deep in sea water, while the holy man ran on the waves ahead, to point out the way.

Then it was that the thing happened which Gralon cannot forget and which keeps him roaming the paths of Brittany in his grief, even to this day. Suddenly he felt as if someone were clinging to his horse, desperately trying to climb up. He looked behind and saw Dahut, a terrible pallor on her lovely face and ghastly terror in her eyes. She pointed to the Devil's Pit. And Gralon saw the procession of all the young men who had died for her, beckoning to Dahut from the depths of the sea. And Dahut wanted to get on Morvark's back and live once more.

But Guénolé said, "Cast her away, O King!"

"Father, I am your only child!" begged Dahut. "I am afraid! Take me with you!"

"Cast her away!" repeated Guénolé.

"I am like my mother," implored Dahut. "For her sake, take me with you!"

But the holy man cried, "Choose between thy

daughter and God, O King! It is written, 'Cut out thy heart, if thy heart tempt thee!' "

The horse, Morvark, suddenly neighed to heaven; and Gralon freed himself from Dahut's arms. Morvark kicked the waves wildly, and the King fell forward upon the neck of his horse. And Guénolé led them to the further kingdom where God needed a good King.

After his death, the King refused to go to heaven, but he lingers on among the people of Brittany, wandering the paths among the gorse, in the golden mist and in the lilac mist of twilight.

And on Easter Day, if the year is going to be a blessed one, you may sit on the rock and gaze far below into the blue-green water, and the spires of Ys, the beautiful, will rise from the depths. And if there is no sin in your heart you may hear the bells, the hundred bells of the hundred spires of Ys, ringing far below in the sea, to the everlasting glory of God.

"GENEVIÈVE! THE HUNS ARE COMING!"

In the town of Nanterre, near Paris, some fifteen hundred years ago, there lived a little shepherdess named Geneviève. She was a very devout child, and on a day when two famous bishops were expected to pass the town, she joined the crowd on the river bank, her seven-year-old heart jumping like a rabbit with excitement. The great bishop Germain came ashore to bless the people, and as he was doing so, his eyes fell upon the little girl and he could not look away.

He walked through the crowd to the child and put his hand upon her head. Geneviève trembled with holy fear. Then the bishop bent down and picked up a rusty coin lying in the dust at his feet. The coin bore a cross and had a hole in the center of it, and he made a necklace of it and hung it about Geneviève's neck. "Never wear any other jewel, little one," he said solemnly, and the child promised that she never would.

After that, Geneviève went to church every day, instead of merely on Sundays, and her mother, Gerontia, became very much annoyed.

"Why can't you go to church on Sundays, like all respectable and sensible girls?" her mother asked in a fury.

"God calls me, mother," answered Geneviève.

"Is that so?" asked Gerontia. "If you were busy helping me sweep and wash I don't think you'd hear God call quite so loudly!"

"Is there anything you want me to do right now, mother?" asked Geneviève.

"You can hold your tongue and not always argue with me!" cried Gerontia in anger, and she struck Geneviève on the head.

At that instant Gerontia became blind, and that was her punishment for slapping a saint. And now Geneviève did all the work about the house. She cared for her mother, she went to market, she carried water from the well. But still she managed to go to church every day, and she never failed to pray for her mother's recovery.

One day as she was drawing water from the well she set the full pail on the edge of the well while she caught her breath. She was thinking with grief and tenderness of her blind mother, and a few tears fell from her lovely eyes into the clear water. She was unaware of it, and returned to the house. While she was setting the table, her mother asked for some water to wash her face and hands before supper, and Geneviève brought her a basin. As soon as the water, blessed by Geneviève's tears, touched Gerontia's blind eyes, Gerontia cried out, "Praise God, I can see!" And Geneviève hugged her mother joyously.

As she grew up, many things happened to Geneviève, and by the time she was twenty-eight she was both learned and good. She lived the life of a hermit in a small house in Paris, where she studied the Bible and copied out and illuminated old manuscripts. She never went out of doors from Twelfth-night until Easter, and she ate only twice a week, on Thursdays and Sundays. When she did go out, during the rest of the year, she visited the poor, cured the sick, and was kind to the wicked. But her neighbors criticized her—the men because she was very beautiful and remained unmarried, the women because she was silent and never talked about herself.

One April morning, Paris was shaken by dreadful news: Attila and his Huns were coming. The people gathered by the small shops, all trying to talk at once; the women crossed themselves and prayed, and the children, terrified, whimpered and cried.

Attila called himself the Scourge of God and bragged that grass never grew again where his horse had stepped. Among the barbarians coming from the east who devastated the west of Europe for centuries and destroyed the Roman civilization, the Huns were by far the most terrible. It was said that every Hun's mother flattened the skull and the nose of her newborn son to prepare him in advance for the shape of his helmet. The warriors never dismounted from their horses until they were victorious, and they looted and sacked and burned and crucified. The people of Paris were in mortal terror, and all the bells of the city were ringing wildly in warning.

The people knew they could not save their small beautiful city, but they could save themselves. They could load their most precious belongings into the hundreds of little boats on the Seine and escape while there was yet time.

Geneviève, kneeling in her bedroom and saying her Lenten prayers, was suddenly aware of the clangor of bells and the tumultuous voices. Someone was calling, "Geneviève! The Huns are coming!"

She recognized the voice as that of the fish monger's wife, who lived three houses down the street. As she stood up, she heard the voice again, urgent and panic-stricken, crying, "Geneviève! Geneviève, the Huns are coming!"

Hastening to the window, she threw open the casement. "Eloise, what's the trouble?"

"The Huns!" cried the stout, kindly woman. "Attila and his Huns are going to attack at any moment! Hurry up and pack your things and come with us in our boat!"

"Wait, Eloise," said Geneviève. "Don't run away yet!"

She closed the window and knelt down again, asking God's direction. And a vision came to her wherein she voyaged through time and saw her beloved Paris as the coming centuries would change it. She beheld it grow in beauty and wisdom, saw it suffer through famine, plague, battle, and riot, and still rise invincible, because of the soul of its people, above all enemies. And she knew that no man was permitted to desert the city whose destiny held so much humanity, so much glory. Geneviève hurried to the window and flung it open. "Hear, ye people of Paris, what God has bidden me to tell you!" she cried. But no one looked up except the fish monger's wife.

"Hurry, Geneviève!"

"Wait," called Geneviève, and she hastened down the stairs and out of her house into the street, hearing Eloise calling the people to wait for her. "You must not run away," Geneviève said to the gathering crowd. "Men and women of Paris, if you pray to God and remain quietly in your homes and in your boats, Attila will not enter the city. I promise you, in the name of the Lord, Attila will not come in!"

A man shouted, "Fool! What do you know about Attila?"

Another yelled, "Stop your chatter! We're wasting time!"

A group of frantic women shrieked, "Down with her! She's a sorceress!"

"Sorceress!" the mob screamed then, mad with terror at being delayed. "Death to the sorceress Geneviève! Throw her in the river! To the river! To the river!"

But Geneviève stood there unafraid and calm. "God is stronger than your fear," she said clearly. "If He watches at our gate, no enemy can force it. And if He blows on our massive doors, they will glide open without keys."

A boatman shouted, "Show us that, Geneviève! Blow our gate open and we shall believe in thee!" And he guffawed.

Geneviève looked at the frightened faces before her. "With the help of God, I will," she said. "Take me to the eastern gate."

The people followed her silently to the great gate which they had closed and barred immediately after the arrival of the scout bringing the news of Attila's approach.

"Unbar the gate and let me outside," said Geneviève. "Bar it again, and some of you mount the wall and watch. If it is the will of God, I shall blow the gate open with a breath, in His name."

The men let her out and pushed the massive gate shut once more, shoving the heavy bar across it.

Geneviève stood alone in the sunlight. "O Lord," she said aloud, "show Thy will, and support Thy servant if she speaks Thy command." She blew on the gate, and the huge bar inside splintered and the gate opened slowly, and Geneviève walked quietly inside the walls. The people knelt in awe, and the elders came down from the ramparts.

"We shall stay with thee, Geneviève," said the elders, "and trust the promise of God."

The men closed the gate and shoved another great bar into place, and Geneviève smiled at Eloise and at Pierre, the fish monger, and returned to her small house in the narrow street she loved.

In the meantime, the Roman general Aëtius had gathered a large army of Romans and of Gauls to fight Attila and his Huns. When he heard of this new army ready to do battle with him, Attila, who had been beseiging Orleans, decided to move northeastward, so that he could fight nearer the Rhine. And Paris lay directly in his path. But he felt strangely reluctant to attack the small city on the Seine, and he could not understand his sense of foreboding. So he offered a sacrifice to his gods and ordered the pagan priest to look closely at the warm entrails and tell him what to do.

The priest said solemnly, "Attila, our gods tell thee to make haste to the northeast and not to pause, for there will be a battle greater than any thine army has yet seen. The river will turn red with blood and a renowned chief will die."

Attila was very excited and was sure that the famous chief would be Aëtius. He commanded his army to press forward, but his men were dissatisfied, for they had expected an orgy in Paris and a few weeks' rest. He told them, therefore, that if Paris were empty they might help themselves to the wine and the loot, since it would mean no fighting and little lost time.

As his horde approached the city, he sent two scouts ahead to observe Paris. They galloped back and reported that all the boats were still there and that they had seen the sails in the sunlight.

"Then the gate is closed," Attila said, "and the people are ready to fight. But Aëtius is waiting for us, and the wine of Paris will be just as cool the day after tomorrow. Forward!"

But two days later the battle of Châlons-sur-Marne was still raging between the Huns and the legions of Aëtius. And not Aëtius but Hilperik died in the fight. Defeated for the first time, half of his Huns dead and the rest in flight, Attila led the remnants of his army across the German marshes to his camp far on the borders of Asia. And the Gauls never saw him again.

The people of Paris knew now that Geneviève was truly a saint, and they made her their mayor. She lived to be ninety and saw many changes in her beloved Paris, but because of the soul of its people, she knew that it would rise invincible above all enemies.

THE FAITHFUL LITTLE SQUIRE

The knight Godefroy had as his squire Robert of Flanders, a handsome, brave, and modest young man. Although he was poor, Robert was cherished by Godefroy for his loyalty and courage. And Godefroy had a daughter named Blanche who was as beautiful as the morning.

Godefroy's wife, anxious because he seemed in no hurry to have Blanche marry, spoke finally to Robert. "I wish you would tell your master," she said, "that he is being sharply criticized for not attending to his daughter's future. He should choose a husband for her."

Robert flushed painfully, for he was hopelessly in love with Blanche, but what chance did he have who was poor and not even a knight? "I'll speak if you wish it," he told Blanche's mother, "but will not my master think me bold and presumptuous?"

"Don't worry about that, Robert," she said tartly. "He cannot go on forgetting his obligations forever!"

So, awkwardly and unwillingly, Robert spoke to Godefroy.

Godefroy listened to his young squire's stumbling speech and tried not to smile. Then he replied, "I'll take your advice, Robert. If you'll name a knight as brave and loyal as you are, and as rich as I am, I'll give him Blanche to wed immediately."

Robert tried hard to think of a perfect knight worthy of becoming the husband of Blanche, but he could not recall one knight who was perfect in every way.

Godefroy asked gravely, "What about Guillaume of Cambrai?"

"He is too old," protested Robert.

"Or Raoul of Hainaut?"

"I'm not sure of his courage."

"Or Raymond of Courtray?"

"He is too dull," said Robert hopelessly.

Godefroy chuckled. "Well, Robert, you, with your modesty, cannot think of a knight whose merit approaches your own. So I shall give you a big estate, which you shall hold in my name, and I shall give you Blanche, because I know you will make her both happy and proud."

Robert stammered, "Do not jest with me, my lord. I know I have been overbold and intrusive."

But Godefroy shook his head. "I'm not jesting, Robert. I'm serious. I swear it. Blanche will have no other husband but you."

"But I'm not even a knight."

"I'll make you one," said Godefroy, "and then we shall have the wedding."

So Robert was given a bath, to signify the purity of his heart. Then he was clothed in a white robe, as white as his innocence, and a scarlet robe, red as the noble blood which he was ready to shed for the sake of God and His church and His poor. He was given brown sandals to signify the earth to which he would return on his death, and he was left alone in the chapel to meditate all night long.

At dawn he was presented with his golden spurs—the symbol of the swiftness with which he, as well as his horse, would answer any just claim made upon his pity and his courage. And they gave him his shining sword, with a cross at the hilt to keep it from ever dealing an unfair blow.

And Robert knelt down, and Godefroy struck him on

the shoulder with the flat of the sword, and embraced him and said, "I dub thee knight, in the name of the Father and of the Son and of the Holy Ghost!"

And Robert and Blanche were married.

But the following day, Robert said to his beautiful wife, "My dear love, I must leave you. Years ago I made a vow to start on a pilgrimage to Saint James as soon as I became a knight. It breaks my heart to leave you, but I must. You understand, don't you?"

"I understand," Blanche answered. "And I would be a wicked wife indeed if I kept my husband from his vow."

But her mother abused Robert, and the other knights joked at his expense.

Raoul of Hainaut, who was jealous of Robert's good fortune, joked more loudly than the rest. "A wise man knows better than to leave his newly wedded wife," he laughed. "I'll wager all my lands that Robert's place in her heart will be filled by another when he comes back!"

Robert was angry. "A wise man does not insult his newly wedded wife by distrusting her!" he said.

"You are very confident," said Raoul with a sneer. "But you would not wager all your new lands on the virtue of your love!"

"I would," said Robert quietly.

"All of your lands against the whole of mine?"

"Yes," said Robert, "although I do not like such a wager."

"Are you backing out already?"

"Sir Raoul," said Robert, "I have complete faith in

my honored wife, and I accept your wager if you promise to keep it secret. And I'll go on my pilgrimage unafraid."

Robert was absent for a year, but at last a messenger came to Blanche saying that her husband would return the following week. When he was fifty miles from home, Robert saw Raoul galloping toward him.

"I have come to spare you unnecessary shame," Raoul said, smiling. "Do you recognize this?" And he showed Robert his wife's wedding ring, which a disloyal servant had stolen for him. "Blanche gave it to me, and I've been wearing it for two months. She confessed that she loved me before she married you but did not dare disobey her father's will. She wishes you to realize what an ordeal it will be for her if you return."

Robert merely stared at Raoul and was mute with sorrow.

"Don't worry about our wager," Raoul said. "I'll let you keep half your land, since you've lost your love."

"Keep the whole of my land," replied Robert in a low voice. "I wish to be under no obligation to you. And tell my wife that I am going so far away that she need not think of me any more." He turned his horse and rode off with bent head.

Delighted at the success of his lies, Raoul hastened back to Godefroy. He told him of the wager, and of his meeting with Robert, showed him the ring, and offered to have Blanche's marriage annulled by the pope so that he could marry her himself.

Godefroy, believing Raoul's story of Blanche's infidelity, sent for her and asked her to defend herself.

She answered, "Father, you may believe what you think true. I shall never marry Raoul. I would rather die. But let him keep Robert's land until Robert himself returns to claim it."

She left the hall, and within a few hours had disappeared. Godefroy caused the countryside to be searched, but there was no trace of her. All the beggars were questioned for miles around, public prayers were held, the knights went on a pilgrimage, but to no avail. Blanche had vanished.

In the meantime, Robert was riding on in his gray pilgrim's garments, heartbroken and in despair, with only his golden spurs as a sign of his chivalry. He had traveled for three days when, near a poor inn, he was accosted after sundown by a very young horseman.

"May I ask, sir, where you are going?" the young man said politely. "I saw your spurs and I wondered whether you would accept me as your squire."

Robert smiled for the first time since he had left Blanche a year ago. The boy was extremely young, with a golden complexion and large, lovely gray eyes, and he moved with an easy grace. "I have met with misfortune, lad," Robert said, "and have neither lands nor money nor any purpose in the world. What is your name?"

"Henri," the boy replied modestly. "But my mother gave me some gold coins when I left home in quest of a knight to serve. If you will allow me to serve you for seven years, so that I may, in turn, become a knight, I shall care for you well. I'll work to earn our living."

Robert looked at the young man's delicate hands and smiled once more. "What kind of work could you do?" he asked gently.

"Try me and see, my lord!" Henri begged.

"Very well," Robert said. "Let us stay the night at this inn, and on the morrow we shall go forth together."

Henri proved to be a delightful squire. He made Robert eat when he wasn't hungry; he made him laugh when he was sad; he finally made him glad to be alive when there was nothing left to live for. Henri slept at his master's feet at night, on the bare ground; yet his ways were graceful and refined. His devotion and loyalty to Robert were equaled by his common sense, and Robert smiled more often now and sometimes patted Henri's small brown head.

They were journeying toward Marseilles, where they hoped to sail for Palestine to fight the infidels. But when they reached the town they found that the crusade was over, peace had been made, and there was no chance of fighting. They could go as pilgrims if they wished, but Robert, just back from one pilgrimage, did not feel like undertaking another at the moment. But they had to eat.

"My lord," said Henri, "if you will permit me, I might try to sell cakes. When I was a little boy, I used to bake them for fun, with my mother's cook, and I think I can remember the recipes. I'll find a small shop."

In another month, the townspeople were crowding

into the small shop for Henri's delicious cakes. A year later Henri suggested that they purchase a large house and make it into an inn, which he would keep while Robert attended the tournaments. "Then you will be recognized as a valiant knight, so that the people will know where to ask for help when they need it," said Henri.

"But why should you work hard all day, while I do nothing?"

"You were a squire, too, my lord," Henri answered. "Did you ever regret the trouble you took for your master?"

"No, of course not," said Robert.

"Well, then," said Henri, laughing softly.

The inn prospered, and Henri bought new armor and a new horse for Robert, and Robert attended the tournaments. They were very happy together, and Robert no longer brooded about the past.

At the beginning of the seventh year a pilgrim stopped at the inn. It was Raoul. Robert did not recognize him, for he was thin and haggard, but Henri was at once interested in him and inquired why, ill as he seemed, he was in such a hurry to reach Palestine. Raoul stated that he had been desperately ill and dying, and that he had confessed to a priest about his lies and his theft of Robert's lands. The priest had ordered him, on his recovery, to go on a pilgrimage for his sins, and to tell the story to anyone who happened to ask. And the next day he took ship in Marseilles.

At the end of the seventh year, Henri said, "My lord,

we have made a fortune now, and do not need to keep the inn any longer. I'd like to ask a favor of you. If I am to become a knight, I must learn how to fight beside you. But before we go to war, take me with you to your old home."

Robert had never mentioned Blanche to his little squire, and Henri had never spoken of Raoul's confession. So they set off on the long journey, for Robert could not refuse his friend; but it was with mixed emotions that he thought of seeing his wife once more.

When they were an hour's ride from Godefroy's castle, Robert sent Henri on ahead, at Henri's suggestion, to announce his coming. But when he reached the castle, he found that Henri had never arrived. Blanche, however, had just returned after seven years in a remote convent, and Robert thought she was more beautiful than ever.

Raoul had confessed again, this time in public, and had given back Robert's land. Godefroy had prepared a great welcoming feast, and Robert should have been very happy, but he was not. He could not understand why Henri had fled without a farewell. Or perhaps the little squire had been attacked by a highwayman and was lying dead behind some rock or thicket. Sorely distressed, Robert looked at Blanche and sighed heavily.

Her gray eyes were dreamy. "Why aren't you happy, my lord?" she asked.

And he answered as he had answered seven years before, "Because, my love, I must leave you."

"Why?"

"I must try to find my little squire. I cannot rest until I know whether he is dead or alive."

"Can it be," she asked, "that you love him better than you love me?"

"You are my love, and he was my friend," said Robert. "It is hard to have to choose between you."

Blanche smiled at him. "Robert," she said, "are you sure you have to?"

And Robert looked into her eyes, and they were Henri's eyes, and he took her into his arms, murmuring, "My love and my friend!"

"If you go on grieving for your squire," she said softly, "I shall have to rub my face and hands with that stain all over again."

And Robert laughed and said, "Never again, my faithful little squire!"

Yugoslavia ❧ ❧ ❧ ❧

THE LITTLE SINGING FROG

MANY YEARS AGO THERE LIVED A POOR LABORER and his wife who grieved because they had no children.

Every day the wife would sigh and say, "If only we had a child!"

And the man would sigh, too, and say, "It would be fine to have a little daughter, wouldn't it?"

Finally they made a pilgrimage to a holy shrine and prayed God to give them a child.

"Any kind of child!" the woman prayed. "I'd be thankful for a child of our own even if it were a frog!"

God heard their prayers and sent them a little daughter—not a little girl daughter, but a little frog daughter. The laborer and his wife loved their little frog child with all their hearts; and they played with her and laughed and clapped their hands with joy as they watched her hopping about the house. But when the neighbors whispered, "That child of theirs is nothing but a frog!" they were ashamed and troubled, and they decided to keep the child hidden in a closet when people were about. They didn't want the little frog girl's feelings hurt, either.

So she grew up without playmates, seeing only her father and mother. She used to play about her father as he worked in the big vineyard where he was a vine dresser. It was marvelous fun for the little frog girl to hop about among the green vines, and she really didn't miss too much not being allowed to play with other little children.

At noontime every day the woman came to the vineyard carrying her husband's dinner in a basket; but as the years passed, the trip to the vineyard began to exhaust her and the basket seemed to grow heavier and heavier. The frog daughter noticed this and insisted on carrying the dinner basket up to the vineyard herself, making her mother sit at home and rest.

While her father ate his dinner, the frog girl hopped up into the branches of a near-by tree and sang to him. She had a lovely voice and she sang very sweetly, and her father, when he petted her, called her his Little Singing Frog.

One day while she was singing up in the tree, the Tsar's youngest son rode by and heard her. He reined in his horse, looked all around, but couldn't see who was singing so sweetly.

"Who is singing?" the Prince asked the laborer.

But the father, ashamed of his frog daughter before strangers, pretended not to hear.

"Answer me," commanded the Prince. "Who is that singing so marvelously?"

But the father answered gruffly, "There's no one singing. It's the wind you hear."

But the next day at the same hour, when the Prince was riding past once more, he heard again the same sweet voice and he stopped again and listened. "See here, fellow!" he said to the laborer. "I know there's someone singing! It's a lovely girl—I'd swear it! If I could find her, I'd marry her at once and take her home to my father, the Tsar!"

"Don't be foolhardy," said the laborer.

"I mean it!" declared the Prince, gazing around eagerly. "I'd marry her in a minute!"

"Are you sure of it?"

"I'm positive," said the Prince.

The poor man looked up into the tree and called, "Come down, Little Singing Frog! A Prince wants to marry you!"

The little frog girl hopped down from among the green branches and stood before the Prince.

"She's my own daughter," explained the laborer, "even if she does look like a frog."

"I don't care what she looks like," the Prince said firmly. "I love her singing and I love her. And I'll marry her if she'll marry me. My father, the Tsar, has commanded me and my brothers to present our brides to him tomorrow. All the brides must bring him a flower, and he promises to give the kingdom to the prince whose bride brings the loveliest flower. Little Singing Frog, will you be my bride and will you come with me tomorrow to the court?"

"Yes, my Prince," she answered, "I will. But I must not shame you by hopping to court in the dust—I must ride. So will you send me a pure white cock from your father's barnyard?"

"That I will," answered the Prince, and before nightfall a messenger brought a snow-white cock to the laborer's cottage.

At dawn the following morning the frog girl prayed to the rising sun. "O golden sun," she begged, "help me! Give me some lovely clothes woven of your golden rays so that I may not shame my Prince when I go to the Tsar's court!"

The sun smiled down at her and gave her a gown of cloth of gold.

Instead of a flower, she took a spear of wheat in her hand, mounted the white cock, and rode to the palace.

When she came to the palace gate, the guards refused to let her in. "This is no place for frogs!" they shouted bravely. "What you are looking for is a pond!"

"I am not!" replied the Little Singing Frog. "I am the bride of the youngest Prince!"

Then the guards were afraid to drive her away, and they let her ride through the gate on the snow-white cock. But as they looked through the gate after her, they saw an astonishing sight. The frog girl, still seated on the white cock, was shaking out the folds of a golden gown. As she dropped the gown over her head, instantly there was neither frog girl nor white cock, but a beautiful maiden mounted on a pure white horse!

The frog girl entered the palace with the two promised brides of the elder princes. They were simply ordinary girls, and beside the lovely bride of the youngest Prince, they looked more ordinary than ever.

The first girl presented a rose to the Tsar. The Tsar looked at the flower, then at her, sniffed slightly, and turned his head away.

The second girl carried a carnation. The Tsar looked at her for a moment and murmured, "Oh, my fallen arches, this will never do!"

The bride of the youngest Prince then handed him the spear of wheat and curtsied, and the Tsar gazed at her with a brightening eye and said, "Ah, this is more like it!" He held the spear of wheat aloft, reached for her other hand, and drew her up on the throne beside him.

Then he spoke to his sons and the royal court: "This maiden, the bride of the youngest Prince, is my choice, for she is both beautiful and wise! She knows the useful as well as the lovely, for she has brought me a spear of wheat! Let the youngest Prince be the Tsar after me, and his bride the Tsarina!"

So the Little Singing Frog, of whom her parents had been ashamed, married the youngest Prince, and when the time came she wore the Tsarina's crown, but her young husband still delighted to hear her sing as she had sung among the green branches in the laborer's vineyard.

THE BEST WISH

Three brothers once possessed a pear tree and took turns guarding it. While two of them went to work, the third stayed at home to watch the tree and make sure that no harm came to it and that no one stole the pears.

An angel was sent down from heaven to test the hearts of the three brothers; taking the form of a beggar, he approached the pear tree on a day when the eldest brother was guarding it. He held out his hand and said, "In heaven's name, brother, give me a ripe pear."

The eldest brother handed him a pear immediately. "I can give you this one," he said, "because it is mine, but none of the others because they belong to my brothers."

The angel thanked him and went away.

The next day the second brother was on guard, and the angel returned as a beggar and again begged the charity of a ripe pear.

"Take this one," said the second brother. "It belongs to me, but I can't give you any of the others because they belong to my brothers."

The angel thanked the second brother and departed.

The third day, when he approached the youngest brother, the boy replied in the same manner.

On the following day the angel, disguised as a monk, came early to the brothers' house while they were all still at home.

"Come with me, my sons," he said, "and perhaps I

can find you something better to do than to guard a single pear tree."

The brothers went with him, and they walked for a long time until they came to the banks of a broad, deep river.

The angel spoke to the eldest brother. "My son, if I were to grant you one wish, what would you ask?"

"It would be wonderful," said the eldest brother, "if all this water were turned into wine and belonged to me!"

The angel lifted his staff and made the sign of the cross, and at once the broad river became wine from great wine presses. Men were filling a large number of casks and rolling them about. A huge industry appeared, with shed, storehouses, wagons, and men running back and forth busily and addressing the eldest brother respectfully as Master.

"You have your wish," said the angel. "But do not forget God's poor, now that you are rich."

They left the eldest brother busy with his wine and traveled on until they came to a great field where flocks of pigeons were feeding.

"If I were to grant you one wish," said the angel to the second brother, "what would you ask for?"

"It would be marvelous," said the second brother, "if all the pigeons in this field were turned into sheep and belonged to me!"

The angel lifted his staff, made the sign of the cross, and immediately the field was covered with sheep. And there were sheds and houses; and women were milking the ewes and skimming the milk and making cheeses. There were men preparing meat for the market, and other men cleaning wool. All of them, as they hurried up and down, respectfully called the second brother Master.

"There is your wish," said the angel. "But now that you are prosperous, do not forget God's poor."

Then he and the youngest brother journeyed on.

"Now, my son," said the angel, "you may make one wish, too."

The youngest brother said quietly, "There's only one thing I pray heaven for, father. And that is a truly pious wife."

"My son, you have asked for the hardest thing of all!" cried the angel. "There are only three pious women in the world, and two of them are already married. The third is a princess who at this very moment is being sought in marriage by two kings. However, let us go to the King and present your request."

So they trudged along to the city where the Princess lived and entered the palace, looking shabby and stained by travel.

The King granted them an audience, and when they had told their mission he exclaimed, "How can I decide? Two kings and now this youth all ask for my daughter's hand the same day! What shall I do?"

"Let heaven decide," said the angel.

"Of course," said the King. "But how?"

"In this manner. Cut three branches of grapevine, and let the Princess mark each branch with the name of a different suitor. Then let her plant the three branches in the garden tonight. Tomorrow you must give her in marriage to the man whose branch has blossomed during the night and by morning is covered with ripe clusters of grapes."

"That is an excellent idea," said the King.

The Princess and the suitors agreed to it; the Princess named and planted the three branches. In the morning, two of the branches were withered and bare but the third was covered with green leaves and ripe clusters of grapes, and the name on the blossoming branch was that of the youngest brother. The King accepted heaven's ruling without question, led his daughter to the church, and had her married to the strange young man. Then he sent them off with his blessing. And the angel led the young couple to a forest and left them there.

After a year had passed, the angel was sent back to earth to see how the three brothers were getting along. Again assuming the garments of a beggar, he went to the eldest brother, who was busy among his vines and his wine presses.

"Please give a poor man a cup of wine," begged the angel.

"Get out, you old rascal!" shouted the eldest brother in a rage. "If I gave a cup of wine to every beggar who came along, I'd soon be a beggar myself. Off with you!"

The angel lifted his staff, made the sign of the cross, and behold! the wine and the presses and the shed and the workers disappeared, and the broad, deep river flowed again in that place.

"In your prosperity you have forgotten God's poor," said the angel severely. "Go back to your pear tree!"

And he went on to find the second brother, who was busy in his dairy.

"Pray give a poor man a morsel of cheese," begged the angel.

"Be off with you, or I'll call the dogs!" shouted the second brother. "I'll give no cheese to a lazy good-for-nothing!"

The angel lifted his staff and made the sign of the cross. And the sheep and the dairy and all the busy laborers vanished, and instead there was only a field where flocks of pigeons were feeding.

"You have forgotten God's poor," said the angel sternly. "Go back to your pear tree!"

Then the angel hurried on to the forest where he had left the youngest brother and his wife, the Princess. And he found them living in great poverty in a little hut.

"God be with you!" said the angel, still looking like an old beggar. "In heaven's name, give me a little supper and shelter for the night."

"We are very poor ourselves, but come in," said the youngest brother. "You are welcome to share what we have."

The youngest brother and the Princess made the old beggar comfortable by the fire, and the wife set three places for the evening meal. They were so poor that the loaf baking in the oven was not made of flour at all but of pounded bark which the youngest brother had gathered from the trees.

"I am ashamed," murmured the wife, "that we have no real bread to offer you, our guest."

"I really need very little," answered the angel, smiling.

But when she opened the oven, there was a browned loaf of wheaten bread, and she cried, "God be praised!" and wept with surprise and delight.

She drew a pitcher of water at the spring, but when she began pouring it into the cups it had changed into sweet wine. And the youngest brother was as overjoyed as she.

The angel said, "In your happiness, you have not forgotten God's poor, and God will reward you!"

He raised his staff, made the sign of the cross, and the poor little hut disappeared. In its place arose a marvelous palace filled with riches and beautiful things. Many servants passed to and fro, and addressed the younger brother as "my lord" and his wife as "my lady."

And the old beggar arose with a smile and blessed them. "God gives you these riches," he said, "and they will be yours as long as you share them with others. Bless you and farewell, my children!"

And the angel returned to heaven to report on the goodness of the youngest brother's heart, while the youngest brother and his dear wife lived in great honor and love.

THE SILVER TRACKS

Of three hard-working brothers, the first was very rich, for his wife was as industrious as himself and they had no children to spend their money on. The second brother was not quite so rich, but he was prosperous. He had one son, and his only thought was to accumulate enough money and property to leave his son tremendously well-to-do. He schemed and slaved, and made his wife do likewise.

The third brother was also industrious but he was very poor, for he had a wife and ten children, and only by working every hour of the day and far into the night could he earn enough to buy food for so large a family. He never took a holiday, but labored incessantly. A simple and good man, he taught his children that the most important things in life were to love God and to be kind to their fellow men.

It chanced that once when our Lord Christ was on earth proving the hearts of men, He came as a beggar to the village where the three brothers lived. He came in a rackety old cart, driving an ancient broken-down horse, and it was cold and raining and night was falling.

The Beggar knocked at the door of the richest brother and said, "I pray you, in God's name, give shelter for one night to me and my poor horse!"

"Get out, you good-for-nothing!" shouted the rich brother. "Do you think I'd give shelter to an old reprobate like you? Be off before I call my men and have them give you the beating you deserve!"

Without a word, the Beggar left and went to the house of the second brother. This brother pretended he was sorry to refuse the Beggar.

"I'd give you shelter if I could," he replied, "but I

can't." Although he had only his wife and his son, he complained, "My house isn't as big as it looks, and I have a great many people dependent on me. If you go on a little farther, I'm sure you will find someone who will take you in."

The Beggar said nothing but turned His horse's head from the prosperous driveway and went on to the miserable little house where the poor brother lived with his wife and ten happy children. The Beggar knocked at the door and asked for shelter.

"Of course, come in, brother," said the poor man. "We're pretty crowded here, but there's still room for you. And we'll stable your horse in with my donkey so he won't be out in the cold and rain. Come in by the fire and dry off, and I'll attend to your horse."

So the Beggar entered the poor man's hut while His host pulled his own cart out of the shed into the rain to make a dry place for the Beggar's cart. He led the Beggar's bony horse into the little shed with his own donkey and fed him for the night from his own small store of oats and hay.

He and his family shared their supper with the Beggar, and afterward they made up a bed of straw for Him near the fire, where He slept comfortably and warmly.

The next morning, pleased with the good hearts of the youngest brother and his wife, the Beggar said to the young man, "You must come and visit me sometime and let me return your hospitality."

"Where do you live?" asked the poor brother.

"You can always find me," replied the Beggar, "by

following the tracks of my cart. You will know them because they are broader than the tracks of any other cart. You'll come, won't you?"

"Yes, I will," promised the poor man, "if I ever have time."

They said goodby, and the Beggar drove off slowly, letting His old horse take his time. Then the poor man went to the shed to hitch up his own cart to his donkey, and the first thing he saw was two large silver bolts lying on the ground. He thought, "They must have fallen from the Beggar's cart!" and ran out into the road to see if the Beggar were still in sight. But the Beggar and the cart had disappeared.

"May heaven grant he has no accident on account of those bolts!" said the poor man to his wife.

"God keep him safe!" she replied.

When he returned to the shed and went into the stall for his donkey, he found four golden horseshoes where the Beggar's horse had been standing. "Four golden horseshoes!" exclaimed the youngest brother. "I ought to return them and the silver bolts at once! But I can't do it today—I'm too busy, and there is so much to be done if I'm to feed the children properly. Well, I'll hide them safely away, and some afternoon when I have a few hours to spare I'll follow the tracks of the cart to the Beggar's house."

That afternoon he chanced to meet his two rich brothers, and he told them about the Beggar.

"Silver bolts!" cried the eldest.

"Golden horseshoes!" cried the second. "Take us home with you and let us see them!"

"Come along," said the poor man, and he showed them the silver bolts and the golden horseshoes. "Brothers," he said, "I wish, if either of you can spare the time, you'd take these things and return them to the Beggar. I have no doubt he needs them."

Both brothers said no, of course they couldn't spare the time, but that they'd like to know where the Beggar lived.

The youngest brother explained, "He said I could always find him by following the tracks of his cart."

"Show us the tracks of his cart!" demanded the eldest brother.

From the shed where the cart had been they followed the tracks out to the road; and the tracks were wider than any other cart tracks and shone like glistening silver, even though it was a dark, cloudy day.

"Are you sure you won't have time to return the Beggar's things for me? I don't like to keep them," said the youngest brother.

"Of course not!" they both answered.

But each in his heart had already determined to go at once and see for himself what kind of beggar this was who had silver bolts in his cart and golden shoes on his horse.

The next day the eldest brother set out early in the morning in a new wagon drawn by a fine horse. The silver tracks led him through woods and fields and over green hills and over rocky hills, until he came at last to a river spanned by a wooden bridge. The bridge was cunningly constructed of beautifully hewn timbers; the rich man had never seen such marvelous wood used on a bridge.

By the roadside beyond the bridge there was a pigsty with one trough full of corn and another full of water. Two sows in the sty, paying no attention to the good food, were fighting, tearing at each other fiercely with horrible grunts and squeals.

Farther on there was another river, and over it a bridge wonderfully constructed of stone. And beyond it was a meadow with a hayrick in it. Around and around the hayrick two angry bulls were chasing each other and goring each other, and they were both bloody from their wounds. The rich man wondered why somebody didn't come and stop them.

Over the next river arched an iron bridge, more beautiful than the rich man had ever dreamed an iron bridge could be. Beyond the iron bridge lay a field with a bush, and around the bush two angry rams were chasing each other and fighting. Their horns cracked as they locked, and their hides were torn and bleeding where they had gored each other.

Over the next river arched a bridge that glowed in the sun like fire, for it was built of shining copper—copper rivets, copper plates, copper beams—and it was blindingly beautiful. By the roadside stood a high crossbar from which were hanging heavy cuts of meat—lamb and pork and veal; and two large bitch dogs were jumping at the meat and then snapping and snarling and biting at each other.

The next bridge was lovelier than all the others, for it was built of gleaming white silver. Very excited, the rich man climbed down from his wagon. He tried the rivets, he shook the railing, and at last he found four loose bolts which he pulled out. The four together were so heavy that he could scarcely lift them, but making sure that no one was looking, he managed to slide them one by one into the bottom of his wagon and to cover them with loose straw to hide them. Then he turned his horse and drove back home as fast as he could. He reached home at midnight and hid the silver bolts in the hay.

The next morning when he went out alone in the dawn to gloat over his treasure he found, instead of four heavy silver bolts, only four pieces of wood. And he was furious, but at whom he was furious he did not know.

A few days later, without saying anything to anyone, the second brother set out to follow the silver tracks and find the Beggar whose cart had silver bolts and whose wheezy old horse wore golden shoes. He planned to bring home some golden horseshoes to his son, for, he thought, not many boys inherit golden horseshoes from their fathers!

He followed the same road and saw all the things his elder brother had seen: the wooden bridge, the stone bridge, the iron bridge, the copper bridge, the silver bridge, and he saw all the angry animals trying to tear each other to death. He did not stop at the silver bridge, for he thought that the next bridge might be golden and that he could break off a piece of it to take home.

Beyond the silver bridge lay a broad valley. And in a broad field stood a man trying to beat off a flock of ravens that were forever swooping down and pecking at his eyes. Near by stood an old man with white hair who was crying to heaven to be delivered from the two oxen who were munching at his white hair as if it were so much hay. They ate great wisps of it, and the more they ate the more it grew out.

A little way on, there was an apple tree heavily laden with ripe apples. A hungry man kept reaching up and plucking an apple, and as he raised each new one to his mouth it turned to ashes.

In another place a thirsty man kept reaching with a dipper into a well, and always, just as he was about to scoop up some water, the water moved away from under the dipper.

The second brother was much amazed at these things, but he kept driving on. Finally he reached the next bridge, and its bolts and beams and pillars were all of shining gold. Greatly excited, the second brother climbed down from his wagon and began wrenching at different parts of the golden bridge. Finally he managed to pull out four long bolts that were so heavy he could scarcely lift them. After making sure that no one was watching him, he dragged them to his wagon and covered them with straw. Then he turned his horse's head and drove home as fast as he could.

As he hid the golden bolts in the barn, he chuckled,

"My son will now be a richer man than my elder brother!"

In the first light of morning he slipped out to his barn, and in place of the four bolts of gold he found four bolts of wood. He flew into a violent rage, but at whom he was angry he did not know.

The years passed, and the poor youngest brother worked day after day and often far into the night. Some of his ten children died, but the rest grew up stalwart and good and went out into the world and married and made homes of their own. At last the poor man's devoted wife died too, and the poor man was finally old and all alone in the world.

One night he sat on his doorstep, thinking of his wife and of his children when they were little, and of all the years he had worked to keep them fed and clothed. And suddenly he remembered the Beggar and the promise he had made to visit him sometime.

"And to think of all the years I've kept his silver bolts and his golden horseshoes!" thought the poor man. "But he'll forgive me, for he'll understand that I've been too busy ever to follow the tracks of his cart. I wonder if they're still there."

And he limped out to the roadside and peered down with his dim old eyes, but there were the silver tracks as clear as ever.

The following dawn he took out the silver bolts and the golden horseshoes and put them in a bag. He hitched his ancient donkey to his battered cart and set out to follow the silver tracks to the Beggar's house.

He saw exactly the same things his brothers had seen many years before: the terrible fighting animals, the unfortunate men, the wooden bridge, the stone bridge, the iron bridge, and the copper bridge, the silver bridge and the golden bridge.

Beyond the golden bridge he came to a garden surrounded by a high wall of diamonds and rubies, sapphires and emeralds, and all kinds of precious stones that glowed like the sun itself. The silver tracks turned in at the gate, which was locked.

The poor man creaked down from his old cart and unhitched his exhausted donkey and set him out to graze on the tender grass that grew by the roadside. Then he took the bag that contained the golden horseshoes and the silver bolts and he went to the garden gate. It was a wonderful gate of beaten gold set with precious stones, and for a moment the youngest brother wondered if he dared knock at such a gate. But he recalled that his friend, the Beggar, lived inside, and he knew that he would be made welcome.

The Beggar Himself opened the gate, and when He saw the poor man, He smiled and held out His hands. "Welcome, my dear friend!" He said. "I've been waiting for you all these years! Come in and I'll show you my garden."

The poor man entered, but first he gave the Beggar His golden horseshoes and His silver bolts. "Please forgive me for keeping them so long," he said, "but until now I've never had time to return them."

The Beggar smiled. "I knew, my friend, that they

were safe with you and that you'd bring them some day." Then He put his arm over the poor man's shoulder and led him through the garden, showing him marvelous golden fruits and beautiful flowers. They sat down beside a fountain of crystal water and listened to the songs of birds. And the poor man asked about the strange things he had seen along the road.

The Beggar looked grave. "All those animals were once human beings who, instead of fearing God and being kind to their fellow men, spent their time in fighting and cheating and cursing. The two sows were two sisters-in-law who hated each other with a terrible bitterness. The two bulls and the two rams were neighbors who fought for years and years over the boundary lines of their farms, and now they must keep on fighting through eternity. The two bitch dogs were sisters who fought until they died over an inheritance left them by their father. The old man whose hair the oxen eat was a farmer who always pastured his cattle on his neighbors' fields. The man at whose eyes the ravens peck was an ungrateful son who mistreated his parents. The man with the awful thirst that can never be quenched was a drunkard, and the one at whose lips the apples turn to ashes was a glutton."

"Well, I can't help feeling sorry for them," said the youngest brother.

The Beggar smiled. "You, with your kind heart!" He said, and went on talking.

The Beggar and the poor man sat there by the fountain, talking together until late afternoon.

"And now, dear friend," said the Beggar, "you must have supper with me, as once I had supper with you."

"Thank you, I will," said the poor man. "But first let me go out and see how my donkey is."

"All right," said the Beggar, "but be sure to come back for I shall be waiting for you."

The poor man went out the garden gate and looked for his donkey, but the donkey was gone. "He must have started home," thought the poor man. "I'll hurry and catch up with him."

So he started back on foot, but he saw no donkey. He crossed the golden bridge and the silver bridge and the copper bridge and the iron bridge and the stone bridge and the wooden bridge, but still there was no donkey. "He must be all the way home by now," he thought.

But when the poor man entered his native village everything looked different. The whole village had changed. Houses he remembered had disappeared, and others had taken their places. He couldn't find his own little house at all. The people he asked knew nothing about it, and knew nothing about him, either, nor about his sons. Finally he did meet one old man who remembered the family name and who told him that many years before, the last of the sons had gone to another village to live.

"There's no place here for me," thought the poor man. "I'd better go back to my friend, the Beggar, and stay with him. No one else wants me."

Once again he followed the silver tracks over the bridges and when he reached the garden gate he was very tired, for he was old and feeble now. The Beggar heard his faint knock and came hurriedly to let him in. And when He saw how tired and feeble the poor man was, He put His arm around him and helped him into the garden and said, "You shall stay with me now forever, and we shall be very happy together."

When the poor man looked into the Beggar's face to thank Him, he saw that He was not a beggar at all, but the Blessed Christ. his friend. And the youngest brother, the good of heart, knew that he was in the garden of paradise.

Brazil ❧ ❧ ❧ ❧ ❧

RAIRU AND THE STAR MAIDEN

NOTHING IN THE WORLD DELIGHTED RAIRU MORE
than to watch the life of the forest, to lean
over a flower and gaze at its loveliness, to lie
beside a leaf-shadowed pool and watch a shaft of sunlight as it shot into the green depths of the water, or to
stand breathless and with a thudding heart when some
wild bird burst into song.

His father often scolded the boy bitterly for what he
considered idleness; and while Rairu suffered because he
was a disappointment to his father, still he was what he
was and could not help it. Before dawn he would slip
away into the forest, and hidden in green thickets, under
the dewy leaves, he would give himself up to the music
of the birds and be lost in beauty.

When Rairu grew into young manhood, he began to
walk alone at night and the surf of stars in the sky filled
him with wonder and joy. Evening after evening he
waited in a secret open place by a small waterfall and
watched impatiently for the clear light of the first star
in the darkening violet sky. As he lay stretched out on
the earth, listening to the low silver song of his waterfall,

it seemed to him that the ill world would be well only when that order which was in the skies existed among men. He thought, too, that of all creatures on earth man was the most destructive, the most wasteful, and the least trustful. If only man's heart could be kind and innocent of hatred, and his thoughts just and clear and as beautiful as a star, then the world would be happier; and man would, perhaps, learn the utter meaning of his own existence.

One night as Rairu lay at the foot of a palm tree, he arose on his elbow suddenly to listen to the heartbreaking song of a night bird. As he looked up through the tall fronds, he thought that the stars sang to the bird as the bird sang to the stars. And he gazed deeply into the sky to see which star, beyond all the others, heard that one bird most surely. And he beheld one softly brilliant star that moved slowly toward the west, far more beautiful than all the others appearing in the darkening heavens.

After that night, when the sky grew lilac-colored, his eyes searched the sky for the Silver One as he listened for the night bird to begin her song. With a stopped heart he heard the lucid singing go up, and he watched as the Silver One listened and trembled. When the star had gone into the west and the night-bird music ceased, Rairu was lonely and sorrowful, as alone as an exile on a far island.

On a day of sun and cloud, Rairu was wandering and thinking about his Silver One, as well as the invisible day stars, when he met an old man.

"Rairu," the stranger called.

The young man looked at him and smiled. "Good day, sir," he said.

"Listen to me," said the old man. "If you could choose, what of all things in the world and out of it would you ask for?"

"The Silver One," Rairu said. "If she could leave her place in the sky and go with me that I might adore her night and day, I would be the happiest man on earth."

"Look you, Rairu," said the old man, "do you go to sleep tonight on that high hill. If you desire the Silver One for her beauty alone, and not that others may envy you her possession, then it may be that your wish will be granted."

"The high hill?" said Rairu.

"Yes," said the old man, and he walked away, singing softly to himself.

Rairu spent the day in the forest, yearning for the night and the stars, and at midday he sat against a tree with his eyes closed, trying to make a song. He wished to tell the world of the beauty of the Silver One, for so few looked to her. But his words did not satisfy him, and he thought his song a poor thing:

When men sorrow and rage,
When the hearts of men grieve,
When arrows of sharp words wound,
When there is none to pity pain,
In the order of heaven there is sweet delight.

In the night hushed and still,
When there is neither weeping nor laughter,
In the nighttime between two empty days,
The Silver One is riding in the sky
Singing hand in hand with her sister stars,
Singing, because the life of men is an empty dream.

When the blue twilight began to darken, Rairu climbed the stony path to the hilltop and lay down to watch the day's end in the western sky. As the colors changed from sea green and gold to orange and flame and back to lucid green, Rairu sang the last lines of the song he had made, waiting for the Silver One:

In the nighttime between two empty days,
The Silver One is riding in the sky
Singing hand in hand with her sister stars,
Singing, because the life of men is an empty dream.

The first faint stars became clearer in the deepening blue, and he was stricken with grief to find that the Silver One was not among them. He searched the heavens, thinking that perhaps she hid behind a leaf, but he soon knew that her sister stars went alone. Long he looked and long he searched, until he grew weary; and he lay face downward on the hilltop and fell asleep with his heart grieving for his lost star.

As he slept, he dreamed that the world was washed in a great white light, a light which was both light and music. As he dreamed, he was lifted high into the heavens and saw far below him myriads of turning spheres of light. Across vast dark spaces and gulfs of blackness flew other and new stars; and from the edge of nothingness to the edge of nothingness, all was music. But his heart ached with sorrow, for in all that star dust there was no Silver One. Yet a sad joy was in him and he felt himself as a tight-stretched golden string that quivered in tune with the music of the flying stars.

Then he awoke, and standing at his side was a maiden clothed in white who looked into his heart with deep love. "Arise, Rairu," she said. "I am the Silver One, and you may keep me with you." And she became small, so small that she might have stood in the palm of Rairu's hand, but she was still very beautiful.

Rairu was filled to his heart's edge with happiness, and he searched for a casket in which to keep his Silver One, but there was none worthy. Then he thought of his gourd, which he had carved with skill, and he cleaned it thoroughly so that not a grain of dust was in it. He lined it with soft green moss and set it on its side in a clean place, and the Silver One smiled and stepped into it.

As Rairu wandered in the forest all day long he took the cover from the gourd now and then to look within and gaze with delight at the eyes of the Silver One looking up at him. And always when he lifted the cover there came from the gourd music so moving that Rairu felt himself a part of the heavens, of the sun and the stars and the moon, a part of the earth and the forest, of the animals and the trees, the birds and the sun-shot pools.

Night and day the Silver One told Rairu strange

things, and day and night Rairu adored her. But what saddened him was her telling him that there would come a day when he would take his eyes from her and think of other things on which she would not look, things which hid from her in dark places and under roofs.

"Then," said the Silver One, "there will be a dividing, and I shall become to you only an aching memory."

And Rairu laughed although he was thoughtful. "No sword, my Silver One, can sever the thread which binds us."

But the Silver One said, "Wait."

One day the Silver One told Rairu that they must visit the heavens for a season. So Rairu sat among the fronds of a palm tree and the Silver One left her gourd and stood at his side. She touched the tree with a little stick and it grew rapidly until it carried them to a place bare and treeless, without flowers or birds. The Silver One told Rairu to wait a little while and she would return. She flew away and Rairu watched her, for her light did not dim, and he listened to her diminished music, for her song did not become lost.

But soon, to his amazement, he saw in front of him a marvelous city with gleaming towers and moving lights of many colors, and about the city danced a procession of young men and maidens, singing and playing instruments. They beckoned to him to follow them, and he did.

He came to a vast hall and his entrance was heralded by a great burst of music, at which all the dancers there began to whirl wildly. Wilder grew the music until it became a caldron of sound that fired his brain, and suddenly from the corners of the hall sprang bats, swine, cold-eyed carrion birds, muddy serpents, and great soft white toads. They joined in the maddening dance, and Rairu's ears cracked. And he hastened back to the place where the Silver One had left him.

She was there waiting for him, but her eyes, still full of love, were shining with tears. Very gently she spoke to him of his disobedience, and Rairu in sorrow and shame knew that the thread was broken and that he must leave the Silver One for a season. They clasped hands then, the more passionately because there must be a parting.

"Go now, Rairu," she said, "and toil and strive, and you will find me again. But in the darkness lean on me, for you know yourself to be weak. Under the shadow of death, my beloved, a dying love is given new birth."

Rairu returned to earth and to his forest, and the memory of the Silver One ached in his soul. He told his fellow men of what he had seen and that he must find his star again. And after struggle and searching he found the clear light of the Silver One, and that light clothed all that he said and did with beauty.

THE PROTECTION OF THE DEVIL

Once upon a time there was a prince whose mother, when he had reached the age of eighteen years, consulted a fortuneteller as to his fate. To her grief, she found he was condemned to die a violent death, and she wept night and day and refused to be comforted.

However, the Prince was brave of heart and declared he would not worry about the matter in the least. "What difference does it make?" he asked his mother. "Death comes to everyone. Whether one dies from sickness or whether one dies from violence, one dies. Why weep?"

But nothing could cheer the Queen and she continued to be sorrowful.

Finally the Prince decided to travel in foreign lands, and he went to his father and mother. "You know well the fate which is to be mine," he said. "If I die by violence in another land, it will, I believe, cause you less pain than if it happens here at home. I pray you grant me your permission and your blessing."

Sadly the King and Queen consented, and the Prince set out upon his journey. He visited many kingdoms and at length came to a city where there was a chapel to Saint Miguel which had fallen into ruins. Immediately he hired workmen to repair it.

Among the images which adorned the chapel, there chanced to be a figure representing the Devil. The workmen painted all the images except this one.

When the Prince inspected the work, he called the head workman to him and asked, "How is this? You have left the image of the Devil in the same shabby condition in which I saw it first. Take it at once and decorate the figure of the Devil as you have decorated all the others!"

Then the Prince traveled to another town and took

lodgings with an old woman. When he had been shown to his room for the night, he sat down to count his money. The old woman, peeping through the keyhole, was amazed, for she had never seen so much money in her life, and she plotted to get possession of it. Hurrying to the authorities, she declared she had been robbed of a great sum of money by a lodger she had taken in for the night. The Prince was arrested and led to trial.

That same night, Saint Miguel said to the Devil, "How does it feel, my friend, to find yourself freshly painted and handsome like the rest of us?"

"It feels marvelous!" replied the Devil. "I haven't felt as well in years!"

"Do you know who is responsible for your good looks?" asked Saint Miguel.

"Yes, a prince who journeyed through our city," answered the Devil gratefully.

"A prince indeed," said Saint Miguel. "The bravest, handsomest young prince who ever passed this way. And now he has fallen into trouble, so that this very minute he is on the way to being unjustly condemned to death!"

The Devil did not hesitate a second. Springing upon his fiery steed, he rode like the wind to the house of the old woman. He seized her and took her before the authorities, compelling her to confess her plot. The Prince was freed at once and the old woman condemned to death in his stead. The Prince's riches were restored to him, but when he turned to thank his benefactor there was no one there.

Not long afterward the Prince chanced to pass again

through the city where he had repaired the chapel of Saint Miguel. As he approached the chapel, he was joined by a monk riding a fiery steed. The monk asked him as to his history, and the Prince told him the whole story of his life.

"Do you know who freed you from your charge and helped you out of prison?" asked the monk.

"To my sorrow, no," replied the Prince. "I have never known whom to thank for saving my life."

The monk threw back his hood and revealed his face. "It was I, the Devil, whose image you ordered repaired and painted like the other images in the chapel of Saint Miguel. Your fate is changed. The old woman met death by violence in your stead, and you are free from the curse. Do you now go home at once to your own kingdom and live in the peace and happiness which your kindness deserves!"

And from this story one may see that even the Devil has a grateful heart.

THE THREE HORSES

Long ago there lived a man who had three sons. The eldest was apprenticed to a blacksmith, the second to a carpenter, and the third to a barber. Joaquim, the youngest son, soon left the barber's shop and went out into the world to seek his fortune.

In his wanderings he came to a kingdom where every night the royal garden was laid waste by trampling wild horses. The royal gardener was in despair, for no under-gardeners would work for him. Every one he hired was terrified when asked to protect the garden from the horses; and furthermore, they soon tired of planting flower beds only to have them immediately destroyed by the horses' hooves. Joaquim applied to the head gardener, who hired him on the spot, for he liked the looks of the boy.

All day Joaquim worked among the flowers in the royal garden, and from the head gardener he heard the story of the horses which came every night to undo the day's labor.

"Let me stay in the garden tonight to protect it," said the boy earnestly. "Your other gardeners have all been cowards, and wild horses will never acknowledge a coward as their master. I have no fear in my heart, and they will know it at once."

The head gardener was more than glad to have Joaquim attempt the protection of the garden, a task he himself had never been willing to undertake.

That night when the wild horses galloped up to the garden gate, their manes flying wildly, there was Joaquim playing soft music on his guitar. The three horses listened, and although they pawed the earth about the gate, they did not enter the garden.

The following morning the head gardener was overjoyed to see that the flowers in the garden were still intact, and the King himself came to walk about among the beds, praising the head gardener.

That night the three wild horses came to the gate once more and listened to Joaquim's music.

The third night, when the horses came they asked for some cabbage leaves, and Joaquim gave them each a leaf.

Then the black horse with the white star in its forehead said, "If you ever need me, simply say, 'Black Horse, White Star, help me!' and I'll come at once."

The white horse with the black mane thanked the boy for the cabbage leaf and said, "If you are ever in any peril, just call, 'White Horse, Black Mane!' and I'll come to your aid."

Then the sorrel horse with the white tail said, "If I can ever do anything to help you, just call, 'Sorrel Horse, White Tail!' and I shall be there."

Then the three horses went away, and the next night they did not come to the garden. The royal garden grew in loveliness day by day, so that the King's beautiful daughter, the Princess Angelita, loved to walk about in it and pluck the flowers with her own flower-soft hand.

Time fled and many suitors came to ask for the Princess in marriage. They were so many, and all so charming, that she could not decide which one she wished to wed, so she sent abroad this proclamation: "I'll wed the knight who will ride at full speed up the stone steps which lead to my balcony and take the carnation from my hair!"

The flight of steps which led to the balcony was very long and steep. The suitors for the hand of the Princess Angelita were dismayed and frightened, but joy filled the heart of the young gardener, Joaquim.

The tournament was held the next day, and many

suitors spurred their horses toward the stone steps which led to the balcony of the Princess.

Joaquim called out, "Black Horse, White Star!" and immediately there appeared the wild horse to whom he had given a cabbage leaf. Springing upon his back, the boy rode halfway up the great flight of stone steps, and all the assembly shouted, for that was farther than anybody else had ridden.

On the second day of the tournament the boy called, "White Horse, Black Mane!" and at once the horse appeared. Mounted upon this handsome new steed, he rode at full tilt two-thirds of the way up the stairway. But still the Princess Angelita did not recognize him as the gardener boy.

On the third day there were many new contestants, for the news had spread abroad and all the knights from all the country around had gathered at the royal palace. Many of them rode well on fine horses, but not one of them could ride halfway up the staircase.

At the very end of the tournament the lad from the royal gardens called, "Sorrel Horse, White Tail!" Immediately the horse appeared, and mounted upon its back Joaquim rode straight up the long steep flight of stone steps which led to the balcony and plucked the pink carnation from the hair of the Princess Angelita.

All the great assembly cheered wildly and shouted, "Viva! Viva!" They asked one another, "Who is this knight?" But no one knew his name nor whence he came.

Finally a young carpenter and a young blacksmith

were found who said that the winner of the tournament looked strangely like their younger brother who had been apprenticed to a barber but had gone out into the world to seek his fortune.

But as soon as he rode up the steps, the Princess Angelita had seen that he was the young gardener, with whom she had long been secretly in love. And so the wedding was celebrated with great joy, and after the ceremony the boy could hear the three wild horses neighing happily at the garden gate before they vanished.

Canada 🌿 🌿 🌿 🌿 🌿

THE BOY OF THE RED TWILIGHT SKY

MANY YEARS AGO THERE LIVED IN THE WEST, ON the shores of the Great Water, a young man and his younger wife. They had no children and they lived alone, far from other people, on an island not too distant from the coast. The young man caught deep-sea fish in the ocean or speared salmon in the mainland rivers, and he was often gone for many days. His wife was extremely lonely during his absence, but she had a stout spirit and was never afraid. However, she found it very dismal in the evenings to gaze only at the lead-colored sky and to hear only the pound of the surf on the desolate beach.

Every evening she said to herself, "I wish we had children, for they would be good company when I am alone and my husband is far away."

One twilight she sat in solitude on the beach, for the young man was far out upon the ocean, catching deep-sea fish. She looked out across the water, and the sky was pale gray. There was never an evening in that country which was not dull and silver, and when the sun had gone into the sea there was no soft light.

The young wife said to herself, "Oh, I wish we had children to play here on the sand with me and to keep me company!"

A kingfisher, with his children, was diving for minnows a little way out in the surf.

"O sea bird with the white collar," said the young wife in a low voice, "I wish we had children like you."

"Look in the sea shells, look in the sea shells," answered the kingfisher, and flew away.

The following evening she sat again upon the beach, gazing westward at the dull gray sky. Not far out a sea gull was riding on the tide with her brood of little ones.

"O white sea bird," said the young wife sadly, "I wish we had children like you to keep us company."

And the sea gull replied, "Look in the sea shells, look in the sea shells."

She marveled at the words of the kingfisher and the sea gull, and as she sat there feeling lonelier than ever, she thought she heard a strange cry in the sand dunes behind her. She followed the sound and found it came from a large sea shell lying in the sand. Picking up the shell, she found inside of it a tiny boy, crying as hard as he could.

Delighted, she carried the baby home and cared for him. When her husband returned from his voyage, he, too, was overjoyed, for he knew that they would never again be lonely.

The baby grew rapidly into a strong little boy and he ran and romped about the island.

One day the young wife was wearing a copper bracelet on her arm, and the child said to her, "I must have a bow made from the copper on your arm!"

She smiled, but to please him she made a tiny bow from the copper bracelet, and two tiny arrows. He went out to hunt game immediately; and every day he went forth, bringing home to his mother geese and ducks, brant and small sea birds.

As he grew older, the fisherman and his wife noted that his face acquired a golden hue brighter than the color of his copper bow, and that there was a strange light wherever he went. When he sat on the beach gazing westward the weather was always calm and there were strange bright gleams on the moving water. But whenever they talked of this, the boy fell silent.

Once the wind blew furiously over the Great Water, and the foster father could not go fishing because of the roughness of the sea. He was forced to stay ashore many days, for the ocean was blown to wildness and the waves dashed high on the beach. Before long, they were in need of fish for food.

Then the boy said, "I will go out with you, father, for I am able to conquer the Storm Spirit."

The man did not wish to go, but at length he yielded to the boy's pleading, and together they set out for the fishing grounds far across the turbulent ocean. They had gone only a short distance when they met the Storm

Spirit raging from the southwest, where the great winds lived.

The Storm Spirit tried to upset their boat, but he had no power over them. The boy guided the small boat through the waves, and all about them the sea grew calm.

In a rage, the Storm Spirit called his nephew, Black Cloud, to help him, and far in the southeast they saw him storming to his uncle's assistance.

But the boy said to his foster father, "Don't be afraid, for I can overcome him too."

And when Black Cloud saw the boy he disappeared at once.

Then the Storm Spirit called Mist of the Sea to come and hid the water, for he was sure the man and the boy would be lost if the land vanished from their sight. When the man beheld Mist of the Sea spreading across the water, he was terrified, for of all his enemies on the ocean he feared Mist of the Sea most.

But the boy said, "Be not afraid—he cannot harm you while I am with you."

And when Mist of the Sea saw the smiling boy sitting in the little boat, he disappeared as quickly as he had come up. In great anger, the Storm Spirit hastened away, and there was no more danger near the fishing grounds.

The boy taught his father a magic song which lured fish to his nets, and before evening the boat was loaded with fine fish and they set out for home.

"Tell me the secret of your power," said the foster father.

But the boy replied, "It is not yet time."

On the following day the boy shot many birds, skinned them, and dried their skins. Then he clothed himself in the skin of a plover, rose into the air and flew above the sea. Beneath him the sea was gray like his wings. He descended, dressed himself in the skin of a bluejay and soared up again. The sea beneath him immediately changed to a blue like the blue of his wings. Returning to the beach, he donned the skin of a robin, the breast of a golden tint like his face. As he flew high, the waves beneath him reflected a color of fire, bright gleams of light appeared on the ocean, and the western sky became a golden red.

Returning to the beach, the boy said to his foster mother, "It is time now for me to leave you. I am the child of the sun. Yesterday my power was tested and it was not found wanting, so now I must leave you and I shall see you no more. But I shall appear to you often in the western twilight sky. When the sky and the sea at evening are the color of my face, you will know there will be neither wind nor storm and that on the morrow the weather will be fair. Although I must leave you, I give you strange powers. Wear this robe, my foster mother. Whenever you need me, let me know your desires by making white offerings to me, so that I may see them from my home far in the west."

He presented to his foster mother a magic robe. Saying farewell to his parents, he soared away westward, leaving them bereft and grieving. But the woman still retains the powers he gave her, and when she sits in the dunes and loosens the robe, the wind blows down the land and the sea is tossed with storm, and the more she loosens the robe, the greater is the tempest.

But in the late autumn, when cold mists roll in from the sea and the evenings are cold and the sky is dull and silver, she remembers the boy's promise. So she makes him an offering of tiny white feathers plucked from the breasts of birds. She tosses them into the air and they become flakes of snow and rise thickly into the winds. They hasten westward to tell the boy that the world is gray and lonely as it longs for the sight of his golden face. Then the boy appears to the people of earth, coming at evening and lingering after the sun has fled, until the twilight sky is aflame and the sea bears gleams of golden light. Then the people of earth know that on the morrow there will be no wind and that the weather will be fair, as the boy of the red twilight sky promised them long ago.

THE TOBACCO FAIRY FROM THE BLUE HILLS

Long ago, deep in the Canadian forest, on the shores of a lake surrounded by large trees, lived happily a man and his wife and their two little children. As the children grew up, they became more beautiful and gentle every day, until the old women of the tribe said, "They are too lovely and good for this world; their home is surely in the next world."

Before the children were twelve years old a terrible plague spread over the land and they perished. Their mother grew slowly weaker, wasting away before the eyes of her husband, who could do nothing to save her.

Now was the man left alone upon the earth in great loneliness and sorrow, and grieving for his wife and little ones, he wished that he, too, were dead. But finally he roused himself and determined to go about doing good. "I shall spend my life helping others," he thought, "and then perhaps I can find peace."

He worked hard, helping the weaker and poorer people of his tribe. All the people of his village, in their high esteem and affection for him, called him Grandfather. He became very old, and although he was happy in doing good deeds, he was still solitary. The days and evenings were long and lonely; and as he grew older and his work grew less, he could only sit alone and dream of his youth and his lost family and absent friends.

One day he sat alone by the lake, thinking. All of a sudden a great flock of birds, like black clouds, came flying from the blue hills in the distance toward the lake shore. They wheeled and circled over the trees, crying strangely.

The people had never before seen birds such as these, and they were very much afraid and took them to be an omen of some strange occurrence. Suddenly one of the birds fluttered and tumbled to the earth with an arrow in its breast. No villager had shot at the flock, and no man could tell whence the arrow had come. Frightened still more by the mystery, they looked to the old man for counsel.

The fallen bird lay quivering on the ground, apparently in pain. The other birds circled about it, uttering loud cries; then they called to each other and flew back to the far blue hills, leaving the wounded bird behind with the arrow sticking in its breast.

The old man was not afraid. "I'll go to the bird," he said. "Perhaps I can heal its wound."

But fearfully the people cried, "Do not go, Grandfather! The bird will harm you!"

"It can do no harm to me," the old man answered. "My work is ended and my life is nearly finished. I am full of sorrow and my sky is dark, and for me it is already the twilight of time. I am alone in the world, I am not afraid of death, so what does it matter if I die?" And he went over to the stricken bird to see if he could help it.

His path suddenly grew dark as he went, but as he neared the place where the bird lay, a bright flame shot down from the sky. There was a flash of fire, and when he looked, the old man beheld the bird completely burned up. Nothing but black ashes remained, and when he stirred the ashes with his stick, he found lying in the center a large living coal of fire. As he gazed at it, it disappeared, and in its stead stood a curious little figure, no bigger than his thumb.

"Hello, Grandfather," it called. "I have been sent to help you."

The old man stared. "Who are you?"

"I am one of the Little People from the distant blue hills," replied the tiny boy.

The old man knew then that he was one of the fairy

people of the mountains, of whom he had always heard. "What can I do for you?" he asked.

"I've been sent to you with a precious gift," said the miniature boy.

The old man wondered, but he said nothing.

Then said the fairy from the blue hills, "You are old and lonely, your work is done, but your life is not yet ended, and you must still dwell a long time upon the earth. You have done many noble deeds and have always helped others, and because of your good life, I have been sent to bring you more contentment. You long always for your dead wife and children, and think of your youth, and now the days are long and time hangs heavy in your heart. But the gift I bring you will help you to pass the time more pleasantly."

And he handed the old man a number of small seeds and said, "Please plant these at once here, in the ashes from which I just arose."

The old man obeyed, and immediately the seeds sprouted and great leaves grew from them, and very soon the place where the bird had been burned up became a large field of tobacco.

Then the fairy gave the old man a large pipe. "Dry these leaves," he said, "and place them in this pipe and smoke them. You will have contentment then, and tobacco will help you pass the time away, and when you are lonely it will be a companion. It will bring you dreams of the future and dreams of the past; and when the smoke curls upward, you will see those you loved as you sit alone in the blue of the evening."

"I am most grateful," said the old man.

"Teach other old men how to use a pipe and tobacco," said the fairy, "so that they, too, may possess it and enjoy it and live out their days in peace."

The fairy boy disappeared toward the distant blue hills and was never seen in the village again. And with his pipe and his tobacco, the old man returned to his dreaming, with far more contentment than before. And this was how tobacco was brought to the Indians in the old days in the Canadian forest.

HOW GLOOSKAP MADE THE BIRDS

Long before the white men came to Canada, there lived a wicked giant who caused great trouble and sorrow, and the Indians called him Wolf-Wind. His home was in the Cave of the Winds, far in the north country in the Night-Night Land. There, men knew, he hid on calm days when the sun was hot and the sea was still, and on quiet nights when not a flower or leaf or blade of grass quivered.

But whenever he descended from the Night-Night Land, the massive trees cracked in terror and the little trees quaked and the flowers trembled and bent their heads close to the earth to hide from him.

Very often he came upon them without warning, and then the corn fell flat and never rose again, the tall trees crashed in the forest, and the flowers dropped dead of fear. And the waters grew white and moaned, screamed and dashed themselves against the rocks, trying to escape from Wolf-Wind. In the darkness of night, with Wolf-Wind abroad and howling, there was great fear upon all the earth.

Once, in those old times, he was in a terrible rage and went forth to kill and devour anyone who dared to come in his path. Many Indian families were living near the sea at that time. The men and women were fishing far off the coast, catching fish to make food for the winter. They had gone far out to sea in small canoes, for the ocean had been calm for a long time and they thought there was no danger. And their little children were playing alone on the shore.

Abruptly, as the sun went down, without a sign of his approach, out of the north blew Wolf-Wind in a howling rage, searching for victims, and roaring as he came. "I am Wolf-Wind, the giant!" he screamed. "I shall kill all the people I meet and eat them up!" His anger increased as he stalked along, splashing and tossing the waters aside in his fury as he descended upon the fishermen and fisherwomen in their frail canoes far out upon the sea. The fishers hadn't a moment to get out of his reach, and the giant caught them all and broke their canoes and killed them. And all night long he stamped over the ocean, searching for more fisherpeople.

In the morning, still angry, he saw the little children of the fishers playing upon the shore, and he knew they were alone, for he had slain their fathers and mothers. "Ha!" he growled, "I'll kill them, too!" And he roared toward land, dashing the waves against the rocks in his fury. As he approached the beach, he howled, "I'll catch you and kill you and eat you up and bleach your bones upon the sand!"

But the children heard him, and they took to their heels and ran and hid in a cave among the rocks and placed a big stone at the mouth of the cave so that Wolf-Wind could not get in. He howled at the door all day and all night, but he could not break down the stone. So he went away, howling, "I'll come back and catch you yet!"

The frightened children stayed in the cave long after Wolf-Wind had gone, for they could hear him still howling and crashing off through the forest. Finally they came out and found that Wolf-Wind had killed their fathers and mothers at sea; and they ran away into the forest for they thought they would be safe among the trees. They hurried to the Willow-Willow Land, where there were grass and flowers and trees. Between the Willow-Willow Land and the Night-Night Land where Wolf-Wind lived, there were hundreds upon hundreds of great trees with thick leaves which the children knew would protect them from the evil giant.

But one day Wolf-Wind returned to find them, and he dashed into the land, killing everyone he met. But he could not catch the children, for the trees with their thick leaves kept him away. The children shuddered as they heard him howling far off in the forest. All during the late summer he tried to find them, but they lived close to the trees; the great branches spread over them, and the leaves hid them, and only the sun from the south. coming from the Summer-Flower Country could look in upon them. Wolf-Wind knew where they were, but he could not harm them. They were always safe while they lived in Willow-Willow Land.

More furious than ever at being cheated of his meal of little children, Wolf-Wind swore vengeance, and he returned again with another giant from the north country who had a powerful charm, the Giant of the Frost.

The two giants tried over and over again to kill the trees that sheltered the children, but the trees only laughed and swayed and creaked.

"You cannot hurt us," said the trees. "We are strong, for we came at first from the Night-Night Land in the north country, and the Giant of the Frost has no power over us." And they were the Fir and the Spruce, the Hemlock and the Pine and the Cedar.

But on the other trees, Wolf-Wind took his vengeance. On the night when the harvest moon was full in the sky, he enlisted the aid of the giant who bore the Charm of the Frost. The Giant of the Frost killed all the leaves, and Wolf-Wind threw them to the ground. One after another fell the leaves of the Beech and the Birch, the Oak and the Maple, the Alder and the Willow. Some came off their branches quickly, some drifted slowly earthward, others died slowly before they fluttered down. But at length the trees stood cold and bare, lonely and empty against the sky, and stillness and sadness settled on the forest.

Wolf-Wind played in silence through the leafless boughs with the giant from Night-Night Land. "Since

I have defeated the leaves that held me away, now I can kill the children whenever I wish!"

But the children moved closer to the strong trees that had come first from the north country and over which the Giant of the Frost had no power. Wolf-Wind could not touch them and they were still safe from both giants.

But the children were filled with sorrow when they saw what Wolf-Wind had done to their friends, the trees. Summer had returned to the south, following the Rainbow Road to her home in the Wilderness of Flowers, and it was very still and lonely in the forest.

At length that time of year came when Glooskap, who ruled upon the earth, gave his yearly gifts to little children. He always came into the land in a sled drawn by his dogs to discover for himself what the children wished for. And the children all came to him to ask for a gift. When the little children whom Wolf-Wind had tried to kill came to Glooskap, they were very sad because the leaves had perished.

"What do you wish?" asked Glooskap, the Magic Master of Gifts, who had great power upon the earth in those old times.

"Nothing for ourselves," answered the children. "But we ask that the leaves that Wolf-Wind killed because they saved us from his rage, be returned to life and put back in their old homes in the trees."

Glooskap was silent for a long time, sitting and thinking and smoking at his mighty pipe, for he was a great smoker.

At that time there were no small birds upon the earth, since Glooskap had not yet brought them into being. There were only the sea birds over whom Wolf-Wind had no power—Sea Gull and Crane, Wild Duck and Loon, Kingfisher and Curlew. These only laughed at Wolf-Wind's anger, and screamed and mocked him as they flew, and hid when he came. There were also the birds that lived with men and gave them eggs and food— Hen and Goose and Duck and Wild Turkey.

Glooskap made up his mind to bring other birds into the world to bring happiness to the children when summer lives in the land, with their lovely feathers and lovely songs. After he had smoked a long time, he decided on a plan.

He said to the children asking for their yearly gifts, "I cannot return to the trees the leaves that Wolf-Wind has killed. But I will take the fallen leaves and change them into little birds. When autumn comes they shall go with summer to the Summer-Flower Land, but in the springtime they shall always come back to you again and live close to the leaves from which they have sprung. Most of them shall nest in the trees under the leaves, and those that nest in the grass shall love the trees and linger in them. They shall all be beautiful in color like the leaves that gave them birth; and they shall rest at times upon the air like a leaf fluttering; and the voice of the air and the laughing waters shall be in their throats and they shall sing sweet songs for little children.

"I charge the children to keep them from harm, just as the leaves have saved the little children from the giants. The trees that Wolf-Wind has stripped shall bring forth new leaves every springtime, so that when summer and the little birds return from the Wilderness of Flowers, the trees shall not be bare. And although Wolf-Wind and the Giant of the Frost may strip them off in the autumn, they will always return in the springtime to make new homes for the little birds."

Glooskap waved his magic wand and at once great flocks of little birds flew up from the ground where the fallen leaves had lain. They twittered and sang and flew back to the trees; and they were of beautiful colors like the leaves that gave them birth. There were Robin Redbreasts and Thrushes, red and brown, from the red and brown leaves of the Oak. There were Hummingbirds and Finches, all green and yellow and brown, from the leaves of the Alder and the Willow, and they glowed like Willows in the sunlight and quivered like leaves in the air. There were Yellowbirds and Canadian Warblers from the golden Beech and the Birch leaves. There were Grosbeaks and Orioles and Scarlet Tanagers of changing colors, red and purple and brown, from the leaves of the Canadian Maple. And all the little birds sang together to the children, and the children were very happy once more.

Glooskap sent the birds away to the Wilderness of Flowers until the rule of the Giant of the Frost from the Night-Night Land was over. But in the springtime the little birds always return and build their nests in the trees as close as possible to the leaves. And all day long

Australia 🖋 🖋 🖋 🖋 🖋

WAYAMBEH, THE TURTLE

OOLAH, THE LIZARD, WAS OUT GETTING YAMS ON a Mirrieh flat, and three of her children were with her, basking in the sun. Suddenly Oolah thought she heard someone moving in the bushes and she listened closely. All at once Wayambeh jumped from behind a bush and seized Oolah, telling her not to make a noise, that he would not hurt her but meant to take her off to his camp and make her his wife. He would take her three children, too, and take care of them.

Oolah had only her yam stick and could not defend herself against Wayambeh's spears and boondees.

When Wayambeh's tribe saw him bring home a woman of the Oolah tribe, they asked if her tribe had given her to him.

"No," said Wayambeh, "I have stolen her."

His tribe was angry: "Her tribe will soon be after her," they said, "and you must fight them yourself, for we will not fight for you. We had chosen a young woman of our own tribe for you, but you had to go and steal an Oolah and bring her to the camp of the Wayambehs. The consequences will be on your own head, for you had no right to steal."

In a little while the Oolahs were discovered advancing across the plain which faced the camp of the Wayambehs. They came neither in friendship nor to parley, but to fight, for there were no women with them and there were no boughs of peace in their hands; they were painted for war and were armed with weapons.

The Wayambeh chief said, "Now, Wayambeh, go out on the plain and do your own fighting, for we shall not protect you."

Wayambeh selected the two biggest boreens, or shields, that he had, and one he slung on the front of his body to cover him and one on the back. Seizing his weapons, he strode out to meet his enemies.

When he was some distance out on the plain, though still not near the Oolahs, he called, "Come on!"

His shout was answered by a shower of spears and boomerangs. As they whizzed through the air, Wayambeh drew his arms inside the boreens and ducked his head down and so was unhurt. The weapons glanced off his boreens and fell harmless to the earth.

Once more he stretched his arms out and held up his head, yelling, "Come on! Try again!"

And once more he drew in his arms and his head from the flying weapons and escaped harm. But at last the Oolahs closed in around him, forcing him to retreat toward the creek.

They flung shower after shower of weapons at him,

and came to such close quarters that he was aware that his only chance was to dive into the creek. Turning toward the water, he yanked off his front boreen, flung down his weapons, and plunged in.

The Oolahs waited, their spears ready to hurl at his head the second he appeared, but he did not appear. They never saw the thief, Wayambeh, again. But in the water hole where he had dived they beheld a strange creature bearing on its back a fixed shield like a boreen. When they tried to catch it, it drew in its arms and its head, and they said, "It is Wayambeh."

And this was the beginning of Wayambeh, the turtle, in the creeks and little rivers.

GOOLAHWILLEEL, THE TOPKNOT PIGEON

Young Goolahwilleel used to go out hunting every day, and his mothers and sisters always looked forward to the emu and kangaroo he would bring home for them to cook and eat. But each day he came home without any meat whatever.

"What do you do in the bush?" they asked. "Obviously you do not hunt."

"I do hunt," he answered.

"Why do you never bring us home anything, then?" they demanded.

Young Goolahwilleel looked anxious. "Because I cannot catch what I follow," he answered. "But you hear me cry out when I find a kangaroo or an emu, do you not?"

"Yes," said his mother. "We hear you cry out each day when you find something, and every day we get the fire ready, expecting you to bring home food, but you bring nothing. Why is this?"

"Tomorrow," he replied, "I promise you that you will not be disappointed. I shall bring you a kangaroo."

The truth was that instead of hunting every day, Goolahwilleel had been gathering wattle gum, and with the wattle gum he had been modeling a kangaroo, a perfect image of a kangaroo, with nose, ears, tail, pocket, and everything. He had even modeled a baby kangaroo in the pocket. And he was very pleased with his work and very happy in doing it.

The next day he went toward the camp, carrying his kangaroo made of gum.

Watching for him, his mother and sisters saw him approaching, carrying the promised kangaroo, and they said, "Ah, Goolahwilleel spoke honestly. He has kept his word and brought us a kangaroo. Pile wood on the fire, for tonight we shall eat meat at last!"

A short distance from the camp, Goolahwilleel put his model down and walked on without it.

"Where is the kangaroo you brought home to us?" called his mother.

"Oh, over there," he said, pointing to where he had left it.

His sisters ran to fetch it, but then ran back, crying, "Where is it? We cannot see it!"

"Over there," he said, pointing again.

They looked at him as if he were crazy. "But there's

only a great figure of wattle gum there!" they said angrily.

"Did I say it was anything else?" inquired young Goolahwilleel. "Didn't I say it was gum?"

"No, you did not," said his sisters impatiently. "You said it was a kangaroo!"

"It is a kangaroo," he said, "a beautiful kangaroo that I made all by myself." And he smiled proudly to think what a splendid kangaroo he had made.

But his mother and sisters did not smile. Instead they seized him and gave him a severe beating for deceiving them. And his mother told him that he would never again be allowed to go out alone, for he played instead of hunting, although he knew very well that they were starving for meat.

"In the future," said his mother sternly, "you will play no more, for we shall all go with you to make you behave and hunt as you should!"

So forever the Goolahwilleels, the topknot pigeons, go in flocks, never alone, in search of food.

DINEWAN, THE EMU, AND WAHN, THE CROWS

Dinewan, the emu, and his two wives, the Wahn or crows, were camping out. They saw clouds gathering and hurried to make a bark humpy. When it began to rain, they all took shelter under it and were fine and dry.

But Dinewan, feeling mischievous, when his wives were not looking gave a kick against a piece of bark on one side of the humpy, knocked it down, and then told his wives to go and pick it up again.

While they were outside in the rain, putting the bark up, he gave a kick and knocked down a piece on the other side, so no sooner were they in again than they had to go out.

He gave a kick here and a kick there, time after time, until finally his wives grew suspicious and decided that one of them would watch.

The one who was watching saw Dinewan laugh to himself and knock down the bark they had just put up, chuckling because his wives had to go out in the cold rain to put it up again, while he was dry and comfortable inside.

So the watcher told the other wife, and they decided to teach him a lesson. They entered the humpy, each with a piece of bark filled with hot coals. Dinewan was lying down laughing, and they went straight up to him.

"Now," they said, laughing themselves, "you shall feel as hot as we did cold!" And they threw the coals over him.

Dinewan sprang up, howling and yelling with the pain, for the hot coals had burned him badly. He rolled himself over and over and ran out into the rain, but his wives stayed inside, warm and dry, and laughed at him.

Belgium 🖋 🖋 🖋 🖋 🖋

THE CHORISTERS OF SAINT GUDULE

THE DONKEY BELONGING TO THE MILLER OF Sandhills had grown old in service and was no longer able to pull the cart to market. The miller was not a cruel man, but he was a thrifty one and decided to sell the donkey for the price of his skin.

"I don't suppose I'll get much for you, Grayskin," he said, "but I'll save the price of your corn anyhow."

Grayskin, standing with hanging head in his stall, said nothing to his master, but thought, "Very well, I am old. But I am still not useless, for I have a splendid voice, and there must be a place in the world for a creature who can sing as magnificently as I. I'll go to the Church of Saint Gudule in Brussels and offer myself as a chorister."

Making sure that the miller was out of sight, Grayskin lost no time in getting out of sight himself and walked as rapidly as he could down the road to Brussels.

As he came to the Burgomaster's house, he saw an old hound sitting forlornly on the doorstep. "Hello, my friend," he said kindly. "You look rather sad this morning. What's the trouble?"

"Hello, Grayskin," answered the dog. "You'd be sad, too, if you were too old and stiff to hunt rabbits for your master any more. He has turned me out with nothing to eat, and I wouldn't mind going hungry if he didn't consider me useless. I suppose my feelings are hurt, for I heard him agree with his wife that I was good for nothing."

"Oh, cheer up, my friend," said Grayskin. "I'm in a similar situation myself. But I'm on my way to the Church of Saint Gudule to offer my services to the choirmaster. I've a splendid voice, if I do say so myself."

"If it comes to voices," said the dog, "I can sing, as well. Last night I sang a lovely song to the moon, and all the people in our street opened their windows to listen, and I don't mean to brag, believe me. I sang for fully an hour, and I'd have gone on longer if some jealous person hadn't thrown a shoe at my head."

"Fine!" said Grayskin. "Why don't you come with me to Brussels? You sing tenor and I'll sing bass and we'll give excellent duets!"

"I'll do that," said the dog, and he and Grayskin went on down the road toward Brussels.

At the edge of the village they saw a cat sitting miserably outside of a house with a face as long as a fiddle.

Grayskin and the dog, having tender hearts, stopped of one accord and asked together, "Hello, cat. What's the trouble with you?"

"Trouble!" said the cat. "Trouble enough. I've just

been thrown out of my home because I took a small piece of bacon from the pantry. I give you my word of honor, it was no bigger than a baby's fist, but the way they fussed you'd think it was a whole pig. They thrashed me and kicked me out to starve. If I could catch mice it wouldn't be so important, but the mice are too quick for me nowadays. They laugh at me. The only thing I can do is to die, and I wish I would hurry up."

"Rats!" said Grayskin. "You come along with us and stop talking nonsense. We're going to sing in the choir at the Church of Saint Gudule in Brussels. Your voice is a trifle thin for my own taste, but you'll make a fine soprano in a trio. Will you join us?"

"You give me renewed hope," replied the cat. "Certainly I'll join you."

And the donkey and the dog and the cat went on together down the road to Brussels. Toward evening they came to a farm, and on the barnyard gate a cock was crowing as if it were dawn.

"Hello," said Grayskin. "What seems to be the trouble?"

"I'm singing my final song on earth," answered the cock disconsolately. "Though it isn't my custom to crow in the afternoon, I happened to sing a song an hour ago, and as I ended it, I heard the farmer's wife say, 'Listen to Chanticleer! He's crowing for sunny weather tomorrow. I doubt if he'd crow so loudly if he knew that he's going into the pot to make soup for our guests!' I don't like the way that woman laughs!"

"Look here," said Grayskin, "do you mean to tell me

you're going to wait patiently until she wrings your neck?"

"What choice have I?" asked the cock.

"With a voice like yours?" asked Grayskin. "Come along with us. We're all wonderful singers, and we're going to Brussels to offer ourselves as choristers at the Church of Saint Gudule. With you, we'll be a quartet, and that's one better than a trio. Won't you join us?"

"Of course I'll join you," replied Chanticleer, and the cat purred and the dog wagged his tail and the donkey flicked his ears and off they all went together down the road toward Brussels.

The stars were just coming out when they reached a dense wood where they decided to rest for the night. Grayskin and the dog lay down beneath a big beech tree, the cat climbed onto one of the boughs, and Chanticleer perched on the very top. From that height he could see over the whole wood and at once he discovered a light twinkling among the trees a little distance away.

"I think there's a house over there," he said to his friends. "Let's go and see—we might find something to eat."

"Or some straw to lie on," said Grayskin. "This damp ground gives me rheumatism in my poor old bones."

"I creak, too," said the dog. "It will do no harm to investigate. Let's go."

The four choristers, led by the cock, found themselves before a brightly lighted little house. In order to reach the windows they made a tower of their bodies, with Grayskin at the bottom and Chanticleer at the top.

It happened that the small house was the home of a band of robbers, who at that exact moment were having a fine dinner. There they sat feasting, and Chanticleer's mouth watered as he watched them.

"Is anybody home?" asked the dog, impatient because the cat's claws were digging into his shoulders as she balanced the hungry cock.

"Sh-h! Yes," said Chanticleer. "Some men are eating a marvelous dinner."

"What are they eating?" asked the dog.

"Everything you can imagine," said the cock. "Sausage and fish—"

"Sausage!" said the dog.

"Fish!" said the cat.

"Ouch!" said the dog.

"I beg your pardon," said the cat. "The cock's feathers were tickling my nose."

"That's quite all right," said the dog in a resigned tone.

"Look here, my friends," said Chanticleer, "wouldn't it be a fine thing if we could share their dinner? I'm starved."

"I've never been so hungry in my life," said the dog. "But what shall we do?"

"Let's serenade them," said Grayskin, "and perhaps they'll reward us."

So the four choristers began to sing with vigor and much expression. The donkey heehawed, the dog howled, the cat meowed, the cock crowed, and they made enough racket to wake the dead.

The effect of the excellent quartet was instantaneous and astonishing. Terrified, the robbers sprang from their seats and ran about the room, shouting with fear, falling over one another, and tumbling over chairs. At that moment the cat sneezed, the cock fell against the window, breaking the glass to smithereens, the dog lost his balance, the donkey gave the frame a good shove, and all four fell into the room. The robbers could bear no more; they yelled and rushed to the door and raced into the forest.

The quartet laughed and set to work upon the rich food with which the table was loaded. After their feast they felt a bit sleepy, so the donkey made himself a bed on a pile of straw in the yard, the dog stretched out on the doorstep, the cat curled up among the warm cinders on the hearth, and the cock perched on the rooftop. In no time at all they were sound asleep.

The thieves, meanwhile, hidden in the forest, waited for the heavens to fall on them. But nothing happened, and they crept back toward their house to find everything quiet and no light in the windows. Finally the chief of the robbers sent his lieutenant to the house to see if all was well. The man made his way into the kitchen and was going to light a candle, but he had no matches. Seeing two sparks of fire on the hearth, he bent to get a light from them.

But the sparks were the cat's eyes, and as soon as the thief touched her, she sprang at him, snarling and spitting, and scratched his face.

With a yell of terror, he dropped his candle and

dashed for the door, and as he rushed out, the dog bit him in the leg. Awakened by the turmoil, Grayskin got to his feet just as the man ran by, and gave him a terrific kick which sent him sprawling into the road. Delighted at the sight, the cock on the roof spread his wings and crowed merrily, "Cock-a-doodle-doo!"

The robber ran like a hare through the woods and practically fell over his waiting friends.

"Is the way clear?" asked the chief. "Can we return?"

"Heavens, no!" cried the robber, panting for breath. "There's a witch in the kitchen who leaped at me and tore my face with her claws, and as I ran through the door one of her creatures buried his fangs in my leg, and in the yard a black monster struck me with a club and nearly broke my backbone! And on the roof a little fiend with wings and eyes like coals of fire cried, 'Stop him! Eat him! Stop him! Eat him!' It's a wonder I've escaped alive!"

The robbers hurried away from the forest and fled to another part of the country altogether. The donkey and the dog and the cat and the cock now had the little house to themselves. They quite gave up their idea of going to offer themselves as choristers at the Church of Saint Gudule in Brussels and lived happily in the little house for the rest of their lives.

SUGAR-CANDY HOUSE

Near a lovely green wood lived Jan and Jannette, who were brother and sister. They played every day in the wood, fishing in the leaf-shadowed streams and stringing necklaces of red berries.

One day they wandered farther from home than they ever had before, and they came to a pretty red bridge over a brook. Across the bridge, half hidden among the trees, they found a little pink cottage built entirely of sugar candy. Delighted, the little boy and the little girl broke off pieces of the roof and popped them into their mouths.

In the sugar-candy house lived an old wolf named Garon. He was lame in one leg and could not run fast, but otherwise he was fierce and strong, and he had a very bad temper.

When he heard Jan and Jannette breaking off the roof of his sugar-candy house, he growled loudly, "Who is touching my sugar-candy house?" And he limped out quickly to see who it was, but the children had hidden in the woods. "Who dares to touch my sugar-candy house?" roared the wolf once more.

And Jan replied:

> *It's the wind so mild,*
> *It's the wind so mild,*
> *That lovable child!*

Satisfied, Garon limped back into his house, grumbling to himself.

The following day, Jan and Jannette crossed over the little red bridge again and broke some more candy from the wolf's house. Out rushed Garon again, his neck bristling and his eyes gleaming with fury.

"Who is touching my sugar-candy house?" he howled. And both Jan and Jannette replied:

> *It's the wind so mild,*
> *It's the wind so mild,*
> *That lovable child!*

"Very well," said the wolf, and he returned indoors, but this time there was a glint of suspicion in his eyes.

The next day was stormy and the dampness made the wolf's lame leg ache; it also made him more irritable than ever and sharpened his hearing. Scarcely had Jan and Jannette reached the sugar-candy house than Garon pounced out of the door and surprised them in the very act of breaking a piece off his window sill.

"Ha!" he shouted. "It was the wind so mild, was it? That wind so mild, that lovable child, eh? Fine lovable children, I must say! Gr-r-r, I'll eat them up!"

As he sprang at Jan and Jannette, they took to their heels and fled through the wood. In spite of his stiff paw and lame leg Garon chased them at a good speed. They looked back once or twice and saw that he was still following them, but they were sure they could outrun him and weren't very much afraid. But suddenly they found their way barred by a river. There was no bridge across it and the water was very deep. And the wolf was hobble-running nearer and nearer!

Some ducks were swimming in the middle of the river, and Jan called to them, "Little ducks! Little ducks! Please carry us over the river on your backs, for if you do not the wolf will eat us!"

Hurriedly the ducks swam up and Jan climbed on the back of one while Jannette climbed on the back of another. So they were carried safely to the opposite bank.

The wolf came to the river, and having seen how the children crossed, roared out in a furious voice, "Ducks, come here and get me or I'll eat you all up!"

"All right," answered the ducks, and they swam to the bank and Garon balanced himself on four of them, one paw on the back of each.

But the ducks had no intention of carrying the wolf to the other bank, for they didn't love him at all and furthermore they objected to his impolite way of asking a favor. In midstream, at a given signal from the leader, all the ducks dived and left Garon struggling in the water. He went down three times and he came up three times, but the fourth time he went down and stayed and that was the end of him.

What became of the sugar-candy house it is hard to say; but doubtless if you could find the wood, and the sun hadn't melted the candy or the rain washed it away, you might break a piece of it off for yourselves.

A DRUM FULL OF BEES

A certain regiment had for its drummer an old man named Donatus. He was a good-for-nothing rascal, but he was a splendid drummer. It was a wonderful sight on parade days to see him marching along with the band and beating his drum with a flourish that was the envy of all the young boys in town.

His companions in the regiment disliked Donatus because he was forever playing practical jokes. He had hoaxed nearly every soldier, and his jokes were more spiteful than funny.

One day he was caught cheating at cards, and was brought before the Captain, who dismissed him from the regiment. With tears running down his face, Donatus begged in vain for mercy. No one was sorry for him, and the Captain, who had forgiven him many times, refused to do so again.

"Captain," said Donatus finally, "if I must go, I pray you to allow me to keep my drum. I've played on it since I was a boy of fourteen, and I don't know any other trade. If you take it from me, how shall I live? But with it, perhaps I may be able to turn an honest penny or two."

"Very well, you old reprobate," said the Captain. "Keep your drum and take yourself off, but be quick about it."

Away went Donatus and his drum, down the first road he came to; and he marched all day until his legs grew weary. He put his drum down in the middle of the road and sat on it, wondering what he was going to do for food and shelter for the night. He turned out his pockets but found he had only two sous and a pack of worn playing cards. Donatus put them back again and, sighing, gazed mournfully at the wood bordering the road.

He decided that among the trees he could at least find shelter, so he shouldered his drum and left the road. No sooner had he entered the wood than he heard a loud humming. He followed the sound and discovered a swarm of bees hanging to the branch of a tree.

"This is fine fruit!" he said, laughing. "I'll pick them —they may come in useful one of these days!" So he took the top skin off his drum, dropped the swarm skillfully into the instrument, replaced the skin, and walked on.

In a while, when it was quite dark, he came to a small house in the wood and knocked at the door to ask for shelter for the night. A peasant woman with a very disagreeable countenance opened the door and looked Donatus up and down.

"Be off with you!" she said rudely. "We want no soldiers here!" And she slammed the door in the drummer's face.

"Now what shall I do?" thought Donatus. "A plague on that she-fox!" And he looked around to find a corner where he might rest.

Suddenly he saw a heap of faggots piled against the cottage wall. Climbing to the top of the heap, he found he could enter an open attic window. He crawled inside and stretched out on the planks to sleep.

The attic chanced to be directly above the kitchen; and as there was a knothole in the floor, Donatus could watch everything that occurred in the room below. There was the peasant woman preparing supper, and the fragrance of the food that arose through the knothole made the drummer's mouth water.

Soon there came a knock on the door. The woman hastened to open it and admitted a man wearing a long cloak. He was the village beadle, and a nephew of the woman's husband. But the husband had such a hatred of beadles that he could not bear to look at one, so his nephew never dared come to the house when he was at home. The beadle's aunt, however, welcomed him, helped him off with his cloak, and sat him down at the table. Before him she placed a roast fowl, a gammon of bacon, and a bottle of wine.

The beadle rubbed his hands. "You're a marvelous hostess, aunt!" he said. "My walk has given me an appetite, and I'll certainly do justice to your good food. To your health!" And he poured a glass of wine and tossed it down.

"Ho, you greedy fellow!" muttered the drummer, who was stretched out in the attic with his eye at the knothole. "I hope you choke!" He watched hungrily while the beadle fell to upon the roast fowl.

Suddenly there was another loud knock at the door.

"My husband!" cried the woman, greatly frightened. "He has returned unexpectedly. If he finds you here, heaven knows what will happen, for you know he cannot bear the sight of a beadle. Jump into this chest and pull down the lid while I clear away the supper!"

The terrified beadle obeyed; he hopped into the chest and closed it, while she cleared the table in a hurry. Meanwhile the husband was pounding impatiently at the door. When the woman finally let him in, he began to scold her.

"Must I wait all night to be allowed to enter my own house?" he thundered.

"I'm sorry, but I didn't hear you knock," she replied. "I was hard at work in the pantry."

"Bring me something to eat!" growled the peasant.

"It always gives you indigestion to eat so late," she said. "Wouldn't it be better to go directly to bed?"

"I'm not sleepy, and I *am* hungry!" he said, and sat down at the table.

Immediately there came a loud knocking on the attic floor over his head.

"What's that?" he asked, springing up. "Is there somebody in the attic?"

"Not to my knowledge," replied the woman. "There's been no one here all day except a soldier who came begging. I sent him away fast enough, I assure you."

"Did you?" said her husband. "I think he's contrived to get into the attic. I forgot to close the window." And he hurried upstairs to see.

There was Donatus, the drummer, who quickly explained his presence and asked the peasant if he might stay the night.

"Of course," said the good man. "Come along downstairs and get warm. My wife is about to get my supper and I'm sure there will be enough for two."

Donatus followed his host to the kitchen, put his drum under the table, and sat down, ignoring the venomous glare of the woman as she slammed down a loaf of black bread and a bowl of milk.

"Is that so?" said Donatus to himself. "There's fowl and wine for the beadle, but dry bread and sour milk for this kind peasant and his guest! We'll see!" And he gave his drum a good kick.

The peasant jumped at the sound. "What's that?"

"Oh, that's only my oracle," said the drummer calmly.

"Your oracle!" said the peasant. "Does he speak to you?"

"Three times a day," said Donatus.

"I'd like very much to hear him," the peasant said.

"With pleasure," said Donatus, and he picked up his drumsticks and beat a fine tattoo on his drum. Aroused by the sound and the vibration, the swarm of bees within began a great humming and buzzing.

"Wonderful!" cried the peasant, delighted at the noise. "What does the oracle say?"

"He says," answered the drummer, "that we have no need to drink sour milk when there is a bottle of wine by the wall, just behind the big chest."

"That's a good joke!" laughed the peasant. "I only wish there were!"

"Tell your wife to look behind the chest," said Donatus.

Unwillingly, and with a black scowl, the woman went to the chest and returned with the bottle of wine. She tried to look surprised, but only succeeded in looking crosser than ever.

"Bring us some glasses, wife!" cried the peasant. "We must drink the health of this amazing oracle! Do you think you can make him speak again, my friend?"

"Of course," said Donatus, and once again he beat a

tattoo on the drum and once again the bees hummed loudly. He leaned down, pretending to listen to what they were saying.

"Well?" said the peasant impatiently.

"He says that if your wife will look in the cupboard she will find a roast fowl and a gammon of bacon which we may eat instead of dry black bread."

"That is a marvelous oracle!" exclaimed the peasant. "Hurry up, wife, and look in the cupboard!"

The woman was forced to bring the good food and set it on the table, but if looks could have killed anyone, the drummer would have been a dead man that night. Before long, between Donatus and the peasant, there was nothing left of the fowl but the bones, and of the bacon nothing but the scrag end, and of the wine not a drop.

"That was a better meal than I've had in a long time," said the peasant, unbuttoning his waistcoat. "Has your oracle any more pleasant surprises, my friend?"

"Certainly," answered Donatus, "but this is the last time, for he speaks only three times a day." And he played the war march of Napoleon while the bees accompanied him.

The peasant listened eagerly, while his wife trembled with terror.

The drummer pulled a long face and looked at them gravely. "Ah, this is very serious. My oracle says that a big black demon is hidden in that chest over there!"

"What?" cried the peasant, jumping out of his chair. "A demon?"

· 318 ·

"Exactly," replied the drummer, "but don't be alarmed. Open the door and the windows and then stand here beside me."

The peasant did as he was told, and the drummer marched up to the chest and threw it open. The frightened beadle jumped up, wrapping his black cloak around him, and dashed for the door. He appeared so suddenly and fled so hastily that he crashed into the peasant, knocking him head over heels. The beadle, too, stumbled and fell, but he sprang up and made for the door, dashed across the yard, tripped on his cloak, and tumbled headfirst into a ditch. There was a splash, an outcry, and then silence.

"Ow," said the peasant, picking himself up and rubbing his knees, "that was a narrow escape! He was all black with flaming eyes and a forked tail! If your oracle hadn't warned us, soldier, he would have eaten us while we slept!"

With a straight face, Donatus agreed, but he was shaking with laughter inside. He slept soundly in the attic that night; and the following morning at breakfast the peasant asked if he would sell his oracle.

"I don't know," said Donatus. "It's worth a great deal of money, of course."

"I'll give you a hundred crowns, which is all I have in the world," said the peasant, gazing fondly at the drum.

"Very well," said Donatus. "It's worth much more, but you have been kind to me and I cannot refuse." He received the hundred crowns and handed over the drum.

Then he said goodby to his host and was going out of the door when the peasant called to him.

"I forgot to ask you—how shall I understand the language of the oracle?"

"Oh, that's easy," said the drummer. "At exactly ten o'clock, not a moment more or a moment less, plant your wife in the ground up to her armpits, then cover her face and shoulders with honey. Then take the oracle up into the attic where you found me. First bandage your eyes, then remove the top skin of the drum. Wait for a quarter of an hour, replace the skin, and take the drum with you to the place where you left your wife. At that precise moment the meaning of the oracle's language will be revealed to you, and you will know as much as I know myself!"

"Thank you, soldier!" said the peasant joyfully. "Good day to you, and good luck!"

"And to you!" said Donatus, and he went away, laughing to himself.

A mile or so further along the road, Donatus saw a laborer working in the fields. "I'll do a bit of digging for you, my friend," he said.

"That's very kind of you," answered the man, giving the drummer his spade. "This is a tiresome job."

"Fine, but let us change clothes," suggested Donatus, "for I wouldn't like to soil my uniform. Here's a crown for you—go to the tavern and buy yourself a glass of wine. When you come back, you'll be surprised to see how much I've accomplished."

So they changed clothes and the laborer went away.

The drummer dug a little but he did not overwork himself, and about half an hour later he heard the sound of hooves on the road. There was his late host, the peasant, galloping toward him as if the Devil were after him, his face purple with rage. He had carried out Donatus's instructions carefully, and had learned fully the meaning of the humming noise within the drum. So had his unhappy wife; for when he returned to her in the garden, her face and shoulders were black with bees.

The peasant reined in his horse and called, "Hello, you there! Have you seen a soldier pass this way?"

"A man, master?" mumbled the drummer.

"I said a soldier, stupid!" shouted the peasant. "A man in a red coat with a wicked face—a scoundrel! Have you seen him?"

"Why, certainly," answered Donatus. "He passed here about three-quarters of an hour ago and went into that wood. You'll never find him, master." And the drummer grinned.

"Why won't I find him?" demanded the peasant angrily.

"He went by a secret way. I saw the road he took and I know how he intends to go, but even if I told you the way, you'd never catch him, for you'd be lost in the wood."

"I'll give you a crown if you'll help me to capture the rascal!" declared the peasant.

"A crown!" exclaimed the drummer. "That's high pay —you must want him very badly!"

"I certainly do," said the peasant, "and I'll break him in pieces when I catch him!"

"Lend me your horse, master," said Donatus. "I'll find him for you and for nothing. Keep your crown. I'd like to see him thoroughly thrashed, for he called me names as he went by!" And the drummer tried to look fierce.

"But can you ride?"

"Can a duck swim?" asked Donatus. "Hurry, or the devil will get away. Wait here for me, and I'll return in less than half an hour."

The peasant dismounted and Donatus mounted quickly and galloped off, chuckling to himself. He rode the horse into the wood, leaving the peasant waiting by the roadside.

A quarter of an hour passed, half an hour, an hour, but the laborer did not return. The peasant stormed impatiently up and down the road, whacking at the grass and bushes with his stick. Suddenly hearing footsteps, he beheld a man in a red coat approaching; this was, of course, the true laborer, dressed in the drummer's clothes. He had drunk several glasses of wine and was very much pleased with himself and the world, and he was singing lustily.

"You thief! You villain!" bellowed the peasant, seizing the unsuspecting laborer. "Where are my hundred crowns? You'd teach me the language of bees, would you? My poor wife is stung all over her face and shoulders and can't see out of her eyes! Knave! Rascal! Liar!

· 322 ·

Take that!" And with each word he brought his heavy stick down upon the poor man's shoulders.

"Easy, master!" cried the laborer, trying to get away. "What's the meaning of this? What do I know about your hundred crowns or your wife?"

"So you'll add lying to your other crimes, will you?" shouted the peasant, striking the poor fellow harder than ever. "Next you'll tell me you've never seen a drum!" And with a mighty blow he knocked the laborer down at his feet.

Then he saw the man's face and realized that he was not the drummer. He turned wearily homeward, followed by the threats and curses of the laborer. "First I lose a hundred crowns!" he mourned. "Then the love of my wife, who will never forgive me her injuries. And now I've lost my horse! Heaven help that drummer if I ever lay eyes on him again!"

As for Donatus, he rode merrily on his way and lived by his wits for the rest of his mischievous life.